# VOYAGE INTO LIMBO

## Patricia Watkins

Down Design Publications
Psychological thriller

First published in this edition May 31, 2014
by Down Design Publications
SA65 9AE, UK
All rights reserved
© Patricia Watkins, 2014
ISBN 978-0-9572104-8-6

All characters in this publication are fictional, and any resemblance to real persons, living or dead, is purely coincidental

www.downdesignpublications.com

# Cover illustration by Patricia Watkins
Printed by BookPrinting UK

Colwyn Yeats, expert sailor and veteran of the war in Afghanistan, is all set to spend his summer working towards his PhD aboard the university's research vessel, but the trip is cancelled at the last moment, leaving him at a loose end.

Fortune arrives when an old college pal appears, and Yeats agrees to act as skipper and navigator on a transatlantic voyage the man and his two friends have planned for the summer.

Misfortune arrives when he's found alone and with no identification on a rocky shore amidst the wreckage of the boat, and wakes up in a rescue helicopter, unable to see, and suffering from amnesia.

Who is he? Where does he come from? He doesn't know, and the authorities can't find out, so what is to be done about him?

OTHER BOOKS BY PATRICIA WATKINS

TRICK OF FATE: Connell O'keeffe and the Pencaer Legacy

DYFED ODYSSEY: Connell O'Keeffe & The Spider's Web
(Sequel to TRICK OF FATE)

THE WAYWARD GENTLEMAN: John Theophilus Potter &
The Town of Haverfordwest

THE WAYWARD GENTLEMAN: John Theophilus Potter &
The Smock Alley Theatre
(Prequel to THE WAYWARD GENTLEMAN: John
Theophilus Potter & The Town of Haverfordwest)

## CHAPTER 1

I struggled to get to my feet, legs and arms flailing, but was going nowhere. My eyes, wide open with fear, strained to see, but a murky grey fog obliterated everything around except the pounding noise. My ears throbbed with it, and its constant roaring and thumping vibrated throughout my whole body, drilling into my head. I gave up and lay there shivering, my clothes clinging to me, damp and clammy, a warm stickiness creeping over my eyes. People, hidden somewhere in the fog, were chattering, but the constant roaring drowned out their words. I reached across to try to soothe the pain in my hand, but someone grabbed hold of it, and I recoiled.

"Let go of me!" I tried to snatch my hand away, but the grip became stronger.

What was going on? Where was I? How did I come to be here? And who was this person holding onto me? I tried again to get free, struggling almost feebly now, but more hands seized hold of me, pushing me back down.

"Easy. Take it easy. Okay? Calm down. Thrashing around like that is only going to make things worse for you."

"Take your hands off me!" I shouted, and lashed out at him.

"Whoa there! Enough of that. We can't have you kicking off in here, or we'll all be in trouble… Hand me that out of my kit, Jack, will you... Yes, that one. Thanks."

I opened my eyes to find myself still looking into a fog, and lay there peering into it, dazed and bewildered.

"It would help if we knew your name."

I tried to get my brain to focus, and turned my head in the direction of the man's voice.

"It would help if we knew your name," he repeated.

"Whose name?"

"Yours."

I was frightened now, and became even more agitated, trying again to stand up, but my arms and legs had been restrained, leaving only my head free, and all the noise, vibration and pain were beginning to terrify me. If only my head would stop pounding so I could think! And if only I could see what was making all the noise, it might help calm me down, but it was all hidden in this fog. I started to gasp for air, unable to breathe, my heart racing.

"I said it would help if you'd tell us your name. Can you do that?"

I concentrated, thinking about the question. "It's… It's…" I began. "It's…" I repeated, then stopped. "I… I don't know my name. It won't come to me. I can't remember it." I began to struggle again, shaking my head violently from side to side.

Someone put a hand on my forehead. "That's okay. No need to panic. You've got a nasty gash on your head that's probably dazed you a bit, but at least you're back with us now. You've taken quite a while to come around." His voice was calm and even chatty. "I have to say it's a good job this lady and her dog found you when they did, or you wouldn't be here now. We're lucky to have caught you in time."

Caught me in time? Found me? Where had they found me? Why couldn't I remember my name? I felt strange, unnatural, not me at all. I did remember them injecting me with something, though. Perhaps they'd drugged me, hoping to get information out of me. Had I told them anything I wasn't supposed to?

Convinced now that they'd drugged me, my heart began pounding so heavily, I was afraid it was going to collapse with the effort, and stop.

I flinched when a hand was put over my eyes, and I tried to shake it away.

"It's all right. Keep still a bit, and let me clean you up here. Your eyes are all gummed up with blood from the cut on your head. I'll get round to that in a minute as well; I need to get all the sand and seaweed out."

Sand and seaweed? I was becoming even more confused. What had happened to me?

He was gentle, and I lay still with my eyes closed while he worked on my eyelids, then started on the cut on my head.

I opened my eyes, expecting the fog to have lifted, but it was still there, too thick to make out any shapes at all, let alone see who these strangers were, and they were behaving far too suspiciously too for me to trust them, especially as I was sure they'd drugged me as well, otherwise there would be no reason why I couldn't remember anything about me. Perhaps they were setting me up, pretending to be friendly, but planning to catch me off my guard, and get more information out of me. Although I'd no idea what I might have that they'd want from me, whatever it was, it had to be something I'd be unwilling to give them voluntarily, and this made it urgent that

I escaped as soon as possible. I tried again to stand up, but someone grabbed my knee.

"You need to keep still there now, okay? We don't want you moving about, doing more damage to yourself... That's better. Now. Can you tell me your name yet?" He took hold of my hand, and I winced.

"Sorry about that. You've got a burn on your hand, and you've also lost your index finger somewhere along the way. It's a bit of a mess, but we'll do the best we can with it for the moment."

"Burn? Lost my finger?" I stopped, thinking about what he'd said. It was so foggy in this place, even I couldn't see my hand, so how could he tell there was anything wrong with it? "How do you know?" I snapped.

"How do I know what?"

"That I... Oh, forget it." I gave up. None of this was making sense. What was he planning to do to me, though? I waited, every muscle trembling, expecting violence, but none came, and apart from the roaring and the thumping, I couldn't hear anything. Even the talking had stopped. Maybe they'd left me alone, surrounded by that reverberating noise. Perhaps the noise itself would be the source of the violence, and I began to panic again.

"Where are you? Come back here. At least tell me what's going on." I raised my head, and peered into the gloom.

A hand patted my knee. "It's all right. We're right here still. How about that name of yours then, eh? Has it come back to you yet?"

"You haven't told me who *you* are, and I'm not giving you any of my own details until you tell me yours."

"It's Mike, and I'd like to be able to call you by your name. Also, I need to find out who you are so we can call your relatives and let them know what's happened to you. It's important, and we can't find any ID on you anywhere."

"Tell my relatives! I'm not dead! Not yet anyway! You're planning on killing me, then telling them?"

"Heavens no! Calm down. We're trying to *save* your life, not end it."

I sighed and turned my head away, more confused than ever. "All you've told me so far is that your name's Mike. Mike what? Who are you? What do you do? Why are you holding me here?"

"I'm with the Royal Naval Air Squadron."

I shook my head. "I don't get it. I can't figure out any of this anymore." I tried to concentrate, but my mind was a blank, and this had me gasping for breath again, hyperventilating, my chest straining for air. I was more convinced than ever now that they'd drugged me. They had to have, and I struggled yet again to free myself. "You can't keep me here like this! I've got to get out of here!"

He put his hand on my chest. "I said to calm down there, okay? Try to keep still. It's all right. Don't worry. It doesn't matter right now. It'll all come back to you soon. Don't sweat it. Tell me anything you *do* know. I want you to keep talking to me. Tell me whatever comes to mind. Have you served in the US army at some time, perhaps? Maybe in Afghanistan? Did something happen to you there? It might help to talk about it."

I was totally bewildered now, and shook my head again. "The US army! Afghanistan! Where the hell did you come up with all this crap? I haven't a clue what you're on about." If only I could see what he looked like -- the woman too. What nationality were they even? Plenty of people spoke English nowadays. Everything in my pounding head was jumbled up. It was no good; I couldn't concentrate, and started gasping for air again.

"Well, first of all you have an American accent, and before you came round you were highly agitated -- something about your men and an IED." While he was talking, he put a mask put over my nose and mouth, and when I breathed it in, it had a faint, sweetish smell, and I shook my head, trying to get rid of it.

"It's all right," he went on. "Relax. You're safe with us. We're in a chopper, and I'm with the Royal Navy Search and Rescue. You were in an accident. You were lying unconscious on the beach in the midst of the wreckage of a yacht, and were rambling away quite a bit before you came to."

"*A yacht*!" My voice sounded muffled. "What yacht?" I felt less threatened now, though. Maybe they weren't going to kill me after all, not yet anyway, and I tried to calm myself, let my muscles relax, and focus on what he'd said. My mind latched onto what he'd said about a yacht.

"Yacht? No, I don't remember. No." At least I could remember what a yacht was. Yachts were huge, ugly cabin-cruisers that tycoons own as tax dodges. "You're crazy! I'm not a tycoon. Do I look like I'm a tycoon? I'd never own a yacht, I'm sure. Wouldn't even want one." The idea even seemed funny, and I giggled.

My breathing was easier now, and he removed the mask. "Can you remember, perhaps, where in the States you come from?"

"No idea. Not all Americans are tycoons, you know."

"I think we're losing him again… Do you remember your name yet?"

"No."

"Do you mind then, if I give you a name, just for the time being? Can I call you Chris?"

"I guess so." Here I was, forced to lie on my back, surrounded by strange people in this roaring, shuddering space, and this man was talking about yachts! Still more agitated, I started hyperventilating again, and he put the mask back over my face. This time I didn't fight it.

"Okay. Now Chris. Listen to me." Mike's voice was calm. "I've checked you out, and found you sustained a nasty head injury, okay? Other than those burns on your hand and arm, and your missing index finger, you've got plenty of other bumps, cuts and scratches as well, and, as you'll already know, of course, you're also visually impaired. Did your yacht go on fire?"

"I told you; I wouldn't want to own a yacht. I don't even like them. Why's that so important anyway?"

"Well, as I said, you were found amidst the wreckage of one. Do you remember anything about your crew? Who your skipper was, for instance?"

"I wouldn't know. Me perhaps. I don't know."

"I think that's unlikely, Chris."

"I'm just telling you what *I* think. I don't know anything about any yacht. You didn't tell me where we are, or if you did, I didn't hear you... You keep going on about yachts."

Mike was talking in riddles, asking me questions I couldn't answer. What was worse, I now seemed to be emerging from some sort of nightmare, and entering an almost more frightening reality.

"I told you, Chris, you're in a helicopter. You were alone when you were found, which is strange, considering you're visually impaired, and couldn't possibly have been out sailing on your own, so the rest of your crew must have been lost somehow, resulting in you washing up on the rocks, and wrecking the yacht back there on the beach. The lifeboat and another chopper are out looking for the others right now. Hopefully they'll be able to shed some light on what happened here -- that's if they're still alive, and can be found."

This time the words "visually impaired" sank in and took on meaning.

"You're saying we're not *all* in this fog in here? I'm the only one? You can see everything clearly?" I tried to sit up, in a complete panic now. "Stop it! For Christ's sake, stop it! What are you on about? What yacht? What about a lost crew? You're saying I'm blind? If you're trying to scare me, you're sure making a damn good job of it, so you can just hold it right there, right now. What have you been doing to me? What's this all about? I'm not staying here, putting up with this!" I tried to clamber to my feet once more, but was still being held by restraints, and couldn't move. "Let me go! You can't hold me prisoner like this. Get me out of here!"

"All right, all right, Chris. Calm down. Take it easy. We're nearly there. Just hang in there. Everything's fine."

"No it's not! Nothing's fine! Everything's all wrong! Maybe you're fine, but all I can see is a damned fog. You've done something to me. You've tricked me, you bastards! I *knew* it!"

Something jabbed me in the arm, and I sank back down again.

"Poor chap!" It was the woman's voice. "What a shame! I do hope…"

--------------------

*The stone pier, jutting out into the water just a few hundred yards away, was empty except for some odds and ends of hauling machinery, a pickup truck belonging to the campus police, and a few beaten-up Sunfishes, Lasers and catamarans* waiting for the weather to clear. It all looked dead and lifeless, the dreary, flat grey of Narragansett Bay washing away even the bright green of mid June.

Maybe it was just my mood that stopped me appreciating the normal beauty of the scene, but I was angry and frustrated because the pier, rain or not, should be bustling with activity as I and my fellow graduate students prepared to leave for a couple of months' research aboard the school's exploration vessel. I wasn't that interested in what had gone wrong. All I knew was that our trip to the southern Indian Ocean had been cancelled, leaving me staring out at the soft-white pillow of fog draped over the upper section of the Jamestown bridge, and wondering what to do now that my whole summer, all set to be spent working towards the final leg of my PhD, had come to nothing.

Not expecting to be spending any of my own money during this time, and for once not having any outstanding debts, I'd splurged by buying myself an antique car, a cream-puff of a '75 Corvette Stingray, lacquer red, so the idea of taking an extended, exotic holiday somewhere was out of the question, and as I'd rented out my apartment too, there was no chance at this stage in the season, of my finding somewhere else to stay in this North American sailing Mecca. One thing I decided I wasn't going to do, though, was to hang around the campus. Having worked so hard for so long to get to where I was, I knew I was in need of a change of pace, and had been looking forward to this research cruise to provide it.

My original plan had been for a career in the army, and after graduating magna cum laude from Westpoint with a degree in environmental science, I'd been sent to Afghanistan, but during my second tour there I experienced something that had left me sufficiently debilitated mentally that I was invalided out.

*With my chosen career brought to an abrupt end, I'd then decided to find an alternative in academia, and given my love of the sea, to get my doctorate in oceanography. Now I'd just finished my second year towards that, and all without taking any real break since I'd first started at Westpoint -- unless I included skippering a cruise across the Atlantic just over three years ago, in which I'd also served as navigator, but that too, had been demanding.*

*I nodded to myself. Yes, I was definitely in need of a change of some sort, but what sort of change was open to me now, I'd no idea. I gave one last look around, turned off the fluorescent lights, set the lock on the door and in backing out bumped into someone on his way in.*

*"Oh! Excuse me." Standing before me was a man who'd already been a grad student when I started at the school, but had left before finishing his PhD. "Hi Steve! Come on in." I opened the door again and turned the lights back on.*

*Steve Callahan was average in every way. His size, looks and build were average, and although of average intelligence as well, was one of those people who are too undisciplined to get off their backsides and ever finish anything. He was a personable man though, and made friends easily, and I quite liked him, although I couldn't say that I'd ever known him that well. Our professor, however, had decided that Callahan wasn't dedicated enough to his work, and had told him to leave and get his act together someplace else, and where he'd been for the last two years I didn't know.*

*He held out his hand. "Col! How are you this long time? I was in the area, and thought I'd come over to say 'hi'."*

*I thought he looked older than when I'd last seen him, strained even, but decided it was just his colouring; he'd obviously just shaved off a quite substantial beard, and while parts of his face were tanned, the lower area around his jaw was a peculiar greyish white, where his beard had been. The* same was true of the back of his neck, where he must have had long hair, now cut short.

He started to say something, but then stopped, coughing nervously, and apologized for holding me up from some prior commitment, something that I was quick to tell him wasn't the case; I was going nowhere in particular, and suggested that as it was around noon time, we head to a local bar down the road, and get us a beer and a sandwich.

"Great! Let's go. My car's outside." There was that nervous cough again, a cough I didn't remember him having when I last saw him, and when I put that together with the newly-cut hair and shaved-off beard, I began to wonder if Callahan's last two years hadn't been the greatest for him. Maybe he'd get around to talking about it.

The bar, verging on the seedy, provided a decent sandwich anyway, and we made our way to a dark corner with our plates and mugs, and cutlery wrapped in white paper napkins.

I knew from my own experience in the army that people can change significantly in two years, and as we chatted, I felt I was talking to a very different person from the student I'd known. He'd developed this nervous cough for starters, and by the time he'd finished eating, had worried his paper napkin into a heap of confetti. He'd become a lot more talkative too, garrulous almost, also in a nervous sort of way.

"Well, Steve, what have you been up to since I last saw you?"

His answer, though, while taking a long time in the telling, still left me with no clear image at all as to what he'd actually been doing, other than spending time with one of the international development agencies in some role or other. It was all rather nebulous.

"Anyway," he told me, "I was at a bit of a loose end at the moment, so thought I'd mosey along down to see how my old pals were doing here on the Bay campus."

I laughed. "And you arrive here, only to find me at a bit of a loose end as well as it happens, and here we are! So what's the reason for your loose end, then?"

"Well, three of my pals and I had planned to sail the Atlantic this summer from Marblehead to Milford Haven, in Wales. We were all ready to leave in ten days' time."

"Something's not happened to stop you, I hope. That's a great experience, crossing the Atlantic. I did it along with some friends right after I got invalided out of the army -- needed to get my head back together, if you see what I mean."

"Yes, I'd heard about that -- a tough period for you altogether, I've been told. Anyway, the man who was going to be our skipper cum navigator, fell last week, and hit his head. It was a bad fall, and since then he's had blackouts, and as a result, can't go, and we can't possibly make it without him, so we're stuck." He sighed, and twirled his beer around in its can. "It's a real bummer. We'd been planning it for ages... Well, that's enough about me. What's the cause of your loose end? You were always such a busy guy -- didn't goof off like I did. I can't imagine you not having your summer all sorted out."

"Ah well, oddly enough, I'm in a position somewhat similar to yours," and I told him about my own ruined summer plans.

Steve gave one of his nervous coughs. "I remember you had the reputation for being one helluva sailor, Col; people were always coming to ask you to crew for them. Word was that you were... let me see..." He smiled. "Competent, reliable, sociable, easy going, good to be with on a long cruise..."

I held up my hand, laughing. "Whoa there! You're too kind," I added in a mocking tone. I got up to get us another couple of beers, and when I returned, Callahan was excited about what he claimed was a great idea that had just come to him.

"I've been thinking, Col. Since your summer is screwed up as well, I suppose you wouldn't consider taking on the job of skipper and navigator for us now, would you?" He coughed again, and began shredding the new napkin I'd brought back with the beer. "I mean, we're a pretty good bunch of guys, although not the greatest sailors in the world, but we've been training hard with our old skipper, who's a real pro, and he was willing to take us, and as you're a professional sailor too... How about it, eh Col? You've crossed the Atlantic once already, and it would seem you've nothing better on the cards right now, so... How about it?" he repeated when I made no comment.

I was thinking. Having been brought up on Narragansett Bay, in Rhode Island, I, like most youngsters living near the water, had learnt to sail at an early age, and by the time I left high school had already built up a reputation for myself in the racing world. As a result, I'd been, and still was asked quite often -- as Callahan had pointed out -- to crew on blue-water cruises, and I'd more than pulled my weight on that particular transatlantic trip, the northern route we'd taken being a less common, and more risky route to follow.

I was also lucky that my family was what was called, 'pretty well heeled,' my father owning a twenty-five-acre estate on the shores of the Bay, near Newport, allowing me to take up crewing offers when they cropped up and other obligations didn't get in the way.

"I know it's not a spur-of-the-moment sort of decision to make, Col," Callahan was saying, "but, again, how about it? What have you got to lose -- all expenses paid too... How can you refuse, eh?"

*"Good question. Well, it's all a bit sudden, I have to say, but... yes. What the hell... I don't see why not."* I gave Callahan a wide grin and raised my beer can. *"Okay, here's to a great transatlantic trip then!"*

## CHAPTER 2

The roaring and thumping had stopped, but I still couldn't remember anything: where I came from, or who I was, and I still could see nothing, the fog as thick as ever, so I jumped when a hand touched my shoulder and a woman asked me how I was. I smiled up at her, and raised my head to answer, but her footsteps disappeared into the distance before I could open my mouth. There were many other people too, coming and going, seemingly in a great hurry, and I wondered who they were, what they were doing and where they were going. Whoever they were, they all passed by, no-one else stopping to take any notice of me -- a body stretched out motionless in this sea of activity.

Lying there, but unable to see where I was, and not knowing what was happening, or what they were going to do with me, was causing me to panic again, and I sat up and began questioning everyone who came close to me, somehow expecting them to know the answers, but none did, of course.

"Please, please, someone, tell me what I'm doing here." I continued to let the words echo through my head, soundless, in fear of recriminations of some sort if I made a nuisance of myself by calling out.

At the same time I let my fingers wander over the blanket covering me. It was of honeycomb texture, lightweight, too lightweight, and I shivered. A bright light was diffused through my fog now. It had the harsh tinge of fluorescent lighting, and I closed my eyes against its brilliance, wondering when all the frightening effects of what had happened to me would wear off, allowing my memory to return, and my eyes to see what was going on around me.

I tried hard to think, but still nothing came back to me, other than the thumping and banging of the helicopter, that I was apparently American, had been washed up on a beach, where I was found by a woman and her dog, and that I was what they euphemistically referred to as 'visually impaired'. This last was more terrifying than the rest, and I lay there, scared, disorientated, my eyes firmly closed, pretending to myself that if I were to open them, the dense, impenetrable fog would have lifted, and I'd be able to see perfectly.

I don't know how long I'd been lying there amidst the bustle of this place, before I felt myself being trundled somewhere else. When I was brought to a halt, so all the movement of everything around me came to a standstill as well. I was alone. My world had come to a stop, quiet, the only sound that of a clock ticking away the seconds. The air smelled of wet mop mixed with stewed coffee and cocoa, and every now and then footsteps approached. There was a clunk and the sound of liquid filling a container, and the footsteps disappeared again into the distance.

---------------------

I called in on my housekeeper, Mrs. Moretti, bursting though the door with such violence that she clutched her hand to her chest in fright..

"Sorry I scared you, Mrs. M. I'm going to be leaving in just a week -- crossing the Atlantic by boat."

"By boat, Mr. Yeats? One of those fabulous cruise ships? Oh Mr. Yeats! How exciting! Great food!" Mrs. Moretti was from Federal Hill in Providence, where you could still go through the back of the store to find live chickens kept in cages, like cans on a shelf. Food was always the first thing that came to her mind; her waistline proved that.

"No, no! Mrs. M. Not a cruise ship, a sailboat, a forty-one footer, about as long as from the front of this apartment to the back."

Mrs. Moretti was incredulous. She shook her head, then shrugged, continuing with her ironing of the white dress-shirts I always wore with my jeans. "When will you be back then, Mr. Yeats?" She shook her head again. "I don't know... crossing the Atlantic in a small sailboat... You will look after yourself, won't you?"

I patted her on the shoulder. "Don't you worry, Mrs. M. I promise I'll be back safe and well, although exactly when, I'm not sure; it all depends on the weather... That reminds me: I should let my father know what's going on too, but he's off in the wilds of Africa at the moment, doing something for the National Geographic... Not sure where... Oh well, I guess it doesn't matter; we can catch up with each other when we both get back..."


For me, another advantage of the proposed voyage was that all the preparations had already been carried out by *others, although I still needed to prove to myself as well that everything had been done to my own satisfaction, so I left Rhode Island early the next morning, and drove my old red Toyota Tacoma pickup-truck up to Marblehead, where a smiling and still nervously coughing Callahan greeted me, all ready to show me our craft.*

*We were the only ones there today, apart from the injured skipper who would be giving me more information about my crew. In preparation for this I'd made up a checklist of questions for him, and was pleased to come away satisfied that any doubts I may have had about adequate preparations and the ability of the remainder of the crew were laid to rest -- the injured skipper gave me glowing reports all round.*

*Callahan and I slept on the boat that night; a pretty boat she was too, although an old lady, having been built quite a few years ago. She was in excellent shape even so, well appointed, and updated wherever feasible, and the following morning I gave her a thorough inspection, which included all the paperwork, from which I found that she'd been hired from a reputable company, and was fully insured for both boat and crew.*

*I was also glad to find there were manual backup systems for all electrically-operated equipment, and the running and standing rigging were virtually new, as were the life-jackets, which had D rings installed in them, all ready for attaching to the tethers. The bolts for attaching the jack line were strong, although the line hadn't yet been set up, and the rails likewise were solid. Navigational charts were included, although I preferred to bring my own, and all necessary electronic, navigational and communications equipment was up to date. The sails too were high quality and fairly light, which meant they could pick up any wind going -- a good thing, as we wouldn't want to end up using the motor too often. So far, so good.*

*There was only one thing that worried me, and that was the lightning-protection system, which needed some work done on it. Having spent some time living in 'lightning alley,' along the north Florida coast, lightning is something for which I have a huge respect, even having to admit that I'm terrified of it, having seen the damage it can do to anyone or anything it chooses to strike, so knowing protection from it to be essential, I'd even jumped over the side into the water to check out the underwater ground plate. Everything there seemed properly installed, but I did have questions about the bonding system.*

*"Steve. Everything else looks fine to me, but can you get the company to give the bonding system the onceover before we leave."*

*"Bonding system?"*

*"Yes, that's the part of the lightning protection system that protects the crew, not just from lightning strikes, but from build-up of static as well... So you'll get that done, will you? Sailing, they say, consists of hours of pleasure, interspersed with moments of sheer terror, and I don't plan on having too many of those moments."*

*Callahan nodded and laughed. "Will do."*

*Other than that, the fuel tank and spare were full, as was the freshwater supply tank; everything, in fact, was working as it should: bilge pump, head, powerful motor, etcetera, and it was Callahan's job to make sure we had enough supplies to keep us going throughout the voyage.*

*Satisfied all was in order, or would be by the time we set sail, we shook hands, and I drove home to Rhode Island, only one thing irritating me -- and which I wasn't going to be able to do anything about -- Callahan's annoying cough. That would be something I was going to have to live with, a small price to pay when I thought of being able to sail the Atlantic again.*

--------------------

It was eerily quiet, and I was still lying there, waiting, but for what, I didn't know. The clock ticked away the seconds, and my mind was still running away with itself, imagining all sorts of horrors and fears of what was to come, all of which told me I had to escape from this place. I was half way over the rails of the bed when, suddenly dizzy, I crashed down onto the smooth, concrete-hard floor, where I lay, its surface cold as glass against my back, and, too light-headed to raise myself up from it, I shivered in the draft.

A brilliant light exploded above my head, making me jump and cry out. It flooded my eyes as though I was staring into a gigantic, frosted sun, and I put my arm over them to block it out. At the same time footsteps were marching towards me, and I put out my other arm to ward off whoever it was. "What are you doing? Where is this? Who are you? What are you going to do to me?"

A man's voice called out for help, and almost immediately I was surrounded by people lifting me back onto the bed. They put several blankets over me, and, still shivering uncontrollably, I clutched them to me, like a child with a teddy bear.

"Hello there, Chris. It's all right. Calm down. You're perfectly safe. I'm Doctor Singh." He put his hand on my arm "Nobody told you where you are? Sorry about that. Someone should have told you. You're in A & E, and I understand you can't remember anything right now."

His voice was slow, soothing. He felt my head, and I winced. "You do have quite a nasty cut and bump here, so we're going to give you a brain scan to see what, if anything, is going on in there, okay? But first, can you see anything at all? Can you see my hand for example?" He moved my arm away from my eyes, and the brilliant light seared into my brain again. I shook my head.

"How long have you not been able to see then? Were you born this way? Had measles as a child, or anything?"

I tried to calm my mind, and behave like the sensible adult I felt sure I must be, or had been before being thrown into this foreign, unseen existence where nothing made sense to me, and where I felt isolated and so very much alone.

"I don't know. I don't think so. I know what things are supposed to look like. I can visualize everything. What's happened to me? What did they do to me? Will it come back all right?" There was so much I wanted to ask.

"Well, as I said, we need to do a brain scan, and we'll get the ophthalmologist to take a look at you and find out what he has to say, okay?" He paused, and I waited for him to continue. Maybe I could question him, and he'd have answers. I was desperate for answers.

He gave me a jovial slap on the knee. "Right then. We'll see what we can do to get you sorted and on your way."

"Thank you. Can you tell me...?" The brilliant light went out, and I was alone again, still needing answers, but once more left waiting in the silence of my fog.

The ticking of the clock impinged on my senses again, and I moved my head from side to side, trying to locate it. It was off to my left somewhere, and I lay there, pulling the blankets about me, clinging to the security offered by their warmth.

--------------------

The time passed quickly, and I was due to meet my crew at Marblehead the following evening, so was taking one last walk around Fort Wetherill, a couple of miles from my home. The sun had set about a half hour ago, and as I walked out to the cliff edge in the twilight, the grey-concrete, weed-surrounded old fort looked eerie and forbidding. I paused at the edge of the cliff, and looked out across the water towards Block Island and the Brenton light.

It was peaceful this evening, but I thought about the night when the 'Captain Lawrence,' an almost new trawler, somehow missed her direction, and landed up on Ol' Noot, the submerged rock at the end of the Beavertail. My father had taken me to see the wreck, but within weeks it was as though she'd never existed; the wind and the waves had mashed her sturdy bones into almost invisible splinters. Much as I love the sea, I, like any good sailor, hold a great fear of and respect for its powers.

Off to my side the moon was rising over Newport, now a mass of coloured lights. Tonight its beautiful bridge was reflected in the water, and behind it I could see the lights of the Naval War College. Newport was where I was born and raised, and by living now on the island just across the bridge, I was able to enjoy all the amenities of my birthplace as well as the peaceful, slow-moving country life of Conanicut -- or Jamestown as most people call it -- at the same time. I considered myself lucky and privileged to be able to both live and work in the area I love. Having sampled other places, I appreciated my home all the more.

It was getting dark now, and the moon wasn't yet high enough to light up the track. Even so, I knew my way well, and took the path back, leading right past the dark, blank entrances to the fort. Once I thought I heard a slight rustle behind me, but wasn't worried. It was probably a rabbit or a raccoon, or even one of the island's growing mink population, although preferably not a skunk. Otherwise, it was quiet.

I'd almost reached the end of the fort complex, and came to a narrowing of the path. Here I picked up speed, and marched along with the confidence of one who knows his way. Next thing, I was sprawling on the uneven path, having been upended violently by a tripwire placed some eight inches off the ground. For a second I thought some idiot had placed a camera tripwire across the path, with the intention of photographing some night creature -- not a good idea, dangerous too for anyone walking along as I'd been doing.

Being a big man, some six foot three inches tall and weighing a muscular one hundred and eighty pounds, I'd fallen heavily on the rock-strewn path, so it took me a minute or two to gather my senses and get up onto my hands and knees. At that moment someone swung a piece of lead piping full force against my right arm, knocking me down again and causing me to cry out.

I waited, tense, fully expecting the next blow to kill me, but it never came, and by the time I felt it safe to stand up again, there was no-one to be seen anywhere. It was dark now anyway, and easy for my attacker to hide from me. Maybe he was behind one of the entrances to the fort, but I'd no wish to go in search of a man armed with a piece of lead piping.

I made my way back to my pickup-truck, cursing loudly, every now and again looking over my shoulder to see if I was being followed, and nursing my now extremely painful arm. If it were broken, then that would be the end of my proposed transatlantic voyage. It certainly felt painful enough to be broken, so instead of going straight home, I drove instead over the bridge to Newport hospital to get it checked, fearful that this trip too might have to be cancelled.

     I was lucky; X-rays showed no broken bones, but where the piping had landed, it had, I was told, bruised the bone, which accounted for the intense pain, but my leather bomber jacket had probably saved it from further damage. I was given instructions on how to deal with it, but omitted to say that I'd be leaving on a transatlantic voyage within the next couple of days, as none of my forthcoming activities would have complied with any of the doctor's instructions. I drove home, trying to forget what had happened, and, looking forward to leaving the next day, wasted no more time trying to analyze what the man with the lead piping had had in mind by clobbering me like that.

---------------------

     They must have given me something in the helicopter to stop me from trying to escape, or being violent, but now it was wearing off, with shock finally setting in as a result of what had happened to me. I was trembling uncontrollably again, and tried to concentrate on something positive, anything, but my brain was acting as though it had no idea what it was supposed to do or think. After all, it had nothing to go on, my memories going back no more than a few hours, and it kept repeating what little it did know like an old-fashioned stuck record, unable to find any solution to my predicament. "Predicament! That's not the right word. This is more than a predicament, you fool. You're trapped, and have no idea where in the world you are, except that you're in an emergency room somewhere. Where? What country? And why?"

The man in the chopper had spoken like the English, but the doctor had an Indian accent. Things like that, I remembered. Why had I forgotten all the important things, like who I was? What could I possibly be doing in the Asian sub-continent? I didn't remember ever being in that part of the world, but that wasn't all; I couldn't remember anything about my former life at all.

The ticking clock became unbearable, so much so that I started to climb out again, desperate to leave this place. Half way over the sides again, though, I came to a stop. How could I escape, and where to if I couldn't see where I was going? Besides -- and it only then occurred to me -- my family must know by now what had happened to me, and where I was, so would be coming to fetch me. The thought calmed me, and I lay back down. Yes, of course, they'd be arriving any minute now to take me home and save me from this hell-hole I'd fallen into. As though in answer to my thoughts, someone came into the room, and I sat up.

"Has my family come to take me home then? They're here already?"

He helped me into a wheelchair. "I no know. I hospital porter." He sounded Chinese.

"Where are we going then, please?"

"Ward three."

"Oh." And within minutes I found myself somewhere where men were talking, chatting. The chatting stopped, and I cringed. They were all watching me; I was sure of it. I was helped into a waiting bed, and curled up facing away from the sound of the voices, wanting to cry. Was I the sort of man who cried? I didn't know.

I woke up, but it took a while for the meagre total of my memories to come back to me. Maybe they'd drugged me again, because I didn't start panicking, even though nothing had changed: I still had no idea who I was; no more memories had come back to me, and scariest of all, the impenetrable fog was still there. I sighed. There was nothing I could do to help myself, nothing, and I lay there, trying to visualize my surroundings. What they looked like, I couldn't tell, of course, but the sounds were of the murmur of men talking to one another. It was normal, everyday chatter about mundane things, not frightening. It was soothing even, and I listened to what they were saying.

"The strawberries are coming along nicely this year. Don't know about my potatoes though. Hope they're better than last year." The voice wasn't that of a young man, and he spoke English with an accent I couldn't recognize.

Not feeling threatened, I sat up.

"Hello there! How are you feeling now then?" It was another man, close by, and he had the same accent. "That was a good sleep you had there. You looked as though you needed it. In fact, he looks a whole lot better now, doesn't he?" There were murmurs of agreement.

I looked in the direction of his voice.

"Well." There was a pause, no doubt because he'd just realised I couldn't see him. "Welcome to our ward. There are five others of us in here, apart from you... None of us in too dire straits, I'm happy to say," he laughed.

They started chatting to me then, their voices friendly, seeming to recognize the turmoil I was in, and anxious to help boost my spirits and make me feel at ease. I was grateful for that, and could feel my brain starting to settle down, prepared now to think more rationally, craving normality, and trying to come to terms with what had happened to it, no longer depriving me of the ability to reason. My problems weren't solved, but a great sense of relief was taking over as I began to accept that I seemed to be in a safe place after all, and I started to relax.

As the man in the next bed had told me, I was in a ward with five others, three on either side of the room, most recovering from minor surgery, so it wasn't long before I knew their life histories, and they encouraged me to tell them mine, but as that covered only a few hours of memory, there wasn't that much to tell. Even so, I found myself desperate to talk about my frightening experience during those hours, from the time I woke up in a helicopter, until the present, and I poured out my story to them.

Eventually I ran out of anything more to say, my memory-box scoured clean of every last detail. I'd finished, and wondered if they'd despaired of my tale ever coming to an end. Who knew? After the first five minutes, perhaps they'd gone back to reading their newspapers, listening to their I-pods, or had even been lulled to sleep by the monotony of my voice. Not being able to look at them as I talked, I'd no way of knowing, but it didn't matter; I'd told my story more for my own benefit than for theirs anyway, and felt much better for it -- a sort of catharsis, I suppose.

"So you've no idea at all how you came to end up on a beach?" said the man in the next bed to me. "That must feel very strange to you."

I nodded. "Yes. It does. It's *very* disorientating."

"You at least have to know you're American though," someone else said.

"Yes, I guess so."

Perhaps the best help anyone could be giving me at this time, was being offered by these men, ordinary people like I was sure I had to be too. Perhaps my accent had kindled an extra interest as well. At least I'd been lucky to end up somewhere where they spoke English, even though it sounded strange to me. In the end, I summoned up the courage to ask what I knew was a sort of movie cliché in such situations. "I know it's a strange thing to ask, but where am I? I don't even know what country I'm in."

I expected laughter, but these men recognized that whatever had happened to me was nothing to laugh about. "Nobody told you where you are, son?"

"All I know is that I'm in a hospital somewhere... I don't know where."

"They shouldn't have left you not knowing like that! You're in Wales, young man!"

"In the beautiful county of Pembrokeshire," the man in the next bed added.

"Pembrokeshire! I've heard of that, I think. I wonder why I'd ever have landed on a beach in Pembrokeshire amidst the wreckage of a yacht." I shook my head, and shrugged. "Who knows?"

The hours passed, and my anxiety about my situation continued to lessen, knowing that my family was sure to find out soon where I was, and would come to take me home. That would jumpstart my memory, and that part of my problem would disappear. All I'd need then would be for the ophthalmologist to tell me the loss of my sight was temporary too, and all would be back to normal again. After all, as I'd told that Indian doctor, I couldn't have been born blind, because I knew in my mind's eye exactly what everything looked like. Given a pen, I could even write, so why shouldn't it come back? It was all probably due to that bump on the head I'd had -- like my amnesia. It couldn't be that long before the bump subsided, and when that happened, both problems, as I said, would be taken care of. In the meantime I had to be patient. My nightmare would soon be a thing of the past, the horrendous trauma I'd experienced, nothing more than an unpleasant memory -- and I relaxed some more.

Now that things had slowed down in my mind, I could hear my stomach rumbling, and wondered how long it had been since I last ate. It could have been days, and I was starving. I must have smelled food, because even while I was thinking about it, my neighbour announced, "Ah! Here comes supper."

Something was rolled in front of me, and something else set down on it. By now I was too hungry to worry about whether other people were watching to see how I was going to manage, and I felt around -- my fingers like a stick insect's legs probing the air, trying to reach another leaf -- and found a banana. I peeled that and ate it. There was also a sandwich, but when I picked it up, the filling, whatever it was, not being held firmly in place as the banana had been by its skin, fell out. I was too embarrassed to attract attention by fumbling around looking for it, so simply ate the bread and butter that came with it.

The drink was tea in a teapot, and, remembering a trick from a movie I'd seen, I stuck my finger over the edge of the cup, and poured the tea into it till it touched my finger, then did the same with the milk. After that, I felt around some more to see if there was anything else to eat as I was still very hungry, but found only a sheet of paper on the tray, although what that was for, I didn't know. It was too firm for a paper napkin, so I left it there.

Eventually someone came to take the tray away. "You haven't filled out what you want for breakfast." She put the piece of paper in my hand.

I looked up, smiling. "Oh! That's what that is. Can you...?"

The man in the next bed came to my rescue. "Come back in a few minutes," he told the woman. "We'll have it filled out by then." He came over to me, and sat down. "Right. Let's see here." He listed the options, and checked off what I wanted. "We get one of these with each meal. That way we get to choose what we want for the next one. We can do that together, if you like."

I was grateful to him for not making a fuss about it, but for being quiet and matter of fact instead, and knowing he'd help me now when I needed it, I wouldn't feel embarrassed asking him.

Supper over, we chatted some more for a while, and eventually the daylight switched into artificial light, and I could tell my roommates had settled down for the night -- one of them was snoring. I lay down and drew the blankets up over my shoulders, then put my hand under the pillow to pull it down closer under my head to make myself comfortable. It came up against something flat, cold and moist, and I snatched my hand away. It felt like a dead thing, and there was no way I could go to sleep with it lying there. I slid my hand towards it again, creeping up on it rather like a cat, testing, patting a tentative paw to see if the mouse it has been torturing is truly dead. It was the contents of the sandwich I'd lost -- a slice of ham -- so I ate it.

Time passed, and I was gradually settling into the hospital's routine. Visitors were always coming to see their relatives and friends in the ward, and I enjoyed listening to them chatting about ordinary, everyday things, something I found helped to calm my attacks of anxiety over finding no improvement in my vision or my memory, and the fear that my family might be having trouble finding me. It was comforting too that my roommates introduced me to their visitors and included me in their conversations, it being obvious that no-one ever came to visit me, and I think they felt uncomfortable, seeing me sitting there alone, unable to do anything, but stare into my fog.

"Someone will be coming to pick me up any day now," I always assured them with a confident smile, and at the beginning I was expecting just that. As time went by, though, I became less confident about this happening, but tried not to show that, it being important to stay positive and cheerful, an attitude to which people responded well, I found.

"I'm just going down to the shop; can I get you anything, Chris? Some sweets or biscuits?"

"No thanks. I'm fine. Thanks for asking, though." I should have liked a bar of chocolate, but how could I ask for anything? I had no money. I didn't even have any clothes of my own. They told me mine were in rags when they found me, so I had to make do with the hospital jonnies. Even my toothbrush and paste came courtesy of the hospital.

"Hello Chris. How are you today?" I looked up, and a woman took my hand. "Alright if I sit down on the edge of your bed here?"

I smiled. "Yes, of course."

"Now, Chris. When you were found, as you know, there wasn't anything at all anywhere to identify you -- no passport, no wallet, nothing at all, even your yacht's identification details were missing. Going by your accent, we contacted the American Embassy in London, and gave them a description of you, but they said no-one answering that description has been reported missing as of now, and not having a name to go on, can't help, especially as you've no other means of identification either. As they pointed out, just because you have an American accent, doesn't guarantee you're a US citizen. The British police have nothing that can help us either, but will let us know if they get any leads."

"No-one's reported me missing? But surely *someone* must have missed me... Maybe, if I *am* American, my family doesn't know where to start looking."

She stood up and patted me on the arm. "Never mind. I'm sure someone will be in touch soon. It's early days yet."

"Yes, I suppose so." Even so, the thought that my family might be having trouble finding me was truly frightening, and I felt my anxiety growing again. How long was I going to have to remain in this state of limbo?

--------------------

*My last evening having turned out so unexpectedly and painfully, I didn't sleep well, so by the time I arrived at Marblehead the following afternoon, I wasn't at my best.*

*Callahan looked at my bruised and swollen arm. "What on earth happened to you, Col?"*

*I told him what happened, making light of it. "So that's it," I ended.*

*"Strange," he remarked. "Why would anyone want to half beat you up? And why aim at your arm? Doesn't make sense. Must have been a nut-case. Have to say you were lucky though. A piece of lead piping can do a whole lot of damage.*

Good job he didn't aim at your head." He coughed, then pointed to another man who had just come up on deck. "Oh! You must meet Joe Gascoigne here. He's our third crew member. Joe, this is my old classmate, Colwyn Yeats"

We shook hands, but it was clear at once that Gascoigne was not at all pleased at having a stranger come in as a replacement. He barely gave me a nod, then went back below. Callahan and I meanwhile -- all the final preparations having already been carried out before my arrival -- sat on deck and chatted. A short time later, Gascoigne, having finished whatever it was he was doing below, reappeared, muttered something about going to fetch a copy of the day's edition of the Boston Globe, and disappeared down the quay. One person, however, was still missing.

"Where the hell is Bob? He was supposed to be here hours ago. I'm going to have to call him to find out where he's got to." Callahan pulled out his cell phone, and called the last member of the crew, Robert Roberts. It rang at least six times before being answered.

"Heh! Bob! What's up? Where are you? Not had cold feet at the last moment, I hope." Callahan gave a nervous laugh and coughed again, and I wondered, not for the first time, if that was something I was going to find particularly irritating, as one thing our sailboat would be short of would be privacy, and as I'd learnt from past experience, in such situations the idiosyncrasies of the crew on a small sailboat can prove much more annoying than they would on a larger vessel.

Roberts and Callahan carried on their conversation for another minute before Callahan rang off, and put his phone away. He looked puzzled. "Strange guy, Bob. Never quite know where he's coming from... Anyway, he's on his way. Should be here within the hour... And about time too. He was supposed to have been here helping us today."

*Roberts arrived at last; Gascoigne reappeared carrying his copy of the Boston Globe and a can of beer, and our crew of four was united for the first time, leaving me a few hours later rather disappointed after experiencing no particular feeling of rapport with any of them. There seemed to be a lack of openness and enthusiasm, which made me think that living together for the next few weeks, or however long it was going to take us, wasn't going to be filled with any great camaraderie -- rather troubling, given that living in such close quarters required being able to get along with one another, and it seemed as though these men barely knew one another, let alone were friends.*

*I noticed something else about them too: apart from Roberts, they seemed singularly unprepared where personal equipment was concerned; their clothes were all wrong for a start. They gave the impression of being more a bunch of amateurs going out after bluefish for the day, and when I went to stow my Musto foul-weather gear in the one lazarette -- the other was locked -- there was no sign of theirs, and Gascoigne was even wearing flip flops, which would be most uncomfortable -- dangerous even -- the moment they got wet, which they'd do the minute we set sail. As the outsider, though, I didn't want to throw my weight around so soon after coming on board, especially as we hadn't even weighed anchor yet, so I kept quiet for the time being, and busied myself with stowing my gear.*

--------------------

Not reading newspapers or watching television, and being where I was -- where one day was like any other -- I was losing track of time, so reached the stage when I no longer knew how long I'd been in the hospital. On top of that I'd not yet seen the ophthalmologist either. I tried to put it all to the back of my mind, but with nothing else to think about, couldn't help but be constantly afraid that I might never see again. I tried not to let myself get depressed about it, but it was hard with nothing to do, other than sit, staring into space, or sleep day after day.

At first they gave me sleeping pills because they said I was restless during the night, keeping others awake by shouting out, but then they stopped, which was better for me at least, in that I didn't wake up feeling groggy. On this morning, though, it was different.
"Chris! Wake up!"
"What! What's happening?" I sat up with a jerk.
"It's all right. I've brought you your breakfast. We let you sleep on, so it's late."
I lay back down again. "Is it? Well, I'm still really tired, so I'll go back to sleep, if you don't mind."
"No. Chris. Come along now. Sit up, will you. You're going to have to wake up, even if it was a pretty rough night you had -- we all had. No wonder you're tired."
I pushed myself up into a sitting position again. "A rough night? Why? What happened?"
"You were all over the place. Getting up, marching around, knocking into things. You were extremely agitated."
"I don't remember anything, although my knee hurts. Did I bang it or something then?"
"You've probably got quite a few bruises. We had to get in a couple of male nurses to hold you down, and give you

something to knock you out. You're a big, strong man, you know."

"I'm sorry -- about giving you a hard time, that is. Did I wake everyone else up too?"

"Yes, I'm afraid you did."

"What was I on about then?"

"It was hard to tell. You were so distraught... Something about everything being gone. You've no idea what that could have been about?"

"Sorry, no. I've no idea. I must have had a bad nightmare, or something." I ate my breakfast, and apologized to my roommates.

"That's all right, son. You've obviously been through a rough time one way or another. We all understood, and felt sorry for you; you were in a right old state there."

Several days had passed since I woke everyone up, and I'd not given them a repeat performance since then, which was a relief all round.

"Hello Chris. I'm Miss Atkins, the person who found you on Druidston beach. How are you now?"

I leaped to my feet, excited to talk to someone who had at least some connection to me, and offered her the chair on which I'd been sitting. "Oh yes! Miss Atkins! How kind of you to come! This is really great! Now I can thank you at last for rescuing me! If you hadn't come along when you did, I'm told I'd have drowned for sure." I held out my hand, and she shook it, then held onto it, while taking the chair I offered her. I sat down on the bed next to her, my spirits rising, and smiled.

"You can thank Paddy, my border collie for that. I was about to turn around and walk home when he ran off. He's usually obedient, but this time he simply would *not* come when I called, and I had to fetch him. I was ready to be most annoyed with him, until I saw you lying there, of course. I'd never have noticed you if it hadn't been for Paddy. You wouldn't remember it, of course, but there are some rocks sticking up out of the sand on that beach, and you were next to one of them, so I couldn't see you. I even had to walk quite a way to see where Paddy had got to, and there he was, standing over you, sniffing at you. I've got him here with me now, so you can meet him properly if you like. He's a Pets As Therapy dog, so is allowed in to see patients.

"Yes of course I'd like to meet him." I put out my hand, and received a friendly lick. I bent down, and Paddy came up close, sitting himself between my legs, so that I could pet him. Touching the dog gave me the oddest sensation of a link between us, and a deep emotion welled up inside me, taking me by surprise. It was something that I found hard to handle. It was as though Paddy, by instinct, understood my innermost thoughts, and could see right into the hidden anxiety behind my outward cheerfulness, and we were sharing a part of each other that no-one else was aware of. His ears were little soft-velvet pads, and I bent right down and buried my head in his neck. The dog I could hug without looking silly, and the physical, comforting contact filled me with a longing for a loving embrace to help me through my ordeal. I held him to me, and felt his warmth and his breath on my face. Paddy, I knew, understood.

"It was lucky I had my mobile with me," Miss Atkins was telling me, "so was able to call 999, and they kept me on the line until they confirmed they were going to get the Air Sea Rescue out to pick you up. Then, while I was waiting for them to come, it all became pretty nerve wracking, because the tide was coming in, so I ended up having to pull you up the beach quite a way, which I knew you shouldn't do in case you do more damage to the victim, but you'd have drowned if I hadn't, so I had to."

I sat back, my hand still stroking Paddy, but happy now to listen to her story of my rescue. I smiled. "You must be quite strong then. One thing I do know, and that is that I'm no lightweight!"

"I suppose I am quite strong for a woman, but then I live on a farm, and it pays to have strong arms... Anyway, they ended up taking us both in the helicopter as well after that."

"All in all, quite an adventurous morning then."

Miss Atkins laughed. "I have to say it's not every day I go for a walk, and find a body along the way."

"Not something you'd want to make a habit of either, I guess... I just wish I knew how I ever got to be there in the first place. I haven't a clue."

"When your memory returns, I'm sure it'll all fall into place, and make perfect sense... I have to say though; that boat of yours was smashed to bits, and the only other thing they found amongst the wreckage was the remains of a guitar. Can you play one?"

I held up my hand. "I don't know, but if I did, then I'm not sure how well I'd do now."

"It's such a shame. Just a few yards difference, and you'd have missed that rock altogether, and would have been fine. It's too bad you ended up hitting your head like that... although things could have been much worse, I suppose." She patted me on the knee. "If you could have heard yourself on that helicopter! What on earth you were on about was a complete mystery to us, but whatever it was, it was obviously causing you a lot of grief... Something about losing your men, and needing to go to their rescue, or something... I'm only telling it all to you now, of course, because they say you're soon going to be just fine."

"They do? They didn't say anything about that to me. Well, that's great news. Who told you?"

"One of the nurses."

"And she said both my memory and my sight would come back soon?"

"That's what I thought she said, but you can always ask her yourself."

"Yes, I'll be sure to do that. Do you know which one it was?"

"Well, I could describe her to you, but I'm afraid that wouldn't help you right now, would it?"

"No. Never mind, I'll ask someone the next time they come round, although I have to say I feel fine. All I need is for my brain to hurry up and unscramble itself – and for whatever's wrong with my eyes to clear up, of course."

Miss Atkins and Paddy left, and I went back to wondering what I was doing in this country in the first place. Did I live here? If so, how long had I lived here? And why did I live here? In return for the small amount of information she'd been able to give me, I hadn't been able to tell her anything at all about myself. It was so frustrating. What did I look like? How old was I? What did I do for a living? What was that about losing my men? Which men? And where did I lose them? Still, the nurse told her I'd soon be fine, and that was the best news I'd heard so far. I did wonder, though, why they hadn't told me as well. Surely they had to know how anxious I was to know that. Anyway, I'd heard it now, and it boosted my spirits more than anything else I could think of.

"I hear I'm going to be fine then -- that my memory and sight are both going to come back soon. That's great! You've no idea how that's been weighing…"

The consultant interrupted me. "Who told you that?"

"One of the nurses told my visitor."

"Your visitor must have misunderstood what the nurse said then. At this time I can tell you only that it's most likely that your memory *will* return at some stage, but we need to wait and see. Amnesia is unpredictable, so we can't make any promises on that score. As far as your sight is concerned, any comment on that will have to come from the ophthalmologist, and to my knowledge you haven't seen him yet, have you?"

"No."

"Well then, best not to count our chickens yet, as they say."

"No, I guess not."

"Well, I do have to say, you appear to be a strong, healthy man in fine physical shape otherwise, and your brain scan came back okay, so that's good news, isn't it?"

I nodded, wishing now that Miss Atkins had not told me what turned out to be the wrong information. She'd meant well by it, though, even if it had raised my hopes, only to have them deflated, so I couldn't blame her. Anyway, maybe it was the nurse who had been mistaken.

"Chris. I have to tell you: Paddy seems to have taken a special liking to you. He even knows which ward to come to now, and heads straight here. He's friendly with everyone, but especially so with you." Miss Atkins put her hand on my knee. "And I always trust his judgment, so I'm sure you have to be someone special."

"Thank you. When you can't remember your past, you have to wonder what your character was. Was it good, or bad?"

"I have to think that even though you've lost your memory, your behaviour and attitudes towards others would stay constant, don't you think? -- setting aside the frustrations you must be experiencing right now, which have to have an effect of some sort, of course."

"I really don't know. It's been hard for me to think rationally at all since all this happened, let alone try to analyze myself."

"What you're going through must be awfully hard to accept, but I think that trying to fight against it can only make things worse, Chris. The time here must drag terribly for you, having nothing to do, and that, of course, allows you to get even more restless, I can see that, but when you think about it, you haven't been here that long, even though it may seem that way, and the wheels of officialdom do tend to move slowly. I'm sure steps are being taken to try to expand the search for your relatives, though."

"Yes, I guess you're right."

I was sitting in the chair next to the bed thinking, as usual. Miss Atkins had been right about my frustration. Most of the other people around me were mobile, as I would have been too, if I could have seen where I was going, but I couldn't, so other than finding my way around to visit my fellow patients in my small ward, I had to stay put, which I did find frustrating, being used to being independent and active, as I was sure I must have been before all this happened.

As a result, my days were passing as though in slow motion. Even so, I thought how strange it is that a person can actually adapt to living within the confines of a mini-world such as the one I was now in; a mini world that throbs with its own unique life, its own version of civilization and its own way of existing, quite separate from the planet of which it's a part; a mini world that people from the big world outside pass and re-pass, ignoring it as they do the moon -- rather like going by a well-known pond every day, indifferent to the peculiar and busy ecosystem hidden beneath its shimmering surface.

I myself, being now in this mini-world, was isolated, safe and protected within its walls. I was a part of its routine, lived by its laws, and, given my limitations and my options, even found a certain comfort in the protection it gave me, despite my frustration. Miss Atkins had also been right though, in that it didn't do to get angry about the circumstances that brought me here. That way, I could easily become bad-tempered and self-pitying, a misery to myself and to everyone else, so I tried to follow her advice, and do my best to bear as calmly as possible with my present -- and surely temporary -- lot, and to be as cheerful as possible.

My positive attitude was rewarded in that I noticed that it was mirrored back to me in the way others behaved towards me -- so much so that I began to find myself becoming almost content. Almost. There was always that fear that my problems wouldn't go away, and that my family wouldn't find me. What would happen then? I didn't dare dwell on those possibilities, although with nothing else to occupy me, it was hard to keep pushing such thoughts away.

"I know it's unusual," Mr. Cartwright, the ophthalmologist was telling me, "but the problem with your vision is being caused by particularly dense cataracts. Given their intensity, and coupled with the burns on your hand and arm, I'm led to believe that you were most likely struck by lightning…"

"*Lightning!*"

"Eye damage can occur in some instances, and such cataracts -- called 'cataracta electrica' -- can form quickly, sometimes within a few days after the event, either caused by lightning or by someone being electrocuted by high-tension wires. They can also take months or even years to show up. In your case, judging by your burns, which presumably were caused at the same time, you were probably hit by lightning not long before you and your boat landed up on the beach. It also fits in with you telling the paramedic on the helicopter that you were probably the skipper. You could well have been... You could even have been sailing singlehandedly. Anyway, this has nothing to do with the bump on your head fortunately. You can't remember what happened?"

"No. I'm afraid I can't"

"That would fit in with my lightning theory too, as people struck by lightning sometimes suffer from amnesia, although it usually lasts only a short time. Yours seems to be lasting quite a bit longer, and that indeed may have something to do with that bump, although the scan they gave you didn't show anything untoward, I'm told. It could also be that your experience was so traumatic that your brain feels unable to cope with it right now -- although that's not for me to say. Well, the good news is that the cataracts can be removed, and afterwards you'll be able to see as well as anyone else who has had cataracts removed."

"You said, 'the good news is'... Does that mean you're about to follow that with, 'the bad news is'...?"

"Not at all. At least not that I can tell."

"And how soon can this be done then? As you can imagine -- the sooner the better."

"Well, unfortunately we don't know who you are, or if you have medical insurance or the money to pay for it. If you did, then the chances are it could be done very soon, privately. However, we do have a National Health Service, under whose auspices you're being treated for free right now. They'll do the surgery for you as well, but you'll have to wait longer, as we have waiting lists, and it depends on the number of people ahead of you on that list... However, given all the circumstances surrounding your case, I'll see about getting it done as soon as possible. How's that?"

"That would be great. Thank you so much! I have to admit it's been a scary time, thinking this was it."

"I'm sure it has been, and quite rightly so, too. Right then. You're all set." He gave me a hearty slap on the back, and left me to revel in my immense relief. Now all I needed was to remember who I was. One down, one to go.

Life was getting easier and more relaxed by the day, what with my good news to keep my spirits up, and now that I was no longer plagued by debilitating panic attacks either, I was even feeling relatively upbeat about my situation. Soon everything would be back to normal. I was sure of it. My grey fog would be lifted, the bump on my head would go away, the effect of the lightning would wear off, and my memory would return. Once all that happened, there would be no need for my family to find me; I would find them.

--------------------

*That evening our newly assembled crew went for what I referred to jokingly as our 'last supper', and while I confined myself to just a couple of drinks, the others were soon knocking it back at a pretty alarming rate. It was our last night on shore, though, so some last minute, celebratory drinks were probably to be expected.*
*Being excited about the upcoming trip, I looked forward to discussing it all over dinner, but was surprised to find that chat on the subject was almost non-existent, probably as a result of their disappointment over their preferred skipper having had to back out, and a stranger brought in to replace*

him. Despite this, I began going over what we could expect to experience on the voyage, and details about the boat where we'd be spending the next few weeks together, hoping to get them talking about it. After all, this trip was the one thing, literally, that we seemed to have in common, given that during our other conversations, we'd not yet found anything else of mutual interest to talk about. It was, though, a heavily one-sided conversation as my crew -- even Callahan -- had almost nothing to add to it.

"So, what's the purpose of our trip then?" I asked when all conversation had stalled. It was a reasonable enough question, as they gave no impression of being the three buddies fulfilling a life-long dream to sail the Atlantic as Callahan had previously portrayed them. The answer was equally discouraging, sounding as it did as though it came from the headline of a small-town newspaper: 'THREE CHUMS BRAVE ATLANTIC OCEAN TO RAISE MONEY FOR LOCAL CHARITY.'

I tried to sound enthusiastic. "Really! That's great! Well, I guess we should make a good go of it then. Which charity are we aiming to help?"

Gascoigne looked at Callahan, who gave me a name I'd never heard of before, but assumed that whatever charity it was, they had to be sufficiently committed to want to sail the Atlantic in aid of it. Roberts, meanwhile, had almost nothing to say, as usual, seeming, as did Gascoigne, to be more interested in watching a Red Sox game on the bar's TV.

In the end it was quite late when we left, and Gascoigne and Callahan disappeared briefly, before reappearing, each carrying a crate of beer and a supply of hard liquor. This time, as their skipper, I did say something. While I wasn't alone in allowing myself, on the odd occasion, to get plastered on a sailboat in that area south of the Jamestown Bridge, where there was no heavy commercial traffic and where I knew every rock and cove, I made it a rule not to allow anyone to be drinking alcohol while sailing anywhere else, especially out in the Atlantic.

I put up my hand and shook my head. "Uh... Uh. Hold it right there guys! I'm sorry, but there's no way you're bringing alcohol onto my boat. You're going to have to take all that back."

Gascoigne glared at me. "What! What's with the: 'my boat' crap? If I want a damn drink during the trip, I'll have a drink, and if you think I'm taking orders from you, you've got another thing coming."

"Uh... okay guys... We need to get something straight here. You thought enough of me to sign me on as your replacement skipper, and, like it or not, I'm now the one in charge, so, as I said, I'm sorry, Joe, but you're going to have to get rid of it. You too Steve."

Gascoigne, who was well away, having got through quite a few beers along with more than enough chasers, turned on me. "Who the hell do you think you are, Yeats? Lord God Almighty?"

Even though I was very excited about making the voyage, my enthusiasm for it did have its limits even so, and Gascoigne's aggressive and in-your-face attitude had just pushed me far enough to reach it; this was no way to begin a transatlantic voyage together. "Right then, if that's the way you feel, I'm out of here. I'll pick up my gear, and you can find yourselves someone else. I'm not facing a mutiny before we've even started," and I began making my way back to the boat to get my things.

Callahan quickly caught up with me, coughing nervously. "Please Col. Don't back out now. We need you. We do. Joe's just in a bad mood -- personal problems. He'll calm down once we get going; I know he will, and as for Bob, he's a bit antsy about the whole thing, I think, but he's a good guy, *pretty level-headed and down to earth... Please Col. Don't quit on us. Have a word with Joe... Look, he's already on his way back to return the stuff, and see: I've already taken mine back."*

By this time Roberts had caught up with us, slouching along, head down, and, looking as though he was trying to remain uninvolved, made no comment at all. Maybe, I thought, it was as Callahan had suggested, and he was having second thoughts about what he'd let himself in for. I let out a sigh. They were certainly not like any crew I'd ever dealt with before: one talked nonstop; another was bad-tempered, and the other was giving every indication he wished he'd not made the commitment to go. I'd been the only one to have even mentioned anything about the boat, sailing, or the voyage the whole evening, and had met with no excitement at all. Anyone would have thought that the Celtics had just lost a game, and we were all about to go home to our own beds, rather than back to share the limited space of a forty-one-foot sailboat for an extended period.

Gascoigne finally joined us. I looked at him for some sort of apology, but received only a shrug. "Okay, you're the boss. I'll mind my own business."

"I don't want you to mind just *your* business. I need you to mind *our* business. We all need to work together as a team, otherwise we stand a good chance of never surviving the crossing."

I looked out over the harbour, and waited, but Callahan simply looked at his feet; Gascoigne was already heading unsteadily back to the boat, and Roberts continued to say nothing, just gazing off into space. There was no knowing what was going on in that man's mind, and Gascoigne apparently thought that telling me I was the boss was all that was needed of him, so that left Callahan -- still with his irritating cough -- who now assured me that, like with a play, the last rehearsal may be terrible, but it would be all right on the night.

Wanting desperately for the trip to go ahead, I persuaded myself that it would be just as Callahan assured me, and everyone would step up to the plate once we got going. After all, the other skipper had spoken very highly of them, so maybe I should just accept that they were suffering from pre-performance nerves. Struggling to find any excuse for their behaviour and attitude, I reminded myself that these guys weren't blue-water sailors, so it was, for sure, quite a big undertaking for them, but it didn't necessarily mean they weren't willing and capable. It was possible too that, as Callahan had also said, Gascoigne had personal problems on his mind at the moment, and maybe he was the sort to get belligerent when he'd had a few too many as well. As I'd now forbidden alcohol on board, that particular problem, at least, should already be sorted out.

I did so much want to go ahead; I'd committed myself to it physically as well as emotionally, and if forced to turn around at this stage and head back home, I'd be back to not knowing how to spend my summer. Besides, where would I live once I did arrive home? I'd nowhere to go, and after taking everything into consideration, and persuading myself that the worst that could happen would be that I'd simply have to put up with their rather unpromising personalities for a short time, I decided to change my mind, and go ahead and take them on their voyage.

"Okay then. Let's do it." And I pushed myself away from the parked car against which I'd been leaning, and followed the reeling Gascoigne back to our home for the following so many weeks.

## CHAPTER 3

It was just after breakfast, and I'd been put in an isolation ward after apparently getting into an argument with one of the male nurses during the night. It seemed I'd accused him of something to do with a crate of vodka, and while everyone else seemed to find it all very amusing, I was most embarrassed over it, because I couldn't remember any of it, so had no idea how I'd acted or what I'd said.

My thoughts on this, though, were interrupted by the arrival of a visitor. She introduced herself as Miss James, and told me she was a social worker. I was delighted. Maybe she'd brought some good news, and I gave her a welcoming smile. "Hi there!"

"Hello Chris. We need to discuss what to do with you -- where to send you."

My eyes opened wide. "Do with me! What do you mean? 'Do with me? Send me?' What are you talking about?"

"Well, Chris -- or whatever your name really is -- as you must realise, because you aren't ill in the sense that you need nursing care such as the hospital is here to provide, we can't continue to keep you here, taking up valuable bed space. Your burns and your hand are healing nicely, and as the hospital can't do anything more for you, we have to find somewhere for you to go -- somewhere where you can continue to be looked after, and your special needs attended to, as it's obvious that you're incapable of caring for yourself." She paused, seemingly waiting for me to say something, but I didn't know what to say.

Thus far, everyone had been very kind to me, and the nurses had treated me with almost affection. It was something I suppose I'd become used to, so this Miss James's abruptness took me by surprise, being totally unprepared for what she'd just told me, and I am sure my face must have reflected that. To make things worse, her tone gave the impression that she was even enjoying having to bring me this news, even wetting her lips in anticipation of my reaction.

That I might have to leave the comfort of my friendly ward had not even occurred to me, and if her aim had been to shock me, she succeeded, as the jolt silenced me, leaving me with my mouth open, but with no idea what to say in reply. I was at the mercy of Miss James, and panic began to rise again for the first time in quite a while. What she was telling me was that my being there was proving to be a problem to them, because they knew nothing about me -- any more than I did -- and that I was helpless, and although this was a truth that I myself had been struggling not to accept, having her express it like that, so openly and bluntly, was overwhelming. Surely my alarm at what she was telling me had to be obvious to her, so where was the sympathy and emotional support to help me deal with it? Was it necessary for her to have been so blunt? Did she even feel in any way sympathetic towards me and what had happened to me? Apparently not, and her lack of understanding added to my sudden and increasing sense of desperation. I blinked.

"... as I think you've already been told," she was saying, her tone cold and efficient. "We've learned from the American Embassy that no-one of your physical description has been reported missing, and without any other means of identification, they can't help. Nobody of your description has been reported missing in this country either. You are therefore what is known in America, I believe, as a 'John Doe'... So..."

She began explaining something to me, but my brain was now dealing with two other things: the fear that was building up in it, and the creation of a mental image of her. She had to be one of that new breed of aggressive, professional young women: smartly-dressed, lipstick moist and fresh, hair shampooed every day to wash away the contamination of those with whom she had to deal. She was probably holding a clipboard too -- no tatty notebook for *Mizz* James. She was still talking, and I tried to concentrate on what she was telling me.

"... normally our response to your situation would be to provide such continuing care as necessary for you and your family or carer in your own home, so you could remain independent within the community..."

I was still imagining her. She probably even had the official government brochure right there on her clipboard, and was quoting from it the paragraph on what to do with those incapable of looking after themselves.

She got her response finally, because a nauseous emptiness started churning in my gut, brought on by what she was continuing to impress on me: I, a strong, healthy, but temporarily blind, man in my right mind -- except for amnesia -- was incapable of looking after myself. Why had she been so unnecessarily brutal in the way she'd pointed that out to me though? There hadn't been any need for that. There surely had to have been a gentler, kinder way of breaking all this to me. That she'd obviously enjoyed the task, though, made me feel like I was every partner who'd ever ditched her -- and there had to have been a host of those-- and she was revelling in the payback.

"... and unfortunately, you've no known friends or relatives to whom we can release you, and you aren't fit to be sent to a home for the homeless... We've held meetings, and have considered fostering you out, but there aren't any provisions on the books for fostering out adults like you... Besides, we know nothing about you -- what you might be. We have no psychological profile of you, and you must understand; we must look at a worst case scenario -- you could be a rapist."

"*What*! Yes. I can see how every woman here under ninety must be terrified of me. I wonder you don't have me chained to the bed, just in case I get up in the night, and make a raid on the women's ward, or worse still, the children's!"

"We do have to be careful you know."

"Yeah, right, lady! Even if I wanted to rape someone, which I don't, I can't even see to pee straight, let alone look around for a victim... Anyway, there's being careful, and there's being downright stupid!"

"Please don't raise your voice at me like that, Chris. As I said: we have to look at a worst-case scenario, and we find we have no option, therefore, but to section you in a psychiatric unit until you can be evaluated. We'd have sent you there a lot sooner than this, but have been waiting for a vacancy to crop up."

"*Section me*? What's that? They're going to do surgery on my brain?"

"No. It means you'll be kept in a secure facility, where you can do no harm to yourself or anyone else, until it's been determined that you're safe to be released back into the care of others. You'll be given a psychiatric evaluation to judge your mental state. In the meantime, hopefully your vision can be restored, and your memory will return. Maybe the one will trigger the return of the other."

"You're going to lock me up in a loony bin as though I'm off my rocker? In amongst nutcases? How could you possibly think I'd ever hurt anyone?"

"I must ask you to refrain from shouting, Chris, and to be careful how you express yourself. It's not politically correct to use such language."

"Politically correct be damned! You know what I mean! I'm as sane as you are, and how would you like to be treated as you're treating me?"

"It's good that I'm not the one giving you your mental evaluation, Chris, otherwise…"

"All right, all right. You win. How long is it going to take before I'm evaluated, as you call it? What if they can't decide about me?"

"I'm afraid I'm not in a position to tell you anything else. That's not within my purview. That'll be up to the psychiatrist."

"What if I refuse to go?"

"In your case, that's not possible."

"It's like throwing me in jail! What have I done to anyone to deserve this? I can't help what's happened to me!"

"It's because we don't know who you are, or if you have a record of criminal or antisocial behaviour."

"Fingerprint me then, and find out."

"We already have. You appear to have no record in this country, criminal or otherwise."

"What about the States then? Have you checked there?"

"No. We don't have the resources to spend an inordinate amount of time on your special needs, Chris. There are others who need our help too, you know."

"When will I have to leave here then?"

"We have transportation arranged for you for this afternoon, after lunch."

"This afternoon! As soon as that?"

"You don't have to worry. You'll be well looked after... Right I'll need you to sign this. An 'X' will have to do in your case. You'll have to do it left-handed too, I suppose."

She put a pen in my hand, and I took it without saying anything more. If she was finding it distasteful having to touch me to show me where to sign, I could have assured her, the feeling was mutual, and then, as it was awkward trying to write with my left hand because of the damage to my right one, and now being highly anxious as well about what was going to happen to me, I dropped the pen.

She handed it back to me. "Chris? I can't wait here all day. Can we get this signed please? Don't just sit there. I have other patients to visit... Chris?"

I fumbled with the pen, and with her help, made what I assumed to be an 'X'

After she left I lay down and closed my eyes. While she'd left me full of fear about being sent to a psychiatric unit, she'd no doubt gone off to get herself a well-deserved cup of green tea and a carrot stick.

Regardless of how agitated I became in the following hours about leaving the safety of my home of the past weeks, that afternoon I found myself being driven through the countryside in the back of a minibus. I was the only passenger, and whoever was driving, wasn't talking, so I was left to the hum of the wheels on wet tarmac, the constant whoosh of passing cars, the occasional siren -- someone else's day ruined -- and my own fears about what was to come.

I must have drifted off for a while, so had no idea how far we'd travelled, and wondered how much further we had to go. I continued to sit there, passing the time by guessing the kinds of vehicles that overtook us: car, motorcycle, bus, or, on occasion, an eighteen-wheeler.

The minibus slowed down now and turned left, and the wheels crunched over gravel before coming to a stop. The driver climbed out, and without bothering to say anything to me, left me sitting there on my own, as though he were making a delivery of nothing more important than a piece of furniture. A couple of minutes later he was chatting with a woman about me -- I could have been deaf for all the tact he used in describing his delivery -- after which someone opened the sliding door. There were birds singing, and sheep bleating in the distance. A big sigh rose from my depths as I was helped down off the bus.

--------------------

*The following morning I got up early, before the others were awake, and made my last inspection of the boat. The jack line had still not been set up, and I made a mental note to ask Roberts to help me with that as soon as he was up. Everything else seemed to be in fine shape, and I was satisfied until I checked the lightning protection, and swore. Nothing at all had been done to it, and it was way too late to do anything about it now. We'd just have to cross our fingers and hope we wouldn't need it.*

*One thing, at least, was in our favour, and that was that we were leaving at just the right time of year weather-wise -- the third week in June -- and the most likely place for us to encounter lightning storms would be if and when we got into the Gulf Stream closer to Europe. With luck, we might avoid* lightning altogether. Luck, though, wasn't the best thing to have to rely on out in the Atlantic.

By the time everyone else was up, I'd finished my survey, and, apart from the lightning protection system, was satisfied with the boat, so, after breakfast, I sat everyone down to allocate specific duties to each one. Other duties would be carried out on a rotation, or ad hoc basis, as needed. I decided that I'd be responsible myself for the boat at night, as this was the time when squalls were most likely to hit, and putting the boat on autopilot at night time wasn't something I liked to do. I saw no point in explaining any of the navigation details to the others, so left that side of things unsaid.

Not knowing I'd be coming on this trip, I'd not had the chance to observe the jet stream pattern ahead of time, but did have the GRIB files and weather maps to help me make educated decisions as to what route to follow. This, of course, I'd have to adjust as we went along. Another thing in our favour -- although it meant we would have to leave as soon as possible -- was that a cold front had just gone through, and that would most likely be followed by some fine weather and a northwest wind. I wasn't sure what speed this boat was capable of, but as the canvas we were carrying was light enough to catch whatever wind came our way, we should make good time.

"How long is this all going to take?"

"It all depends on conditions and the boat's speed capabilities, Joe. We'll get there when we get there. I'm not making any promises. One thing though, I think we should get going."

"What? Right this minute!"

"Yes, Steve. Right now. So let's untie ourselves and head out."

And within the hour we were out of the harbour, our voyage begun.

## CHAPTER 4

"Come along now, Chris dear. Out you come. That's it. This way. Very good." The woman's tone was unnaturally upbeat and encouraging, as though she were leading a child into the kindergarten for the first time, and it made me cringe. It was as though she were really talking to a child, patronizing me, making me feel like an inferior being, no longer a competent, intelligent adult, and I began to wonder what was in store for me in this place.

The hospital nurses had always treated me as a normal adult -- even flirted with me -- and I was tempted to take this woman up on her attitude, but decided it wouldn't be a good way to start by antagonizing those on whom I was going to be -- and I hated to even think of the word -- dependent.

"Here we are then Chris. I'm Miss Carmichael. I'm the manager. Do come on in." She opened a door, and put her hand on my back, ushering me into a room. "There. Would you sit down here for me please." She took my arm, and led me to a chair. There was a rustling of paper, and a vague smell of mustiness.

"Now, let me see. It says here that it's already been explained to you why you've been sectioned. As you must understand, we know nothing about you whatsoever, so before we can allow you anywhere where you can do harm to others -- or to yourself, of course -- we need to assess your mental state. Your unique position is such that we've had to bypass normal procedures in your case, but I hope to have you out of here as soon as possible. I'm told that, thus far, you've shown no signs of aggression -- apart from losing your temper with your social worker -- or of aberrant behaviour, which we must take as being a good sign, but to be completely satisfied, we shall be carrying out a full psychiatric assessment during your stay with us. Do you understand?"

"I guess so, but how soon will you be able to do this assessment, and if you find me to be a normal, healthy-minded person, which I'm pretty sure I am, what happens then?"

"The longest we can keep you here is twenty-eight days. Unfortunately, your assigned psychiatrist isn't here full time, and won't be able to see you for another couple of weeks or so. The assessment will then be considered and, all being well, you should be out of here within the twenty-eight days, providing we receive the psychiatrist's report in time. As to what happens to you afterwards, I'm afraid that's not up to me to decide, but it's obvious you're in no position to take care of yourself if released into society, so decisions will have to be made by your social worker, Miss James."

"Oh."

"Now, I should explain to you as well that you're to be given your own private room. Normally, non-violent patients are put in a ward with five others. However, you've been classified as 'vulnerable', and so for your protection you've been given your own room... We can't afford to let you wake up other patients with your nightmares either, can we?"

"Why have I been classified as vulnerable? Vulnerable to what? Why do I need protection?"

"Unfortunately, given the nature of the establishment, situations can arise. Normally, they're minor in nature, and easily dealt with. However, your inability to see puts you in a position in which you may not be able to avoid becoming involved in such a situation."

"You mean… No, I'm not even going to go there. It sounds ominous. I'll have to assume you'll not let anything happen to me here."

"That's precisely why you're getting your own room. The chances of anything happening at all are, of course, minimal, but as you can understand, we have a duty of care that requires us to take all precautions, no matter how infinitesimal they are. Your room is just for sleeping in. At other times, you'll be in a communal room along with others, who, for the most part, are here voluntarily, and can go outside if they wish. You, of course, will need assistance wherever you want to go. Right. I'll send for someone to take you to your room. Do you have any questions, Chris?"

"Not that I can think of right now. I don't know what sort of questions I should be asking as I don't know what to expect at all, especially after what you've just told me. Maybe I'll have some later. Is there anything I *should* be asking you now?"

There was a knock at the door. "Ah! Here's Alec. Come in Alec. This is Chris, Alec. Would you take him to his room, please. Give him a while to settle in there. Let me see; it's now five o'clock. Supper's at six, so that would be fine. Chris is unfortunately unable to find his own way around, Alec, so perhaps you'd collect him at six, please, and take him down to the communal room for supper, and see he's taken care of. Thank you."

"Certainly. Okay, Chris. Let's go, shall we?" Alec took my arm, and led me from the room. Miss Carmichael had not answered my question. Was it convenient for her not to? I was beginning to imagine all sorts of horrors.

The corridor was noisy, and people were coming up close to me, invading my space, unnerving me.

"He's new here, isn't he? Who is he?"

"This is Chris, Lisa, and yes, he's only just come to stay with us a few minutes ago."

"What's *his* problem then? Why's he got sunglasses on in here? That's silly. He looks daft. Is he a paranoid schizo?"

The warm breath of someone peering into my face wafted against my cheeks, and I backed up.

"Lisa, why don't you go on down to the communal room? That's where you were going, weren't you? Oops! Sorry Chris. I should have told you there was a step here. We need to go upstairs. Are you okay?"

I found the banister, and clung onto it. "Yes. I'm fine. No problem." There was though -- a big problem. Everything was so new, so strange, and the people around me weren't normal people, behaving in a rational manner. I was disorientated, and finding it hard to breathe again. "Control yourself, Chris, or whoever you are," I ordered myself under my breath. "The last thing you want is to be medicated. What faculties you still have, you need to hang onto -- intact."

"Here we are then, Chris. This is your room. You don't have any personal belongings, it seems, but get yourself settled in anyway, and I'll be back in an hour to take you down to supper, okay?"

"How about giving me some idea of the room's layout before you go... Just so as I don't break my neck tripping over things." I tried to sound light-hearted.

"Oh? Oh yes, of course." Alec gave me a rundown of the room and its contents, which were minimal. "We've given you an en suite bath too. The regular bathroom's too difficult for someone like you to find – it's down the corridor a ways… All right. I'm off now, and I'm going to lock the door, okay?"

"Lock the door? Why? I'm not going to go on a rampage, or anything."

"No, I know that. It's for your protection. You don't want anyone coming in and bothering you, do you?"

"They can do that?"

"Well, yes. In this unit, the patients are mainly depressives and mild schizophrenics. They're entitled to come and go around the place. As long as they're on their medication, they're fine."

"And what if they're not on their medication?"

"Well, it's up to us to see they are. Besides, if anyone did come in, we'd catch it on the CCTV camera in here."

"You mean you're watching me! Even in the bathroom?"

"Yes. It's for your own safety."

"Oh… well… Thanks."

"Right. I'll be back in a little while, then. In the meantime, you can get yourself settled in."

I heard the door close, and the click as it was locked, making me feel as though I were in prison, then found the bed and lay down. It was a very narrow bed, and too short for me to stretch out fully, so I must be quite tall I decided. I got up, found the door to the bathroom, and measured myself against it. There was hardly any space between the top of my head and the top of the door, so I had to be at least six feet three inches tall, I calculated.

I went back to my bed, and lay there, thinking, going over my new situation. My safety? Vulnerable? CCTV cameras? A prisoner in my own room? Where on earth was I this time?

---------------------

*For the first few days I didn't push either the crew or boat. The latter was weighed down with supplies, which added considerable weight, and I didn't want to put too much strain on the rigging to begin with. As I'd predicted, we were lucky with the weather, and it had given the others a chance to settle down to some sort of routine without having to cope with any emergency. That we'd have similar luck throughout the voyage would be too much to ask for, but if and when danger did strike, I hoped I'd be in a position to deal with it.*

*In these first few days too, I'd been able to form more definite opinions about the character of my individual crew members as well, although I still couldn't claim to have succeeded in getting to know any of them to the extent that I'd have liked.*

*Whatever Gascoigne's personal problems were, they didn't seem to have diminished in any way, as he was still morose, and when not taking his turn on watch, spent his time below, reading or listening to whatever he had on his iPod. Thus far, he was contributing the bare minimum too, and hadn't offered to do anything over and above what he was assigned to do. What he did in his onshore life I didn't know, and nothing about him gave any clues as to the kind of occupation he might have as a day job. After several attempts to be friendly, I finally gave up, and now spoke to him only when necessary, which he seemed to prefer anyway.*

*Callahan on the other hand, talked non-stop, and by now I'd given up listening to him. For some reason he'd developed a hatred of all international aid organizations, calling them meddling busybodies that pour money into developing countries without ever carrying out feasibility studies, with the result that they wasted the public's charity gifts and did more harm than good. Some of the examples he gave were, if true, quite frightening, but after expressing surprise the first few times, I'd by now become bored with his constant gripes, especially since he'd begun repeating himself like a circular tape. He was so hyper too, I thought that if I'd had tranquilizers on board, I'd be tempted to feed them to him to shut him up.*

*To save my own sanity I'd forced myself to ignore his nervous cough, which was enough to drive anyone crazy. He did carry out his duties as crew member, though, but obviously not concentrating on what he was doing, was careless and kept making mistakes -- as with forgetting about the lightning protection system -- and this irritated me as I constantly needed to double-check everything he did.*

*The one I liked best was Roberts. I had the feeling that under different circumstances he might be an interesting man to get to know. Every now and again he showed flashes of humour and dry wit too, but otherwise still gave the impression he was worried about something, although what, he never said. At least I felt I could trust him and rely on him in an emergency -- something I couldn't say about the other two.*

--------------------

I must have fallen asleep as it seemed no time at all before Alec was back to take me down to supper. After negotiating a staircase and a couple of corridors, we eventually arrived in what I assumed was the so-called communal room where everyone else, allowed the freedom to roam around, was gathered. It was very, very noisy in there, and as Alec led me through a minefield of people, chairs and tables, as though escorting me through a crowded airport terminal, I already felt overwhelmed by it all.

"Here we are, Chris. I'll put you at this table. You'll be sharing it with Kevin, Beth-Ann, and Sophie -- all about your age... Everyone, this is Chris. He's just joined us, so I'd like you to make him welcome, and help him if he needs it."

He sat me down in a chair at the table, but my stomach had tied itself into such a knot of anxiety, I didn't even want to think about eating supper, and although the room was obviously crowded, I was sure I'd never felt so lonely and isolated before.

Alec had left already, and if there were others sitting at this table -- which I assumed there had to be, as he'd introduced me to them -- they said nothing, and knowing they were there, but keeping silent, made me feel even more isolated. Should I say something? Or was I supposed to wait until they greeted me? I was sure they were staring at me, but afraid to appear as though I myself was staring at any of them, I looked down towards my lap. Still nothing. It was unbearable. I had to say something, and looked up.

"As Alec said, I'm Chris. How about telling me who you all are, starting with who's sitting on my left?"

Right then a hand was placed on my shoulder, and I turned.

"Hello Chris! Are you comfortable, love? Don't worry. You'll soon settle in. We'll do our best to make you feel at home. The staff here are very kind. I've brought you your supper and a cup of tea. I've put them down right in front of you. Okay?" She thrust a knife and fork into my hand. "I'll be back later to see how you're getting on. You others, do please make Chris welcome, won't you?"

"Thank you. What is it?" But she was gone. "Anybody like to tell me what I've got on my plate?"

"Wow! Spooky!" It was a female voice.

'Vulnerable,' the manager had called me, and it was obvious that these people, inhibitions on the back burner, were infantile if nothing worse, and it occurred to me that this could result in bullying. I had to sound confident. "What's spooky?"

"You are!"

I didn't know why, but I'd equated their silence with aggression, so needed to get them on my side by keeping them talking. "Why? How?"

"Not being able to tell what's on your plate. How are you going to get to eat it?"

"Well, you could start by telling me what's on it. That would help, and I can't see anything spooky in that, can you?"

"It's cold ham, lettuce, tomato and bread and butter."

"Hi! Thank you. You must be Kevin."

"Go on then. Eat it, why don't you?" It was the same one who'd told me I was spooky.

"Heh! Give me a break here, folk. I'm getting to it as fast as I can."

"How did you get that way? I mean, that you can't see."

"Are you Sophie or Beth-Ann?"

"Sophie." So the one who found me spooky, had to be Beth-Ann.

"I was struck by lightning, Sophie."

"Wow! Cool!" Sophie again.

At least they were talking now, which was something, even if they were being cruelly blunt -- like small children.

"Actually, it wasn't that cool. In fact, it was pretty hot."

"That's funny!" Beth-Ann laughed. It wasn't a pleasant laugh. "You're funny!"

"Well, that's better than being spooky, I guess."

"You're American," Kevin announced. "Where are you from in America? My parents have a place in Florida. They spend the winter there."

"I don't know where I'm from, but where in Florida do your parents have a place?"

"Longboat Key."

"Oh, over on the Gulf side. Nice."

"You've been there?"

"I don't know."

The ice was broken at least, and I could feel their aggression drain away. Maybe it was going to be all right after all.

I'd been at the psychiatric unit for a week now, and each new day I had to start from scratch, trying to get to know my fellow inmates. There was no continuity, and my table mates were as suspicious of me at each new meeting as they had been at the first. I'd discovered too, that keeping myself in their favour meant playing childish games with them, and as these people weren't small children, but adults, they could get quite rough, and I dreaded it, but then I was, after all, in a psychiatric unit. Given the option I'd have much preferred being locked in my room, but as long as no-one was getting violent, that wasn't allowed -- not good for my mental state to be alone, I was told.

I also discovered that if I was going to be able to cope at all on a social level with these people, I'd need to develop a sense of humour about not being able to see -- difficult in that I was still trying to adjust to it in so many other ways as well. This meant that as long as they were being good-natured in their behaviour towards me, no matter how blunt or hurtful, then I'd have to learn to take it in the way it was intended.

Here, though, they behaved, as I said, like small children, rather than normal adults, and, like small children who throw a temper tantrum after being denied something, they could switch to aggressive bullying when things didn't go their way. This meant that, unable to see what was going on, I had instead to be constantly alert to any change in the atmosphere around me, and it was turning me into nervous wreck.

During that first week, I was told I'd be going on an outing somewhere that day, along with a group of other patients. The idea of being treated like other people not in their right mind, and being forced to walk and eat in public as one of them, made me cringe, and I balked at the idea, telling Alec I didn't want to go.

"Don't worry, Chris. It'll be fine. I'll be in charge of the group, and you can hold onto my arm."

"Please, no, Alec. Let me stay here. I really don't want to go." But he insisted, and an hour later I was in the bus.

Everyone was all hyped up with excitement, making it incredibly noisy, and those next to me kept leaping up and down, constantly jostling me. I'd no idea where we were, or where we were going, and wondered how Alec could possibly have thought that dragging me along like this was going to help me in any way. I was utterly miserable.

Eventually we piled out of the bus, and traipsed along for a while. I asked Alec where we were, but he had his hands full, making sure we all kept together, and didn't answer. Several times we came to a stop, and from the comments I heard on one occasion, it would seem we were passing a fairground, and some of the group were trying to persuade Alec to let them go on the rides.

Afraid to fight against it -- so making myself look as though I too was out of my mind -- and to my utter humiliation, I was set on a roundabout horse, where I spent what seemed like an eternity rising up and down, surrounded by screams of delight, the tinny sound of fairground music, and the smell of diesel fumes.

Later, we arrived at a place where we were to have lunch. I could smell frying fish and French fries, but wasn't in the slightest bit hungry, my stomach in too much of a knot, thinking about what other patrons would be thinking of us, and able to hear all too clearly their frequently unkind comments. For once I even felt protective of my fellow inmates, and was tempted to come very loudly to their defence; it wasn't their fault that Nature had dealt unkindly with them. If I could have seen my surroundings, I might well have done that, but given that I couldn't, and was in the middle of tables, chairs and all that was piled on them, I thought better of it, imagining the local newspaper headlines that might result: *"Blind Madman comes to Defence of Fellow Inmates, and causes Chaos."*

"You sit down here, Chris. I'll be right back. I'm just going to order lunch for everyone. Fish and chips okay?"

I nodded, but the cacophony of voices, scraping chairs, plates and cutlery, background music and outside traffic was turning into a blur in my head, and, starting to hyperventilate, could feel panic rising...

"Aren't you going to eat your fish and chips, Chris? You're going to be hungry if you don't."

"He's just been sitting there all this time, Alec, and he won't even answer us when we talk to him."

"Why would you do that, Chris? You're not in a bad mood just because I made you come with us, are you? That's not very sociable, is it?... Chris? I said, you're not just being awkward, are you, and refusing to eat your food too?"

I blinked. "What? I... uh... No-one's asked me anything that I know of, and why would I be awkward, as you put it? Refusing to eat my food? What food? I didn't know there was any there, and yes, I'd have eaten it if I'd known it was."

"Well, it's probably cold by now, and we're ready to leave. I'll get them to put it all in a doggy bag for you, and you can eat it on the way home in the bus."

"Thank you."

--------------------

We'd been at sea for about ten days, and I was sitting up on deck, not on duty specifically, but doing what I always did anyway, and that was looking for any signs something was coming loose, or not doing what it was supposed to do. My eyes on this occasion focused in on a stanchion that should have been rigid, but which was wobbling in its socket. To tighten it I needed a wrench, and remembering from my inspection of the boat that the tool box was stowed in the for'ard cabin under Gascoigne's bunk, I went below. He was lying there as usual, listening to his iPod.

"Excuse me a sec, Joe. I just need to get under your bunk for something."

"What! You keep out of my closet." He leaped off the bunk, and stood between me and the door, legs spread, arms folded, a belligerent expression on his face.

"But I need to get something from the toolbox in there. Besides, it's not your closet."

"What do you need? I'll get it for you."

"No, I can get it myself, thanks." I bent down to reach for the door, but he immediately planted himself right where I couldn't open it.

"I said I'd get it."

"Lay off, Joe. All I want is a wrench." I made another attempt to open the door, at which he suddenly kneed me in the groin, dropping me to the floor, and causing me to let out a loud yelp. Callahan and Roberts came racing down the companionway ladder, but Gascoigne had slammed shut the door of the cabin, locking them out, while I lay there clutching myself, groaning.

He kicked me in the ribs. "I'm sick to death of you ordering us around."

"Joe! For Christ's sake!" Steve was yelling from the other side of the door. "Stop it! We need him! What the hell are we going to do if he can't navigate? Use your head, man. You want to spend the rest of your life wandering around the Atlantic?"

Gascoigne gave an unpleasant grunt, and stood back, but it was a couple more minutes before I recovered enough to clamber to my feet. Physically I was in much better shape than he was, and was tempted to clobber him, but, anxious to avoid a fisticuffs on board a small boat in the middle of the ocean, I refrained. I was, even so, furious.

"Open the damn cabin door, Joe. Now!"

He opened it, allowing Steve to come in, and I bent over to open the closet, only to find the reason for his reluctance to have me open it myself. On the night before we set sail, after I'd fallen asleep, he'd obviously crept out, gone back to the bar, and come back with a crate of vodka -- presumably chosen because I'd be unable to smell it on his breath.

I pulled the crate out of the cupboard. There were ten half-gallon bottles left, which meant the man had already consumed the other two in our ten days at sea. I looked at the haul: no wonder he spent so much time in his bunk, as well as being morose and belligerent.

"This has to go." I lugged the heavy crate up the ladder, and was about to heave it overboard, when he lunged at me.

"And I say it's not going. What are you going to do about that, eh Yeats?" He punched me on the cheekbone, spinning me around, and knocking me forwards over the rail. Punching me with the crate still in my arms, though, had an effect contrary to what he wanted, because as I pitched against the rail I dropped the crate, and it fell into the sea, sinking at once.

"No! You bastard, Yeats!" The next minute the two of us were having an all-out fight, and as I was bigger, stronger and fitter, he lost, and ended up unconscious on the deck, no-one else having raised a finger to break up the fight.

I rubbed my knuckles. "Gee. Thanks for all your help, guys. Nothing like supporting your skipper."

I went below, washed my face and hands, then went back up on deck. Apart from a bruise on my cheek, I wasn't hurt, although I was still feeling the after-effects of the kick in the groin that Gascoigne had given me, so when he came around, I just sat there on the deck, staring at him until he got up and went below.

Now, for the first time since we'd set sail, I wished I'd not taken on the job after all, and there was still much of the Atlantic to be crossed. The thought came to me to turn around and head back to Massachusetts, but I was afraid that doing so might cause a mutiny with everyone against me, so continuing with the voyage seemed the lesser of two evils, and I put the idea out of my mind.

Steve coughed.

"Oh belt up!" I stood up, stepped over him, and went up as far for'ard as I could go, and stood there for the next hour, holding onto the rails on either side, and riding the bow up and down as it ploughed its way over the swell. It was cold there, and while I held onto the rail with my one hand, I put the other in my pocket to warm it, and expecting to find my cell phone in there as usual. It was wasn't there! I checked all my other pockets, but it was definitely gone, and I went back to Callahan and Roberts. "Has either of you seen my phone anywhere?

They shook their heads. "No."

I looked around, but it was nowhere to be seen. I knew I'd had it in my pocket right before my set-to with Gascoigne, so the only possibility was that it had slipped out and fallen overboard along with the vodka. I sighed. Could there possibly be anything else that could go wrong?

Even more fed up, I went below and lay down on my bunk, my hands behind my head, contemplating what I'd gotten myself into, and staring at the bulkhead against which my feet were resting.

When I'd come on board, I'd pinned up some photos of my friends that I'd taken on the day they'd held a special going-away party for me. I looked at their smiling and laughing faces, and wondered how they would feel if they could see me now. I tried not to think about what had just happened with Gascoigne, and let my mind think back to that day instead.

Being a native of the Narragansett Bay area, I had many friends there, mostly in the sailing community, and had been delighted to discover they'd decided to hold a going-away party for me. It would be the same as any of the other parties we often enjoyed on the Bay, the idea being that we'd all meet up on Dutch Island in the middle of the West Passage, and have a clambake, accompanied, of course, by plenty of booze.

Usually, we each took our own food and beer or liquor. On this occasion, though, I was to be treated, and as my own boat had been already prepared for the people renting my apartment, and I didn't want to mess it up again, I was ferried to the rendezvous in one of my friends' boats.

It wasn't far to Dutch Island, and when we arrived, someone had already been there for hours, heating up the stones and gathering seaweed for our clambake. As the morning went by, everyone else found their way to the island, and before long there were at least two dozen of us bunched together on a few square yards of the tiny isle -- alcohol already flowing freely as usual -- having left our offerings beside the stones, now heated through to a high enough temperature to cook everything.

Already the smell of steaming seaweed filled the air, and soon everything from corn on the cob, soft-shell clams, or "steamers," and small quahogs, or "littlenecks" as we called them, to lobsters, sausages and potatoes were arranged in the seaweed, and a large tarpaulin placed over the top to hold the heat in and cook everything.

My daydream was interrupted by banging behind my head. Gascoigne was up to something, probably suffering from alcohol withdrawal and hitting his head against the wall as a result. The harder, the better, I thought, and went back to my reminiscing.

It takes quite a while to cook a clambake, and during that time we swam, climbed around the island among the blackberry thorns and bayberry bushes, and got as high as kites, while our boats pulled at their anchors against the fast-flowing tide.

Thus the afternoon had passed, and we amused ourselves like a bunch of teenagers, and when all was cooked, gorged on all the goodies in our clambake. By the time we were through, the sun was setting on one side of us, and the full moon rising on the other, and we lounged around, waiting for *the effect of our afternoon's intake of liquor and food to wear off a bit, before wending our way back home.*

*I was glad now that on that day I'd taken my camera with me, and taken the trouble to create a photographic memory of the party -- photographs that I intended, even then, to take with me on this voyage.*

*The banging in the for'ard cabin had stopped, and the boat wasn't filling with water, so presumably Gascoigne hadn't been trying to sink us all out of spite, but I knew I could trust him even less now.*

--------------------

There were no more outings, for which I was thankful, but having to spend my days in that Tower of Babel called the communal room was getting increasingly difficult for me to deal with, my impatience with everything growing daily, especially when it came to their rowdy games in which they expected me to take part.

"Okay, guys. That's it. Give me a break, will you?" I put up my hands. "Come on. That's it. Enough. Give me a break, I said."

"He wants a break! He wants a break! What sort of break shall we give him?"

There was a sudden and dramatic change in the atmosphere, and someone punched me in the stomach, knocking me to the floor. I was afraid to shout or cry out, though, knowing that if I did, like dogs with a squeaky toy, they'd raise the level of attack, but the adrenalin was flowing now, their boisterous behaviour having deteriorated into outright aggression, and I remained there on the floor, curled up in foetal position, trying to protect myself, while complete chaos seemed to have erupted around me.

"Okay. That's enough! Cool it! Enough I said!" Alec came to my rescue, but then they turned on him as well, like sharks at a feeding frenzy. An alarm bell went off, and I stayed curled up, with my arms over my head, because although no-one was any longer taking any notice of me, there was every chance of my being trampled on in the mêlée, and I could feel my panic rising...

"Are you all right, Chris?... Chris?" It was Alec's voice.

"Uh... Yes, I guess so, but no thanks to you. How come you waited so long before stepping in? Surely you could see one of your so-called situations was brewing... And you didn't even come when someone clouted me. Where were you? I thought you were supposed to be watching us all."

"Well, I'd have got to you sooner, Chris, but we're a bit short-staffed right now, and a couple are off sick today as well, so we're stretched thinner than usual, and I can't be in two places at once. Anyway, you're not hurt, are you? So no harm done."

I brushed myself down. "I don't know what you count as 'harm', but I sure know now what was meant by telling me I was vulnerable. I don't feel safe at all here anymore."

Another carer came up. "Here, Chris. Drink this; it'll help you calm down."

I put up my hand, and accidentally knocked whatever it was out of his hand. "Sorry, I didn't mean to do that, but I don't need medication. If you want me to calm down, just sit here and talk to me for a few minutes."

"I'm sure we'd all love to sit around and chat with you, Chris, but we have other people to attend to as well, and don't have time for that. Would you like to go to your room for a while though? I can arrange for that, if you'd like."

I nodded. "Yes, I guess that would be better than nothing." And I ended up locked in my room for my own safety.

What had happened left me feeling even more scared and isolated, and I'd have given anything to be able to talk to someone of sound mind -- to have a normal conversation. I couldn't imagine ever having been bullied like that before, and was forced to admit to myself that it had truly frightened me, and left me wondering how I was going to be able face them again.

I stayed sitting on the edge of my bed until Alec came to fetch me for supper.

"I'd rather stay and eat it here, Alec, if you don't mind. I don't want to go down there amongst that lot again."

"Oh, you don't need to worry, Chris. Everyone has calmed down now. They'll have forgotten all about it."

"Maybe they have, but I haven't."

"I'm sorry, but you *will* need to eat in the communal room like everyone else. We can't go making special exceptions for each individual. Besides, you need to get over this. Pull yourself together."

"How about it then if you join us at our table for your supper? That would take the pressure off a bit."

"I'm sorry, Chris. I can't do that, but I'll keep an eye on you. Call out if you feel you're in trouble."

"You know very well I can't do that. If I show I'm afraid, they'll really have it in for me. Even *I* know that much."

"How about if I see if I can arrange for you to talk to our psychologist? Would that help you? Right now though, her schedule is running a few months behind, but I can put you down on the waiting list if you like."

"What on earth use is that? If I need help, I need it now, not in a few months' time. Besides, I hope to be gone from here in a few weeks, so as I said, what use is that?"

"Well, it's that or nothing, I'm afraid," and he led me down to the communal room again.

--------------------

*After the day of my set-to with Gascoigne, nothing went right. Making it even more difficult for me was that I had the impression that they all seemed to think the fault had been mine, although no-one came out and said as much. Whatever the case, the atmosphere aboard the boat was now abysmal, and I was feeling virtually isolated in my role as skipper and navigator. Even the boat itself appeared to have become jinxed, in that although it had been in such fine shape to start with, it now kept on producing a niggling succession of mostly minor, yet annoying little problems, none of which the rest of my crew ever noticed, leaving it up to me to be responsible for everything, and making me feel as though I might as well be sailing the Atlantic single-handed, for all the use they were. I'd even come to think of them as passengers, not crew at all.*

*One incident, though, was neither minor, nor niggling, but that wasn't the boat's fault in this case. I was taking my allotted four-hour sleep at the time. It was Callahan's watch, and he was supposed to be at the helm, when I was woken by the boat rolling, the head of the mast creating a wide and dangerous arc as the boat wallowed from side to side. It was,* in fact, because I was almost tipped out of my bunk, that I was woken, and I raced up on deck to see what was going on.

Callahan, not heeding what he was doing, had allowed the boat to go so far off the wind that she was sailing almost parallel to the waves, causing her to rock dangerously as each wave hit her broadside. I could see another one approaching that could easily cause her to broach, or capsize, and yelled at him to head her up. "Now!" I shouted when he hesitated. "Hurry man!" But he didn't seem to know what I meant, so I rushed up and grabbed the wheel from him, all the while watching the wave coming nearer, and struggling to deal with the mainsail at the same time, while my crew sat there, not knowing what, if anything they were supposed to do.

"Quick, Help me out here!" I yelled at Gascoigne, and watching the angle of the oncoming wave, fired off instructions regarding the mainsail. The boat responded quickly, and instead of the wave causing her to capsize, or do a complete rollover by hitting her broadside, she pitched into it instead, safely, but still steeply, drenching everything in the process.

"I thought you were supposed to know what you were doing," I yelled at Callahan. "Did you even think about what you were doing? What the hell did any of you think you were doing? Trying to drown us all? Look! Your hatch is open too, Joe. If I hadn't come up when I did, the boat would now be on its side, with all of us floundering in the sea. I can't stay at the wheel twenty-four seven. I need to sleep some time... You scared the living daylights out of me. I've got to be able to trust you... And by the feel of the boat, I'd say we've taken on a helluva lot of water. That's your job, Joe. Go see to it... Now!"

Gascoigne looked at me, expressionless, offering no apology. At least he took my harangue without attacking me for it. Instead, he simply brushed past me, and headed down the companionway to the cabin below as though nothing had happened. I looked at the other two, but it was like looking at a couple of zombies, with Roberts staring vacantly out over the rolling sea.

I now wished more than ever that I'd backed out when I'd had the chance that night when I'd nearly said goodbye to them in the restaurant car park, back in Marblehead.

It turned out that, because the hatch was open, gallons of water were dumped straight into the cabins, soaking everything, including our bunks, and the lower deck was awash. But at least the bilge pump was working, now that it had been switched on, and I was thankful that I'd made a point of putting my precious guitar in its waterproof case, or that would have been ruined.

Excessively tired and emotionally drained after all this, I'd have given anything for a good, worry-free sleep, but stayed at the wheel until the seas calmed down, afraid to leave the boat in their hands. Now that the crisis was over, I was surprised that even Roberts hadn't appeared to notice the danger. Were they all on drugs, or something? After all, Gascoigne had managed to hide his liquor stash from me, so maybe they'd hidden drugs on board as well.

While sitting there in silence at the wheel, another thing occurred to me, and that was that when I'd been woken up by the rolling of the boat, I'd noticed something else as well: they were all talking together, even Gascoigne. They had, moreover, been in the midst of an animated discussion, a real discussion -- an argument almost -- and I began to ask myself if this was what they always did while I was asleep, saving their other personas for when I was present. If this were the case, why would they consider it necessary to hide anything from me?

As a result, I now began to feel even more isolated, and was finding myself becoming as non-communicative as

*Gascoigne. It was an uncomfortable situation in which to be, and I wished the trip over as soon as possible, as now there was no enjoyment at all, the great grey Atlantic rollers adding to my disillusion with this trip.*

--------------------

It was the morning after the fracas, and Alec had come to my room to take me down to breakfast. I felt groggy, and wanted to go back to sleep.

He took hold of my arm, and pulled me up. "Come along Chris. I'm not surprised you're a bit tired this morning. You had quite a night last night, didn't you?"

"What do you mean? 'quite a night'?"

"Could be that what happened yesterday triggered it, but we had to come here to your room in the night to see to you after catching you on your CCTV, kicking off. You were very noisily and pretty crudely refusing to do something someone was ordering you to do. It seems they'd done something to you as well, and were backed up against the wall, frightened out of your wits, making it hard for us, because you seemed to think we were the ones attacking you."

"I wasn't violent towards you myself, was I?" I was really scared now that they would keep me here permanently if I started exhibiting any strange or aggressive behaviour.

"No, but we had to stay with you and keep an eye on you till you calmed down and we could get you back to bed and to sleep. You don't remember anything about any assault on you, or who these people might have been?"

"No to both questions, I'm afraid. Did you medicate me, though? It sure feels as though you did."

"No, we've been told to let you work your way through these things as long as you don't get in any way aggressive -- something about allowing your brain to try to sort itself out."

After that, I wished more than ever that they'd hurry up and get my assessment over as the longer I had to wait, the more I was afraid they'd find something wrong with me mentally, and end up keeping me here indefinitely. If they did wait too long, I was convinced they'd find me as insane as all the other inmates, as it was becoming ever more hard to get my brain to find stability.

After that one experience of being attacked, I never knew what was going to happen next, so remained ever on the alert, listening to changes in tone and for signs of more boisterous behaviour, which I now knew often preceded an attack of aggression. The slightest thing, I learned, could trigger what Miss Carmichael had called, 'a situation', and knowing that I couldn't simply walk out of the room and get out of the way when it happened, led to me being in this constant state of agitation. Even more now, I wished I could talk to someone! Even a normal visitor would have done, but I never had any visitors, and they were so short-staffed, appointments with professionals so far ahead, I was afraid I might really lose my own sanity before they ever got around to evaluating me.

The situation being as it was, I realised that hard to accept as it was going to be, I was on my own, and that it would be whatever strength of character I had that would have to sustain me and prevent me from succumbing to my fears. I'd heard of inmates absconding from psychiatric units; now I understood why.

The day of my assessment arrived at last, and I found myself sitting in front of another desk. It was a different room from Miss Carmichael's, this one smelling of a mixture of aftershave and fresh coffee. As on the day I first arrived, there was more paper rustling. "Hello Chris. I'm Dr. Fairchild."

"Oh! You're a woman!"

"Yes, Chris. Why? Do you have a problem dealing with women? It says here you weren't comfortable with Miss James. Do you prefer men?"

"Oh no! Please! Don't get me wrong. I don't have anything against women, if that's what you're thinking already. I was just expecting you to be a man for some reason, that's all."

"Are you nervous, Chris?"

"Well, yes, of course I'm nervous. Whatever conclusion you come to about me will determine my future, and I'd think that would be enough to make anyone nervous, wouldn't you?"

"Tell me a little bit about yourself, Chris."

"What do you want to know? Or, rather, what do you want to know that you don't already have written down there in front of you?"

"Maybe something about your likes and dislikes."

"That's hard for me to say. I can't remember what I used to like doing, and my recent memories seem to be all filled with dislikes. As you can imagine, not too many nice things have happened to me since I got myself into this situation, although obviously I'm happy that my cataracts are going to be removed soon -- I just wish they'd hurry up and do that."

"Would you like to talk about your dislikes?"

"Well, apart from this whole situation that I'm in, I obviously disliked the occasion when I was attacked here."

"Attacked? Who attacked you? When? I see here that you're prone to blackouts or hallucinations which you can't remember afterwards." There was more rustling of paper. "But I see nothing here about any attack, so this had to have been one of your hallucinations, don't you think, Chris?"

"That was no hallucination! Besides, if and when I do hallucinate, I don't remember anything about it afterwards as you've just pointed out, and this I remember all too clearly. It has to be in your notes there somewhere that I was punched by one of the patients here, and ended up on the floor in the middle of an angry mob. I'm not a coward, but it was a scary situation to be in, and I've since been afraid of it happening again."

"Are you *sure* it wasn't in your imagination, Chris? As I said, there's nothing here at all about you being attacked, or punched, as you say."

"*What*! It became a free-for-all! Don't they report things like that? Ask Alec. They turned on him too."

"Let's talk about something else, shall we? What...?"

"No. Let's not. Right now you're thinking I suffered an hallucination, or maybe that I have a persecution complex, or something. That's just not true."

"Yes, all right, Chris. There's no need to get worked up about it."

"I won't, just so long as when Alec comes to get me, we straighten this out with him. I don't understand why there's no record of it. I don't want you thinking I'm imagining things."

"All right then. How about you tell me what you think happened. Would that help?"

"I don't just *think* it happened. It *did* happen!"

"All right then, tell me what happened."

So I told her. It was impossible for me to know if she believed me, or not, but there wasn't anything I could do about that. I'd simply have to hope that Alec would corroborate my statement.

"Do you know anything about what's going on in the outside world?"

"Obviously I don't get to read the newspapers, but I did hear on the TV in the communal room that there's been a massive oil spill, and there are fears it might spread to the nearby coastline. That would be a terrible shame, and in a way I'm glad I can't see the damage it's doing to all the wildlife."

"What would you do if you could do something about it?"

"I honestly don't know. I know nothing about oil transportation, although, strangely, I seem to have a knowledge of the types of geology in which oil can be found. I suppose I'd try to help with the cleanup, like a lot of other people."

"Do you ever lose your temper, Chris?"

"Yes. Doesn't everybody?"

"Do you get violent when you lose your temper?"

"Only if someone attacked me first. I'd never get so cross that I'd clobber someone without provocation, if that's what you mean... although I'm not sure what I'd do if I saw someone mistreating a child or an animal... but then, I'm not sure anyone would know what they'd do in situations like that, do you? I'd certainly try to stop them, but I disapprove strongly of gratuitous violence, if that's what you mean."

"Do you feel the whole world is against you?"

"You mean, do I think everyone has it in for me? So you *are* thinking I suffer from a persecution complex! The answer is 'no'. Do I feel sorry for myself right now? Yes, I do. I think anyone in my situation would, but I don't consider it's anyone's fault. No-one did this to me. It's just my bad luck; it could have happened to anyone."

There were other probing questions, particularly with regard to my amnesia and that I'd been suffering from nightmares, flashbacks or hallucinations; they didn't seem to know which.

Paper rustled yet again. "All right, Chris. I think that's all I need to ask you. I'll get Alec to come and fetch you."

"Thank you."

The instant I heard the door open, I launched into him. "Alec, why is there no record of me being punched, and of you being attacked at the same time?"

"Oh that? If we made a record of every minor incident like that, we'd be forever writing reports, and we simply don't have the time for that."

"You call that minor? What on earth do you call a major incident here then? But you're not saying it didn't happen, are you?"

"Oh no. It happened, but no-one got hurt. Why do you ask?"

"It's all right Alec. Chris was afraid I didn't believe him, when he said he was punched."

"Oh, I see. That's all it was? Okay Chris. Let's go, shall we?"

"When will I know the result of my assessment?"

"I'll deliver a report to Miss Carmichael within the next week or so."

"Thank you. Goodbye."

"Goodbye Chris -- and good luck."

---------------------

*When we had started out on our voyage, I'd planned on going fairly far south, keeping well clear of the Great Circle*

*Route with its problems of storms, fog and ice, but not far south enough to get caught in a Bermuda high. I'd thought too to perhaps take advantage of the Gulf Stream, assuming the wind was right and we didn't get caught up in too many of its quirky eddies, which could get us into trouble. Now, though, hoping to speed things up and get this voyage over as quickly as possible, I began edging as far north as I dared, while still trying to stay on the good side of the lows, and dodging potential bad weather where possible -- almost an impossibility in the Atlantic. Luckily, the winds were in our favour, and not having experienced any bad storms so far, we were making good time, and now, after a number of days' sailing, were nearing the southwest coast of Ireland.*

*I'd just finished taking my four hours off, and had to admit that during that time I had, as usual, been in a deep sleep, so had set my alarm, not trusting anyone to remember to wake me up. Roberts had been on watch while I was asleep, and the boat on autopilot.*

*Still not yet fully awake, I clambered up the companionway ladder onto the deck. It was deserted. Assuming Roberts was in the head, I thought nothing of it, but then, when he still hadn't appeared after fifteen minutes, I went back down to see if he'd gone straight from the head to his bunk. He wasn't in either place. He'd disappeared!*

*I shouted to the other two, but when they joined me on deck, they were as mystified as I was. Roberts was nowhere to be found -- a disaster of the first magnitude.*

*"He must have gone overboard," Callahan remarked, giving his usual nervous cough.*

*"Of course he's bloody-well gone overboard. And we don't know when he went either. I know he's been gone at least twenty minutes, but he could have gone any time in the last four hours!"*

I brought the boat about, but knew it was useless to try to find him. The Atlantic was frigid, and he'd be long-since dead. Besides it was almost dark now. Even so, I felt I had at least to search for him, and spent the next four hours attempting to retrace our steps, knowing that was impossible. Of course there was no sign of him. In the meantime, I tried to raise the Irish Coast Guard, but, to compound matters, our entire communication system had died, including backup, and nothing would bring any of it to life. There wasn't anything to do, but continue on our way, and call in at the nearest port to report the event, and I set a course for Cork.

I wasn't a man to lose my composure at the slightest thing; it was one of the reasons people liked to have me as a crew member -- because I stayed calm in a crisis. Never before, though, had I ever been on a boat where someone had been lost overboard, and now, as skipper, I felt responsible, although I'd in no way acted irresponsibly -- not that I could think of anyway.

I spent hours anguishing over it, asking myself if there had been anything I could, or should have done to prevent such a disaster, but even though I came to the conclusion that I couldn't have prevented it, it didn't help, and I felt anxious in a way I'd never felt before.

Not being able to summon help either, was adding to my anxiety, and I couldn't wait to get to Cork to be able to unload my burden, imagining over and over again the sceptical reception we'd receive when we tried to explain that a man had fallen overboard in broad daylight, and none of us had even noticed! Would they believe us? Would they even think we'd murdered Roberts? And the thought was eating away at me.

Callahan, with his nervous cough, tried to calm me. "Look, Col. It's not your fault. Bob must have leant over the side for some reason, and lost his balance, poor guy."

"I can't think why that could possibly have happened. It isn't as though the sea was particularly rough, and he should have been tethered anyway. You can't remember him screaming, or anything? Not that that helps us any now, I guess."

"Didn't hear a thing," Gascoigne said. "But then, when I'm plugged into my I-Pod, I don't hear anything else… Too bad. A nice guy too."

"I don't give a shit how nice, or how nasty he was. The truth is that we've lost a man overboard, and that's a total disaster! And I still think the authorities are going to be sceptical when we try explaining it to them."

Callahan patted me on the shoulder. "Well, there's nothing we can do now, Col, except get to Cork asap, and see what happens."

"Even so…" I sighed. This had all become too much, even for me, the supposedly level-headed, calm man.

--------------------

Another week passed, and I was really worried because I'd heard nothing further regarding any of my problems.

"These things take time," Alec told me, but I was on tenterhooks all the same.

My assessment report having reached her desk at last, I was back in Miss Carmichael's musty office again, and it was almost impossible for me to contain my anxiety while she rustled papers and muttered sotto voce comments to herself in readiness to giving me the news. In the meantime I gleaned a little bit more information about the room. There was a smell of wet dog. It didn't seem as though it was still there, though, and I wondered if it had been hers, or another therapy dog like Paddy had been. I missed Paddy's visits – Miss Atkins too.

"Well, Chris," she said after what seemed like an inordinate amount of time, "I'm delighted to let you know you've been found to be of sound mind, no threat to society, and to be suffering from general dissociative amnesia with symptoms of post-traumatic stress disorder resulting from some unknown traumatic experience or experiences."

"Thank God for that!... That I'm of sound mind, I mean, although it would be nice to know where all the rest comes from."

"Right, Chris, we're over that hurdle. I've already spoken to Miss James, and she's arranging for you to be taken to a respite home, where you can stay for a maximum of six weeks. Hopefully, some of your physical problems will be resolved by then, or your relatives will have found you, but we'll have to wait and see. At the moment there are no vacancies anywhere, but we'll make sure you get the first place available."

"Thank you."

To be found of sound mind, and not considered to be a threat to anyone, including myself, brought home to me how afraid I'd been that I might not have passed the test. Even with that no longer hanging over me, though, as long as I stayed here in the psychiatric unit I still faced the risk of being attacked, and waiting for the day I left this place was becoming almost unbearable in that I still was obliged to keep myself in favour with those around me.

As I said before, I never knew when the atmosphere was going to change, the characters of the patients being so volatile and dependent on so many variables. Anything could set them off, and only the previous day Beth-Ann had smashed everything on the table, when told to take her medication. I dared not refuse to take part in their games either, as that could set them off too, but it was mentally exhausting, and the only escape was to ask to be taken to the peace and quiet of my own room. Even that was never granted, though, unless the atmosphere was getting to be what they liked to call 'boisterous'. The lack of understanding on the part of the carers was beyond me -- or, if it wasn't a lack of understanding, then perhaps they were being forced into slavishly following official guidelines, regardless of the situation. Either way, it was taking its toll on me emotionally, if not physically, and I was finding it hard not to succumb to it all, and sink into depression.

During this waiting period, another situation came up; Kevin took a liking to me, and insisted on telling me all about himself.

"I can't stand to see things suffering. If I see something suffering, I just have to put it out of its misery."

"Well, there's nothing wrong with that, I suppose, Kevin. I'd put an animal out of its misery too, if I thought it was suffering, and not likely to survive."

"Yes! I killed a seagull once. It's wing was broken and couldn't be fixed, so I hit it on the head with a rock, and killed it... Then our neighbour got all riled up with me, because I killed her cat. I told her it was suffering, but she didn't believe me. I could see it in its eyes; it was just asking me to put it out of its misery."

"What was wrong with it? Had it been run over, or something?"

"No. I could just see it in its eyes. It came into our garden, and came up to me, and was rubbing itself against my leg, begging me. So I picked up a spade and killed it."

"Oh... How about telling me instead about some nice things you've done, Kevin."

"I just did. Then, everyone got really mad with me, because there was this kid..."

"Kevin, I really don't want to hear this. Why don't you go find out how long it'll be till lunchtime, yes?"

"Oh, okay." For once, it was a relief to be left, sitting, staring into space with nothing to do -- or at least until my other fellow inmates decided otherwise.

Kevin decided that not only did he like me, but wanted to act as my protector as well, and asked permission to take me outside with him. This was granted, so we started going for walks together around the grounds. I had to admit that this was a welcome change to being confined to that awful communal den.

I think it must have been Kevin's voice that made me assume he was a rather skinny guy. It had a high-pitched, reedy tone to it, so I was surprised when he put my hand on his arm to walk me around. The man was built like a tank! "Do you do weight lifting, Kevin? You strike me as being a mighty strong guy. Wouldn't like to tangle with you," I joked.

"Oh yes. Feel my biceps, then." He took my hand and put it on his muscle, and he was right; he *was* strong, and I imagined the carers would have quite a time of it if he ever got out of control.

"I'm a very gentle giant though, Chris. I'm very caring, and I'll take care of you."

"That's very kind of you, Kevin. I appreciate it." What else could I say?

After that he saw to it that when we were in the communal room, I wasn't bullied, which I did appreciate, because when he saw trouble brewing, he steered me clear. There was a price to pay, though, as he seemed to have found in me an ersatz psychoanalyst, talking to me constantly about his problems. It wasn't an easy role for me, as I had to be careful not to give my layman's opinions, thus risking affecting his behaviour adversely.

He also wanted to know everything about me as well, asking me question after question, as though my situation was of particular concern to him. Sometimes his questions were unsettling, making it difficult for me to keep giving him upbeat answers, which he frequently countered with "Yes, but…," and it was uncanny how accurately he could pinpoint my true feelings, fears and anxieties.

"Yes, but what if you never get your memory back? Never find out who you are, or about your loved ones? You must be awfully lonely, not having someone close to you -- a relative or someone. I don't know what I'd do if my parents weren't always there for me. I couldn't handle it."

He was right. I didn't have anyone close to me to turn to, and to have him express it outright like that, caused my stomach to lurch downwards. "Yes, I'm so glad you have your parents to be on your side, Kevin. It must make it a lot easier for you."

"What about your sight too, Chris? What if, when they go to do the surgery, they discover there's damage to your retinas, or something, and you'll never ever see anything again? What'll you do then?"

"Can we talk about something else, please Kevin? If I always look on the downside, I'm going to be depressed, and that won't do... I can smell flowers. What are they?"

"I don't know. They're spikey things. I don't know much about flowers. I'm more interested in people and what makes them tick. I've been told I'm empathetic, you know. Too empathetic, some say… Going back to you though, Chris, you've no money, no job, no prospects, no real name even. You don't have anything as far as I can tell. What are you going to do when they turn you out of the respite home? What'll you do then? How will you survive? It makes me shudder to think of it."

"I'm sure that, in this country, no-one would ever turn me out onto the streets, Kevin. After all, I wouldn't be able to move any further than their own doorstep. Besides, they just wouldn't do it... How about telling me where we're walking. I get the impression it's more like a park than a parking lot, am I right?"

"Yeah. Lots of trees and shrubby things -- flower beds and all that. Tell me, Chris. What's it like to not see anything? I've tried walking around with my eyes closed, just to imagine what it's like for you. I couldn't live like that..."

My protection was coming at a high price, and now I didn't know which was worse: being bullied by the others, or being depressed by Kevin. It was as though he was taking an almost obsessive interest in my welfare, and that, of itself, made me uneasy.

--------------------

*To my added consternation neither Gascoigne nor Callahan seemed to show any particular emotion over the loss of their shipmate, nor did they show any particular anxiety over the fact that we now all had to face questioning by the authorities -- most likely highly sceptical authorities at that. For me, this tragedy, and all it was going to entail, had made it even more difficult to bear, because the worry was keeping me awake when I should have been getting my sleep, and fatigue could lead to mistakes, and the middle of the Atlantic Ocean* wasn't the place in which to make mistakes. As navigator, if for no other reason, it was essential that I stayed alert, and not allow us to sail into trouble, especially as my so-called crew were of no help at all, leading me to wonder, not for the first time, why on earth their other skipper could have been so enthusiastic about their nautical expertise.

To add even further to my problems, the wind had changed, making me tack frequently, so reducing the number of miles covered, and increasing the length of time it was taking us to reach Cork. One thing I was sure of, though, and that was that even if the authorities didn't prevent us from continuing our voyage, as far as I was concerned Cork would be it; I was going no further, and with this prospect of an official enquiry hanging over me as well, the whole trip had now become a complete nightmare.

Time now seemed to crawl, and we had covered barely another two hundred miles after losing Roberts overboard. I'd just come off yet another of my sleepless four-hour rests, and was sitting up on deck, prior to taking over from Gascoigne. I was struggling to focus my brain in readiness for my night watch, when Callahan poked his head out of the companionway door, and asked me if I wanted a cup of tea.

"I'd prefer coffee, please, Steve. Strong. Thanks."

A few minutes later he appeared with the steaming and welcome mug of coffee, and I sat there with my hands wrapped around it, feeling chilled throughout my body -- caused by fatigue, as I was well dressed. It was a pity, I thought, that I wasn't now due for my four-hour time off, rather than just had it, as the warmth of the coffee was making me feel sleepy, and given the chance, I was sure I could now have a good sleep finally. In fact, I was so tired I thought that if left alone at the wheel the way I felt, I ran the risk of falling asleep on my watch. I even began to wonder if I was navigating properly; it didn't do to let the mind wander when trying to take all the variables into account.

This wouldn't do; I could put us all in danger if I literally fell asleep at the wheel, so decided to ask Callahan if he'd mind filling in for me for an hour or so. Even one hour would help. It was something I'd not done at all during the rest of the voyage, so it wasn't a case of my slacking off, and I did have the safety of us all in mind. It was fairly plain sailing at that moment too, so I went ahead and asked him.

"Sure, Col. You look as though you could do with a bit of a shut-eye. Go on. It's not quite dark yet, and I'll call you when it is."

I put the boat on auto, and went below. Despite feeling incredibly drowsy, however, I was so anxious, I still couldn't fall asleep, and just lay there, eyes closed, trying to relax. Above me, I could hear the murmur of their voices on deck. They were talking earnestly again. The only time I remembered them carrying on any sort of lengthy conversation such as this -- let alone one with the business-like tones I was hearing now -- was when we nearly had our roll-over. I listened, but the sound of the wind in the rigging allowed only the odd word or two to reach me.

"I wish we knew... hit... take place." It was Gascoigne's voice. "Damned if I... Skibbereen... assignment... don't even know who... where the hell... target... let us..."

"They haven't told... how soon even... get ourselves killed..."

"... worry, Steve... ricin... syringe... easy... not suicide..."

"...navigate... contact Ireland... Yeats knows we ditched Bob?... spiked his coffee well... can't afford to let him... too damn clev..."

"Yeah... sleeping... baby..." Callahan's nervous cough.

I slipped quietly off my bunk and crept towards the companionway. Roberts had not fallen overboard! They had murdered him! Ricin! There was only one thing that ricin was used for that I knew of -- assassinations! Georgi Markov had been murdered with it using the point of an umbrella. No wonder Callahan had drugged me! I wasn't supposed to hear any of this!

I listened carefully. They were talking to someone else now, which also meant that they had put the communication system out of order specifically to prevent me from reporting Roberts's death, and had now resuscitated it so as to make contact with some other people, presumably also in on whatever it was they were planning to do.

Now Gascoigne was telling his contact that he'd let him know when and at what co-ordinates they would need to be picked up. He was speaking more quietly now, but I could still hear some things: "Ireland... Ricin again... Ditch Yeats before he..." They were going to murder me as well! What the hell had I gotten myself into?

I still couldn't pick up everything, so crept as close to the bottom of the companionway ladder as I dared without being seen.

"As for damned Yeats, the bastard needs teaching a lesson after ordering me around like that with that damn Bostonian accent of his, and then giving me the clobbering he gave me over the vodka, and I'm going to make sure he gets it. Just dumping him overboard is too good for him. Im going to see to it that he..."

"You forget, Joe," Callahan interrupted him. "Yeats is a pro. He doesn't need us at all. We should really stick to orders, tie him to the anchor, and shove him overboard when we reach the pickup point. If we don't, he's perfectly capable of sailing this thing to the Antipodes on his own, let alone the few miles left now to Cork. Think about it; he'll scupper everything if he gets there."

"He won't be capable of getting anywhere if we leave him the way I plan to leave him. He can go through hell for all I care, before he finally kicks the bucket."

"Well. You're the boss, Joe. I just take orders, so whatever you decide, I'll go along with, but I still think it'd be safer if we made sure he goes under and doesn't come back up..." Callahan coughed. "By the way, you don't suppose, do you, that he's heard any of this by any chance? That he's woken up, and been listening to us?... although I did give him a pretty stiff dose. Even so, if he has even the slightest suspicion about what this damn voyage is really all about, he's the sort that'll do everything he can to stymie us -- you forget, Joe; I know this guy... Yeah, maybe I'd just better go check on him, just in case... I don't trust him not to..."

"What! I thought you said the bastard was sleeping like a baby! Goddam it!"

I heard someone lunging towards the companionway, and tried to scramble back into my bunk, but it was too late.

"What the hell? Goddam you, Yeats! Steve! Come down here! Now!"

I stood backed up against the side of my bunk, fists knotted, waiting for Gascoigne's attack, but, my reactions slowed by the amount of narcotic in my system, I was caught off balance when he grabbed hold of me and knocked me backwards, my head banging against the bulwark, stunning me.

"The bastard's been listening in to everything!" Gascoigne roared, and still holding onto me, pulled me towards him. "I've a good mind to chuck you overboard right now after all."

Callahan gave yet another of his nervous coughs. "We can't do that yet. We can't get to the pickup point unless he navigates for us."

I wrenched my arm away from Gascoigne. "He's right. You're going nowhere without me. You may have murdered Bob Roberts, but right now you need me. As Steve has so generously pointed out, I'm your navigator, and for your information, I've no intention of taking you anywhere near any damn pickup point, so you might just as well go ahead and pitch me overboard right now anyway. I'll not help you commit any act of terrorism, and I'm heading straight for Cork. What you do after that is up to you."

"Oh yes you <u>will</u> navigate for us, Yeats. At least, you will unless you want me to chop off your fingers one at a time. We've trained too long for this to let some damned war hero like you ruin it now."

Gascoigne pulled a flick-knife out of his jeans' pocket, snapped it open, and tried to seize hold of my arm again, but I was holding onto the edge of my bunk with both hands, so raised both legs, and rammed him in the stomach with my feet. He grabbed hold of one of my legs, while Callahan seized the other, and with me now on the floor, they dragged me over to the navigation table, where they forced me into the chair.

"Now! You swamp Yankee bastard! Set a course for these coordinates." Gascoigne slapped a piece of paper down in front of me.

I shook my head, and Gascoigne, who had hold of my right hand, slammed it, palm down, on the table. "Now!" he shouted at me, and before I could say or do anything, he drove the point of the knife down on my index finger, severing it completely. "How's that for starters, eh, Yeats?"

--------------------

The news arrived at last that I'd be going to the respite home the following Sunday. It was now Wednesday, and even though I wasn't sure what a respite home was, I was convinced it had to be an improvement over the psychiatric unit. For all his good intentions, Kevin's attentions were becoming ever harder to live with, so getting away from him would be a relief in itself.

It was Saturday night -- my last night in the psychiatric unit -- and Alec was taking me up to my room as usual. "I hear you'll be leaving us tomorrow, Chris. Good for you. I know it's not been a pleasant time for you here, but you're obviously a survivor and made of strong stuff. You've handled it all very well, and it's been a pleasure to know you."

"Thank you."

"Not at all...Well, good night. Sleep well."

"Good night, Alec."

I sat down on my bed, undressed down to my underpants, in which I slept, never having acquired any pyjamas along the way, and let out another sigh. They came from deep down inside me, and I was glad the CCTV camera in my room had no listening device -- at least, I assumed it didn't.

I went into the bathroom. There was no bathtub, presumably because they were afraid I might try to drown myself, but there was a shower, and after yet another of Kevin's depressing sessions in which, as usual, he'd kept reminding me about my uncertain future, I felt I needed one. Falling asleep while thinking about all his dire predictions, all of which I knew were reasonable possibilities, was impossible. I removed my underpants, and turned on the shower.

"Hello Chris."

"Kevin! What are you doing here? How did you get in?"

"I've been waiting for you -- waiting for Alec to bring you. Poor Chris. You can't even find your own room without help. It's just too sad."

"Oh, please, Kevin. Enough already. No more. I know what my life is like. I really don't need you to keeping impressing it on me…You shouldn't be here, you know. What if they see you on the CCTV camera? And Alec's locked the door too. How are you going to get out?"

"I don't need to get out, and I've covered over the CCTV camera. I've thought so much about you these last weeks, Chris, and I've decided I like you far too much to allow you to continue to suffer as you do."

"What the heck are you talking about? Yes, my life's a bit difficult right now, but I wouldn't call it suffering. You don't hear me complaining, do you?"

Kevin put his ham-sized hand on my shoulder. "Ah, Chris. Of course you're suffering. I've watched you on the CCTV camera when you're here in your room. I heard you just a few minutes ago, sighing. I watch you struggling with your handicaps every day. I know you don't complain. That's what makes you so heroic."

"Heroic! Nonsense Kevin. Heroic I most certainly am not."

He put his arms around me, and gave me a hug. I'm a big man, but Kevin was built like a bear, and almost took my breath away. I was beginning to get scared too. Why had he covered the CCTV camera? How had he been able to spy on me? And what was it he'd just said that sounded so ominous?

"What are you doing here, Kevin? Surely you didn't come just to tell me I'm heroic. What's this about not allowing me to continue to suffer? I hope you…"

"As I said, Chris. I've been thinking a lot about you these last weeks. It just isn't right that you're made to suffer like you do. It's so unfair, especially for someone as nice as you, and I've come, as your friend, to put you out of your misery." He clutched my shoulder as though to make me understand the depth of his concern for me.

I was backed up against the entrance to the running shower, and what he'd told me earlier about his neighbour's cat now took on a new meaning. "Heh! Hang on there, Kevin! Put me out of my misery? For Christ's sake! What the hell are you saying? You've come here to kill me?"

I put up my arms to ward him off, and felt something brush past my upheld hands. The knife was so sharp I didn't even feel it, but immediately felt my blood starting to pour out, warm and sticky. Kevin had slashed my wrists.

"Kevin!" I backed up, fell over the step into the shower, and ended up sitting on the floor, water pouring down on me, washing away my blood down the drain. I was too shocked to shout for help. No-one would hear me anyway, and the emergency cord was over near the bathroom door.

"You made that easy for me, Chris. I'd been wondering how I was going to get to do that. I'd figured out, you see, that that would be the kindest way to have you die. You'll basically just go into a deep, comfortable sleep… And please don't say I'm killing you. That sounds terrible. What I'm doing is called euthanasia, Chris."

"Kevin! I don't give a shit what you call it! I don't want to *die*!" I tried to stand up, but he'd joined me in the shower, and was standing over me, pushing me down. The floor was slippery too, making it impossible for me get any purchase with my bare, wet feet, which simply slid out from under me.

"There, Chris." Kevin stroked my head with his bear paw. "Don't worry. It's all for the best. I'll stay with you till the end. I'll keep you company. I couldn't watch you suffer anymore. I'm doing this for you. I like you too much to see you carry on with the horrible existence you have…You're too good a person. I couldn't let it happen. Please don't struggle, Chris. It'll make it harder for you. I want this to be peaceful. I've thought so much about this. At least your last moments will be calm, and you'll know you have a true friend at your side. You're so beautiful too, much too beautiful to deserve to lead the life you've been leading."

I was still struggling to get up, but with Kevin standing over me, along with the slippery floor, it was impossible, and I sank back down. "Oh my God, Kevin, please! No! I beg you. Don't do this. Pull the emergency cord! Please!" I tried to push him away. "How can I explain it to you? Whatever life I've got, I prefer it to being dead. Please pull the emergency cord. Please, Kevin."

I could already feel the effects of losing so much blood, and was feeling dizzy. If I blacked out, it would be the end of me, and I made another tremendous effort to stand up, but my blood was flowing steadily, and it was already beyond me. It wouldn't be long before I fainted. Was this going to be the end of me? Bleeding to death in a shower in a mental home somewhere in Wales, with a maniac petting me as though I'm a beloved dog he's putting to sleep?

"Kevin. Please listen to me. Please." I tried to get my brain to think of rational arguments to present to him, but it had gone into panic mode, and I could think of nothing except that I was going to die.

He was speaking to me. His tones were soothing, but I was no longer listening to the words, and my energy was draining fast. His hand was on my shoulder, smoothing it, and considering his size, I was aware he was being as gentle as he knew how. He was right in one regard, though; it was, in an odd way, peaceful. I was going to die, and that was all there was to it, and my brain switched off, leaving me floating in a strange limbo in which time no longer had meaning.

I felt Kevin move so that he was now sitting next to me under the shower, his arm around me. He pulled me towards him so my head was resting on his shoulder. It was almost comforting, and I began to drift in and out of consciousness.

There were other voices now, and I tried to concentrate on them.

By the sound, it seemed Kevin was in tears. "You understand, don't you? I had to do it. Poor Chris. I felt so sorry for him. I could tell he was begging to be put out of his misery. I didn't want to do it. I love him, but it's because I love him I needed to do it. You wouldn't keep a pet in his state, would you? It's so very sad." He was stroking my head again, and weeping. "Look at him. He's at peace at last, or nearly so. Just give him a few more minutes with me. It'll soon be over, and he'll be gone from us."

He clutched me tighter, and buried his face in the top of my head, rocking me in his arms. "Oh my poor dear, beautiful Chris! So sad! So very sad it has to be this way."

I drifted off again, then revived when I heard Alec's voice.

"Kevin. You've done what you feel you needed to do. Why don't you leave Chris to us now? You wouldn't want him to die, lying there in a shower, would you? Let us at least take him and put him in a nice, comfortable bed where he can die in peace. You can come too. That's it. You can give me the knife now; you don't need it anymore. Thank you, Kevin."

I tried to raise my head, but it was firmly clamped to Kevin's shoulder by his huge hand.

"There, you see Kevin? Chris agrees. Come on. The shower has gone cold. You wouldn't want this for him, would you? He must be most uncomfortable on that hard, wet floor with all that cold water pouring down on him. We know you have his best interests at heart, so let us take him. We can do now what you can't. You've done all you could to help him."

Kevin moved away from me, and began laying me down with immense care, until my head was resting on the shower floor.

"That's right, Kevin. You've done the right thing. Come with us. You can help us prepare a special bed for Chris," and the sound of Kevin weeping retreated into the distance.

--------------------

*I sat up on deck, hunched over, clutching my mangled hand, and finding it hard to accept that Callahan could have veered so far from his life as an ordinary grad student, that he'd shown no qualms about having tricked me into coming on this trip, already knowing how they planned to make use of me, and then helping Gascoigne cut off my finger.*

*Having thought over the pros and cons of taking them to where they wanted to go, I was now at the wheel, and headed towards the coordinates they'd demanded. My reasoning for going along with them had been that if, once there, they did set me adrift as Gascoigne had threatened to do, I still had every chance of reaching land in time to notify the* authorities. The other alternative was, of course, to refuse to navigate no matter what Gascoigne did to me. The problem with that was that, although they were unaware of it, I knew they were already close enough to the rendezvous for their co-conspirators to have little difficulty finding us anyway, in which case I'd nothing to gain by subjecting myself to even more torture.

I looked around, and decided that there was, perhaps, one other option worth considering as well, but we were so close to their rendezvous now, I'd have to act quickly, and hope that there were was other shipping sufficiently close by to notice.

The sea was relatively calm, the wind light; Gascoigne was sitting on deck, head down, preoccupied with fiddling with some electronic device that I could only partially see, so couldn't tell what it was, and Callahan was lying on one of the deck cushions, gazing up at the sky. Maybe, I thought, just maybe, I could pull this off. I let go of the wheel. "I need to go to the head."

Gascoigne glanced up. "Hurry up about it then."

I left the unmanned boat turning slowly into the wind, and climbed down the companionway steps. Once on the lower deck I went aft to where Gascoigne's bunk was, pulled one of the red parachute distress rockets out of the closet beneath it, tucked it under my jacket, clambered back on deck, and started to head for'ard.

"Heh! Where do you think you're off to? Come back here!" Gascoigne shouted at me.

"I noticed a bolt coming loose up near the bow, and need to check it out."

I went as close to the bow as I could, then, my back to both men, pulled the rocket out from under my jacket, and set about trying to fire it, something that could be tricky at the best of times, but now made even more difficult because of my injured hand, which prevented me from getting a firm grip on the tab. I was still fumbling with it when Gascoigne lunged at me.

"What the hell do you think you're doing? Steve! Help me here... Quick!"

I used all my strength to prevent Gascoigne from wrenching the flare out of my grip, and as I'd already proved on the voyage, I was much stronger than he was, but now with the rocket in my left hand, and my right one in no state for me to put up any sort of fight, it was inevitable that when Callahan grabbed hold of my ankles and yanked me off my feet, my plan was going to fail. Unable to hold onto the flare, I watched it first fall to the deck, then roll, unfired, into the sea.

I saw Gascoigne's fist coming, but with Callahan still holding onto me, couldn't avoid it, and when I came to, I had my back to the mast, my hands tied behind me.

Over the following hour I saw all hope of reporting anything to the authorities disappear as the two men methodically destroyed all my navigation tools, and smashed the communication system along with everything else that might help me navigate or call for help, and a short while after that a powerful RIB roared into view, two men on board.

Looking at it as it came alongside, I recognized it as the civilian version of the Zodiac Hurricane, used by Navy Seals and the US Coastguard, and powered by two huge 250 hp engines. This was no amateur operation!

By this time Gascoigne and Callahan had stripped our sailboat of everything bar the sails and steering mechanism, and while the two other men waited, staring at me and laughing, my last two crew members prepared to abandon both the sloop and me, its one remaining occupant.

Gascoigne's last act before leaving was to take my guitar out of its case. He held it up. "As a gesture of generosity, I'll leave you this, although you sure ain't going to *play it like you used to, I bet."  And he tossed it down the companionway stairs.*

*I watched it disappear, and as it smashed against the bulkhead felt a jab in my arm, and looked up to see Callahan holding a syringe.*

---

I was back in hospital, having been told I almost didn't survive Kevin's attempt at a mercy killing, and had been there just over a week, when Alec came to see me.

"Hi Chris! Good to see you coming along so well. I hear you'll be going into the respite home in a few days -- only two weeks later than originally planned. Not bad considering, eh?"

I'd been hoping someone from the psychiatric unit would come to see me, and my fury at what they'd allowed to happen to me had been festering in the meantime, so I was more than ready to show just how angry I could get.

"How did what happened, get to happen at all? How was it that someone like Kevin was allowed anywhere near me? He's totally insane! I'm sorry, but someone goofed up big-time, and it nearly cost me my life. It's inexcusable."

"Yes. It's true. Mistakes were made, but lessons have been learnt."

"*Mistakes*! Is *that* what you call them? *Lessons have been learnt*? What sort of lessons do you teach in that place? Hands-on practicals, with me as the guinea-pig? Did you take notes, then write papers on me? Gee -- this lesson taught us that we fucked up royally with the poor slob! How could you possibly have let Kevin run free like that, given his history? How did he get to watch the CCTV cameras? Spy on me in my room? How did he get hold of that knife? And how, after all that, did you conveniently manage to arrive in time to only just save my life? Were you watching the whole process on CCTV, leaving it to play out as long as you dared, just so you could see what lessons you could learn by letting me almost die?"

"Yes, I can see that you might consider it a failure in our duty of care to our service users, Chris, and feel justifiably annoyed."

"*Failure in your duty of care! Service users*! Is that all I am? A goddamned service user? Annoyed? I'm damn livid! Heads should roll because of your abysmal failure in your duty of care to this service user!"

"Yes, well, of course, the investigation is ongoing, so I can't say much, except perhaps that someone was remiss in not operating according to his or her remit."

"*Remiss in not operating according to his or her remit*! What the hell does that gobbledygook mean? Remit in my book means sending payment for a bill you've received."

"In this country it means the work someone is supposed to do."

"Oh! You mean their job description. I just love the euphemistic jargon: 'duty of care', 'remit'. Very fancy -- and in my book, totally meaningless. And I'd say it's not a case of *perhaps* someone was remiss; someone was *definitely* remiss. Was Kevin even taking his medication?"

"Well, I didn't come here to discuss that. I thought you might like to know how, in fact, we did end up saving you."

I could see I wasn't going to get anywhere with Alec, who was obviously intent on protecting himself and the psychiatric unit by hiding behind official jargon. I'd pretty much said all I intended saying anyway, so capitulated. "Okay.

Go ahead. I suppose you're going to tell me anyway. How did you?"

"Well, the staff – that's the staff not on duty -- were sitting in the staff room. The boiler is right next to us, so we hear when it kicks in and goes off. It's summertime, so there are no radiators to heat, so the only heating to be done is of water for washing, showers, etcetera. Then someone noticed it wasn't turning off, and as no-one was -- or should have been -- showering at that time of night, we wondered why it was still running. Someone then went to look at the CCTV cameras, and noticed yours wasn't showing up, and none of the other showers were in use, so we immediately came to investigate, and found…Well, you know what we found."

"I'll admit you were pretty savvy in the way you talked Kevin into relinquishing his post as my saviour. It could have gone either way. Where is he now?"

"In a secure psychiatric ward for the foreseeable future. Anyway, how are you? Everything healing all right? I'm told there was no nerve or ligament damage to your wrists."

I wiggled my fingers. "Yep. Everything seems to be working okay, although I'm told there'll be some scars that'll give the impression I've tried to do myself in. Maybe I should get a written statement from you in case someone asks in future."

Alec laughed. "Right then…. Well, I'm off. Glad you're okay."

"I'm serious about getting a statement, by the way. I don't want people thinking I've tried to off myself." But Alec had gone already.

--------------------

*It was daylight, and I was in my bunk, although how I got there, I didn't know. I clambered up on deck. The boat wasn't on autopilot, the sails were furled, and there were two figures seated there, but they were neither Callahan nor Gascoigne; they were inflated dummies, dressed in bright-yellow, foul-weather gear. The last of my crew were gone, and I was adrift, alone, both sky and sea leaden, the latter heaving into infinity in all directions, no other sign of life anywhere, and it was raining.*

*I'd no idea how long I'd been unconscious, and after the initial shock my immediate reaction was to find out where I was, and call for help, but that was impossible, because all my navigation and communication tools had either been taken, if portable, or destroyed, if not. Out of sight of land, with the sun hidden behind the overhanging nimbus cloud, I'd no way of knowing where I was headed, or where to head for, and no way of sending out any sort of distress signal because all the flares had been removed also. The anchor was gone too, as was my valuable camera, along with all the digital photos I'd taken of us all during the early part of the voyage.*

*I searched around for my own personal property, but all that was missing as well: my passport, wallet, driver's license, money and credit cards. As Gascoigne had threatened, I'd been left with nothing. They'd abandoned me on a drifting sailboat, in the middle of the Atlantic Ocean, with nothing but food and water, with the dummy figures there presumably to prevent any observant pilot flying overhead, or anyone else, from thinking the boat was deserted. They'd even destroyed the photos of my friends that I'd taken at the going-away party just before I left. Only the thumbtacks remained.*

*For once, I didn't know what to do. The reason why I'd been left in this situation was irrelevant; I couldn't do anything about it anyway, having no means of notifying anyone about what my former crew members were plotting. That would all have to wait as the most important thing for me now was to work out how to get out of this situation, for if I failed, I was going to die.*

## CHAPTER 5

Another move, and this time to the place called a 'respite home', where I was dropped off without ceremony, and handed over to someone else. I knew everyone was doing their best to accommodate my 'special needs', as they called it, but was also aware that I didn't belong to anyone and that, as such, no-one was anxious to accept responsibility for me, being only too grateful to pass me along like a hot potato. Each time this happened, though, I grew more and more lonely and isolated, and it was hard not to simply disappear like a snail into its shell, and not open up for anyone. If I did that, though, I'd be hurting no-one but myself; I had to continue to reach out in each new situation, so each time, again like a snail, I opened up and put out my antennae, and did my best to communicate with those unseen strangers all around me. It was difficult, and getting more so each time, needing great willpower to break down the barrier separating me from the rest of society.

I was immensely surprised, therefore, when I arrived at the respite home, and a man came up to me, grabbed hold of my hand and gave it a hearty shake.

"Chris! Welcome! I hear you've had a rough time. You don't mind me calling you Chris, do you? They didn't give you a last name. I gather Chris isn't your real name anyway." He was leading me away from the entrance as he spoke. "Come on into my office here. I'm the manager. My name's Devonald Ashby, by the way. Feel free to call me Dev. Would you like a drink? How about a beer? It's that time of day. I'm not allowed to offer drinks to our guests outside my office, but I consider this my private domain."

"A beer would be great, thank you. I don't know when I last had one."

"Excellent. I have my own little stash here. The bottle okay?"

"Perfect."

"So... You'll be with us for the next six weeks, then." Dev held a chair behind me, and put his hand on my shoulders, motioning me to sit down.

A window was open, and a slight breeze carried with it the smells and sounds of the outside world. Some sparrows were squabbling nearby. In the distance, a motorcyclist was testing out his engine by revving the motor -- sounded like a Harley -- and there was a slight smell of fertilizer in the air.

"We have some other guests here, that I think you'll get along with. A couple of our older guests are a bit forgetful, shall we say, but we also accommodate other people who need help when their carers, who also need a break, go away, and so when that happens, their patients come to stay with us. You'll get to meet everyone gradually anyway, and there aren't that many here -- just ten -- so we'll try to make it so you can find your own way around."

"That would be great. Can I go outside too?"

"I don't see why not. Our garden is fairly small, and with no major pitfalls that I can think of, so I'm sure you'll soon figure it out. I'll get someone to go with you the first couple of times. Oh! While I think of it: someone has been asking for you -- wanted to know when you'd be arriving, so she could come to see you. A Miss Atkins. You know her?"

"Oh yes! She was the one who saved my life on that beach, where I wrecked the boat. I'd love to see her again. Can we let her know I'm here now?"

"Of course."

For me it was an uplifting few minutes. It had been so long since I'd chatted with a normal person in a normal, adult way, and I left Dev's office feeling calmer than I'd done in weeks.

My room was comfortable, and also had an en suite bathroom, and the whole atmosphere of the place was calm and relaxed. Once confident of knowing my way around, I could come and go as I pleased, and everyone was only too willing to take me in the right direction when I got lost, and, most important to me, to have a chat. I settled in.

I felt even better when, a few days after my arrival, Miss Atkins came to see me.

"I'm so sorry I haven't been able to come to visit you sooner, Chris, but it's quite a long way here, and I've been helping out on the farm in my spare time, as Dad hasn't been well. I've brought Paddy to see you too."

We caught up on everything that had happened since I last saw her, and she was, of course, outraged at the Kevin saga. "It's almost unbelievable that they could have let that happen to you. It would seem obvious that this man was somehow making them believe he'd taken his medication, when he hadn't. I've heard of that happening. Because they're behaving normally, they think they've been cured, so don't need to take their pills anymore and, of course, they relapse. I've heard too that so many of these people can appear on the surface to be quite sane and rational. The human mind is a strange thing. I hope I never end up somewhere like that for any reason; I'd be scared out of my wits -- as you were."

"Well, Miss Atkins, I don't think you're going to have to worry on that score, and look at it this way anyway: if you did end up there, you'd probably not be with it enough to be scared. For me it was different. I still had my wits about me, and that allowed me to consider my situation all too well."

Miss Atkins patted my hand. "Well, you're all over that now, thank goodness, my dear. I'd have come to see you in the psychiatric unit, but as I said, Dad hasn't been too well, so I've been doing some of his chores."

"I hope he's better now."

"Oh yes! He's a tough old bird despite his age. Had a bit of bronchitis, but that's all over with now, and he's back at work on the farm again. I'd like to get him to wind down a bit -- have fewer animals to deal with -- but he thinks he can go on forever."

It was so emotionally uplifting for me to be chatting like this, feeling about as normal as I could possibly feel, considering everything -- although, of course, I still hadn't heard anything about having my cataracts removed, and, longing to be able to see again, was wondering just how much longer I was going to have to wait.

Miss Atkins and Paddy visited me a couple of times a week after that, which was most thoughtful of her, seeing that she didn't really know me, and I enjoyed our time together -- time in which I could carry on an intelligent conversation, find out what was going on in the world, exchange humour, and have a good laugh, because she could also be quite funny.

My affection for Paddy was growing too. After all, if he'd not found me that day, I definitely would have been drowned by the incoming tide. I had the feeling he was becoming especially fond of me too, so having them both visit me gave a great boost to my morale.

No matter how great the improvement here at the respite home, though, the memory of what Kevin had almost succeeded in doing to me wasn't something I could brush aside easily, and being able to hug the dog, and bury my face in his fur showed me what a sad state I was in, it being so important to me, not only to be loved by a dog, but needing to satisfy my own yearning for affection by hugging it in return -- and I missed them when it came time for them to leave.

In the meantime I was gradually getting to know the other guests, and even the simple fact of being called a guest, rather than a service user, made me feel better about myself. Even so, the people at the home were there because, like me, they were unable to look after themselves, and I found that they tended to be a bit depressed and morose about their situation, so that alone made Miss Atkins's visits that much more welcome.

"Today, Chris, I've come with an offer." Miss Atkins's voice had a particularly upbeat tone. "I've already made enquiries, and have been told you can take me up on it, if you'd like to. How would you like to come and live with me and my father? They say your stay here is limited to six weeks, so, what do you say? I do work, mostly full time, but my hours can vary. My father's out in the fields during the day, but I'm sure we'll be able to find interesting things for you to do anyway... We'll get you out and about too; all this inactivity is starting to show. Besides, Paddy here will be around to keep you company, and you two seem to be particularly attached to each other... Oh, and our farm has been inspected by the authorities, so we can offer what they call, 'an approved home' for you. How's that?"

"I don't know what to say, Miss Atkins. It's so very kind of you. Are you sure, though, that you're not just asking me because you know I've nowhere to go once I leave here? I wouldn't want to impose on you, or be a liability either."

Miss Atkins patted my knee, something she did quite frequently -- that, or taking my hand and patting it. "Believe me, Chris; I can't think of anything that would make us happier. A new and handsome young face around the house would be great -- just what my father and I need to brighten our lives -- and my visits here over the past weeks have convinced me you're just the sort of person we'd be only too glad to share our home with. I mean it. I speak for my father too. We'd be delighted if you'd accept our offer."

I gave her a broad grin. "How soon?"

Within the hour I was in her car, heading back to the Pembrokeshire coast, and saying more than I'd said in weeks. I was talking to a normal person in a normal surrounding -- a regular passenger in a regular car -- and I was so elated, poor Miss Atkins had no chance to get a word in, even if she'd tried, but she didn't seem to mind at all, and I prattled on.

Once home, Mr. Atkins came out to greet us, and I was introduced. I unloaded the trunk, while father and daughter carried the bags into the house, before I too was brought into my new home.

It was well into Fall now, but there was a light, warm breeze, bringing with it a smell that was familiar to me. It was the sea. Paddy was barking with delight, and Miss Atkins told me to be careful, because he'd presented me with his ball, dropping it at my feet, and waiting for me to throw it for him.

I found it, and picked it up. "Okay if I throw it this way? I don't want to break any windows before I've even begun my stay," I laughed. Given the okay, I threw the ball, and Paddy scampered off to fetch it.

"You've started something now," Mr. Atkins said.

"I think that's something we're going to have to put a stop to, though. We don't want you doing a header because you've stepped on his ball, do we?... Come." Miss Atkins took hold of my hand and led me into the house.

"This is our kitchen. Mind the step here... I'll show you around. As you'll find out, it's a large room, and we have all our meals in here. Our big farmhouse kitchen table is in the middle, and everything is arranged around it. This is where we have our meals. This is the big oven-cum-stove. We don't light it in the summer, but it keeps everything cosy in winter. We'll be lighting it up soon, so you'll need to be careful when we do -- it can get pretty hot, and can give a nasty burn if you're not careful. This here is the fridge. Feel free to help yourself. The milk and juices are on the bottom shelf of the door..."

"Once my cataracts are removed, of course, I won't need for you to have to tell me where everything is. I'll even be able to help you and Mr. Atkins then... Help pay for my keep."

"Oh, I'm sure you'll be able to do a lot of things anyway, once you're familiar with everything, Chris. I can't tell you how happy we are that you've come to live with us!"

"The same goes for me too, you know. I'm finding it hard to believe just how lucky I am."

She then took me upstairs to the guest room. This was to be my room in my new home.

---------------------

*Not knowing how long the boat had been drifting, or in which direction, meant I'd no idea where I was. It could be that I'd drifted into the arm of the Gulf Stream known as the North Atlantic Drift, in which case I could end up either closer to the United Kingdom or to the Canary islands, depending on which branch I was in.*

*My brain was in overdrive, bombarded with possible scenarios, none of them favourable. There was no point in setting the sails because, depending on wind direction and whether I close-hauled it or broad-reached it, or whatever I did, I could wander around indefinitely, until I ran out of food and water. The best thing, I decided, was to just let myself continue to drift in the hope the clouds would clear, allowing me to try navigating by the sun and the stars.*

*The sea being relatively calm, another two days went by without any emergencies, before the sky cleared, and I was relieved to see I was at least pointing in an easterly direction, although that was still no guarantee, of course, that the boat had been drifting that way. I hoisted the sails anyway, in the hope that eventually I'd reach the west coast of Europe, although which country of Europe, I'd no idea. With luck I'd sight land before too long -- not too long, or I'd run out of drinking water.*

*In the meantime, it seemed as though I was the only person left in the world, having seen nothing at all in the way of shipping or even aircraft, although, now the sky was clear, I could see planes cruising in the same direction at about forty thousand feet above me, so they were clearly still quite a way from their destinations, wherever those may be.*

*Whenever I could, I snatched precious minutes of sleep. Although I'd slept through at least one night after Callahan had given me that jab of whatever it was, the sleep* being a drugged one, it had left me feeling sluggish ever since, so I forced himself into a strict routine.

I settled into this, although even this was accurate only insofar as I could guess the passage of time, because, along with everything else, they had stolen the valuable Panerai Radiomir wristwatch my father had given me for my twenty-first birthday.

With nothing else to think about now -- thoughts of official enquiries regarding the loss of Roberts no longer being uppermost in my mind -- I began going over what this whole trip was about, and my own role in it. As I'd already discovered, of course, my only purpose had been merely to make sure they arrived safely at a pre-arranged rendezvous off the southwest coast of Ireland, with no intention of ever going to Milford Haven in the first place. The only reason they chose that destination had to have been because aiming for it would take us past their true destination.

The one thing I couldn't understand was why they'd murdered Roberts. Had he got cold feet about the plot for some reason, and refused to go along with it? Maybe that was why he'd always looked so worried.

Distressing too was that I'd spent all that time in the company of men who fully intended, right from the start, to murder me too, once they had no more use for me. Why hadn't they then just pitched me overboard as well, while I was drugged, although from what I'd overheard Gascoigne say during that conversation, he obviously thought that throwing me overboard was too good for me, and that leaving me to die was a greater punishment for having knocked him unconscious over the vodka incident. He could, of course, still be right in that, because, depending on what happened to me now, perhaps tossing me overboard might have been kinder. Only time would tell which would have been the better fate.

*Like prisoners of old, locked in the dungeon of some castle somewhere, I started marking off the days by making scratches on the bulkhead, where my photos had been. Having no pen or pencil with which to do this, I used one of the remaining thumbtacks, still stuck in the wood.*

*It was another few days before I sighted land, and I headed towards it with almost feverish gratitude, despite having no idea what sort of coastline was going to greet me, or even to which country it might belong. It would, I hoped, at least consist of a sandy beach, and not a vertical cliff-face or dangerous rocks sticking out into the sea.*

*Now that I could see land low down on the horizon, the skies once again began to cloud over, but as long as I had that coastline in sight, I didn't mind. That sliver of land was my anchor, my goal. Sometimes it almost seemed as though it was nothing more than a mirage painted there, never changing, never coming closer -- I was the nautical version of the man in the desert, seeing the oasis in the distance. Even so, I held it, like a beacon, in my sight. After all, it was my only hope of ever being on land again.*

*Another day, and at last, not only did the skies clear, but my coastline mirage began to show itself in detail. It was coming closer, rising higher over the horizon, and my spirits, depressed as never before, began to rise along with it.*
"*Looks like I'm going to be able to step on terra firma again after all, although whose terra firma will it be? And I'll be landing without any passport, ID, or money. Oh well. All I'll really need is to be able to make a phone call.*" *Even the weather had, like my spirits, warmed up, and the breeze, out of the southwest, no longer had a mean bite to it, but an almost caressing, gentle touch.*

--------------------

That evening I was lying on my bed in my new home, hands behind my head, thinking. Ever since I crashed into that rock, my life had been a rollercoaster of stress and fear, alternating with high expectations and hopes that were dashed almost before they'd had a chance to take shape in my head. Now, though, I'd entered a new and as calm a phase as I could expect, given my circumstances. At least I was somewhere where I knew I'd be safe and in the care of people who had actually chosen to have me live with them, no longer at the mercy of people running an institution, who saw me only as another patient or service user to be dealt with as a part of their job.

Nothing would be truly right with my life, of course, until I was returned to being the person I'd been before all this started, but until then, I could be content, living like a normal person in the home of Mr. Atkins and his daughter, as a part of their family, complete with family dog that, like his owners, had already accepted me with enthusiasm.

I got up and opened up the sash window, letting in the salt-laden breeze. There was even a tang of seaweed in it. I leaned out of the window, and felt a light drizzle blowing onto my face, bringing with it a smell that stirred something in me, a mixture of pleasure and a sense of home and belonging -- but then, with no warning, an irrational surge of fear overtook me, and I tried to shake it off, leaning further out of the window and sucking in the air, struggling to think only of the sense of pleasure, but was starting to panic, my stomach cramping into a familiar knot: I was experiencing yet another of those dreaded bouts of panic that overwhelmed me every now and then with that unexplained fear, and as I did so often, wished I knew what it really was that stopped my brain from remembering everything. How was it even that they knew at the psychiatric unit that I suffered from general dissociative amnesia and post-traumatic stress disorder? Did they know things that I didn't? All they'd told me was that I had violently disturbing nightmares in which I talked, or ranted about things I knew nothing about, or had periods in which I did nothing but stand or sit as though in a trance, but had no recollection of either kind of episode afterwards, and I feared my brain would never right itself.

I remained standing there at the window, my breath coming in great heaves, as though I were suffocating...

"Chris? Are you all right, my dear? You're very quiet in there."

I blinked.

"Chris? Is it okay if I come in?"

"Uh... Yes... Yes, of course, Miss Atkins. Do come in. I... I was just standing here at the open window, listening to the sounds of the country. I imagine it's beautiful here, and is that the sea I can hear?"

She joined me at the window. "Yes it is. And yes, it is beautiful here, although it can get a bit wild sometimes when the wind comes in from the southwest. Are you ready to come down and have some supper? You must be hungry."

"Yes, that would be great, thank you."


I'd lost track of how many weeks it was since I lost my sight, but I'd still not heard from Mr. Cartwright, the ophthalmologist. Surely it couldn't be long now, though, before my cataracts were removed, especially as my case was being considered an emergency. Then all, well not exactly all, of course -- I still needed my identity back -- would be well, and I'd be leaving to return home to my real life, whatever that was. It was hard to remain patient, but knowing I'd soon be able to see everything for the first time since my accident, kept me feeling upbeat, and I lay on my bed, listening to the waves on the shore in the distance, and allowed myself to wonder how I'd approach my blindness if I'd never been able to see.

Maybe it wouldn't be so bad, because I wouldn't know what I was missing: all the colours; all the shapes; all the movement of the world around me; the stars around the galaxy; the earth around the sun; the moon around the earth; birds flying; Ingmar Bergman's black stallion galloping across the meadow -- yes, things like that I did remember, oddly enough. I thought of other sights I'd never have known: flowers; a spreading oak; wheat flowing in the wind like waves on the ocean; the ocean itself.

It didn't bother me to think about this, of course, because I was in a position to contemplate it all objectively, as none of it applied to me; I'd seen before, and would soon be seeing it all again. For a brief moment, though, I did allow myself to think: "what if I never…?" but immediately brushed it away; such a possibility didn't bear thinking about.

I continued to lie there awake in the calmness of the night countryside, listening to all the little sounds: the odd squeak or grunt from the farmyard below, a hen complaining in the barn, an owl in the distance. It seemed so strange to me that, despite being unable to remember the details of my own life, other knowledge still remained etched on my mind, and I wondered yet again what it was that had been so terrible that my brain blocked it all out. Had I committed, or witnessed some terrible crime? At the other end of the scale, maybe some terrible crime had been committed against me, but there was no point in conjecturing. There wasn't anything I could do about it anyway. Instead, I concentrated on looking forward to the day when I'd get my sight back, and laughed out loud. My optimism was back, and my brain nestled down into the pillow, starting to rebuild its shattered cocoon.

## CHAPTER 6

Mr. Atkins, although a man of few words, was nevertheless pleasant, and made me feel most welcome, and I imagined that if his daughter was in her early fifties, which I guessed her to be, then he must be at least in his late seventies, but was still doing a full-time job on the farm.

"Can you hold that down there for me a minute, Chris? That's right... Perfect."

Elation can be triggered by such minor things, and to be doing something as simple as holding down a two-by-four was helping significantly to boost my morale, especially as one of the effects of my recent experiences was that I'd lost confidence in my ability to do anything. It was something I needed to regain as soon as possible, so was grateful to Mr. Atkins for being matter-of-fact, and getting me to do things he, if not I myself, was sure I was perfectly capable of doing.

I worked with him until noon, but that afternoon he'd be tending to the cattle, and decided this was one situation where he didn't think it was safe for me to be around. "Steers can get pretty pushy, even without intending to," he told me, so, with Miss Atkins being away at work, I went up to my room intending to relax, but spent most of the time worrying yet again about my family -- assuming I even had one -- and their apparent inability to find me. Maybe they were even thinking that I must be dead by now.

I lay there till I heard Miss Atkins arrive home, then went down to greet her.

"Oh! What a day! It seems there's been another earthquake in China, and the person I'm working with kept prattling on about plate tec... something or other."

"Plate tectonics?"

"Yes! That was it, Chris! You know about that then? Hmm. You're quite a mystery one way and another, aren't you?"

I smiled. "Yes, I guess I am at that... I could explain continental drift and tell you about the Mid Atlantic Ridge too. Strange, I know, but I've no idea why I'd know all that... Anyway, can I help with anything?"

"Yes, you can set the table for me. It would help if you'd peel the potatoes too... Here's the parer."

I wondered briefly whether she didn't trust me with a sharp knife in case I cut myself, or didn't trust me with a sharp knife for more sinister reasons. After all, no-one really knew what sort of person I was in my previous life, and in a way she could have been taking a risk, inviting me into her home as she'd done. The psychiatric unit had been so wrong about Kevin; they could have been equally wrong about me. Perhaps I was a paranoid schizophrenic after all, although I'd no idea what it would feel like to be one.

--------------------

*It was just after noon judging by the position of the sun, and my blue sky had begun to show a heavy, almost black wall of cloud rising above the horizon on my starboard side. There was no mistaking it: it was a thunderhead. At almost the same time, my gentle zephyr of a wind faded away, leaving the sails luffing uselessly, the boom starting to swing to and fro. I was becalmed, and without the engine, all I could hope for now was that the tide and the currents would take me inshore, and once within visual navigating distance, guide the boat into some safe haven. I was still a good eight or nine miles from my oasis, though, and a lot could happen in that distance.*

*The ominous cloud was getting larger, and advancing on me like a monster out of a science-fiction movie. It was clear I was in for a heavy thunderstorm, and avoiding it was out of the question. It was heading straight towards me, and soon I'd be engulfed in it. It was already being ripped through with continuous shafts of my dreaded lightning, and that Callahan had forgotten, or hadn't bothered, to get the boat's protection system overhauled, now assumed overwhelming importance: I was a seductive beacon, the only thing sticking up out of the ocean, beckoning a bolt.*

*I tried to persuade myself that it might bypass me, although common sense told me there was no hope of that. I also knew that lightning can travel a long way -- time to get below. I ducked my head to go down the companionway ladder, when the air exploded, surrounding me with a brilliant, fiery, all-engulfing light.*

---------------------

I wasn't only settled in at the farm by now, but was calling Miss Atkins by her first name, "Gemma". One thing for which I was grateful was that although she tended to fuss over me a bit more than I felt necessary, she was never condescending. She did expect me to help where I could, and to this end taught me to do whatever she thought was within my capabilities. I was a quick learner, and it was rare that she had to show me twice. I spent much of my time helping Mr. Atkins out on the farm as well, something that I enjoyed in particular, as he was calm and methodical, allowing me to do all the heavy work, something which, because of his advanced years, he was finding increasingly difficult to do himself. In this way I was building up my strength and my confidence, and began to feel truly healthy again, no longer the physical wimp as my muscles returned. Even some visitors remarked on how much better I looked than when I first arrived.

Whenever there was time, Gemma took me for walks along the path above Druidston beach, but not having seen it either before or now, it couldn't help jog my memory.

"I'll tell you where I'll take you one day, Chris. We must go to Tenby. We'll make a day of it, and take a picnic."

"Sounds great. I'll look forward to it."

The weather was perfect and, as promised, Gemma took me to Tenby, where the first thing she did was to buy me some new clothes. My old ones, she said, looked as though they'd come from a charity shop, which they probably had. First she bought me a couple of pairs of well fitting, expensive jeans. For tops, she planned to get T-shirts, but I balked at that. "I don't like T-shirts."

"What sort of tops do you want then?"

"I always wear white dress shirts."

"White dress shirts! What? Even with jeans?"

"Yes."

"With a tie as well?"

"No, I always wear them with the neck open, and the sleeves rolled up."

"You're sure about that?"

"Yes." Why I was so positive I'd no idea, but knew that was what I wanted anyway, So I came away from the store wearing a pair of my new jeans, a white shirt, a good quality leather belt, and a pair of Timberland boots. She gave the store my old clothes to dispose of, and I stepped out looking, I hoped, a new man, and holding in a carrier bag another pair of jeans, two more white shirts, a pair of sneakers, or trainers as Gemma called them, underwear, a pair of swimming trunks, and at long last, pyjamas.

"That was a lot of money for you to spend on me, Gemma. You're very kind to me. Thank you. I *do* appreciate it, you know."

She put her hand up against my cheek. "You're well worth it, my dear -- and you should see yourself now in your new clothes. You're such a tall, handsome young man, you know, and I'm very proud to be seen with you, particularly as several people have already assumed you're my son, something I especially like the idea of." She took my hand, and squeezed it.

The rest of the day we spent at the beach, and as the preceding months had taught me to appreciate the little things, I realised on the way home that I'd now reached the stage where, as long as I didn't think too hard, I could even persuade myself I was happy.

Time was passing, and my life had assumed a comfortable and regular routine, something that suited me well. Change and new situations were hard for me to cope with, I'd discovered, and caused me to be overly anxious and agitated, so as long as everything remained fairly static, my emotions stayed on an even keel as well, and I could cope more easily. I could tell too that Gemma was growing fond of me in a motherly sort of way. It was obvious she found pleasure in my presence, and while I naturally made every effort to be a good guest -- considering their amazing kindness to me -- I still tried not to put on any sort of act just to please her, but to let myself be myself, whoever that was. Whatever the result, the Atkinses seemed happy with it.

Gemma was even perfectly open about how delighted she was that I'd come to live with them. She thought nothing of coming up to me and putting her arms around me to give me a hug, and to reach up and kiss me on the cheek. It reminded me of what she'd said in Tenby about people thinking I was her son, and had the feeling that, if she did have a son of her own, she'd treat him in exactly the same way as she was treating me. She could be bossy as well, but I didn't mind; there was even a certain comfort in it.

I had to hope, though, that she didn't allow herself to become too attached to me because, as she surely had to be aware, as soon as my cataracts were removed, I'd be in a position to start finding out for myself exactly who I was, and no matter how comfortable I was here in her care, my stay was a temporary one, and I did need to get back to my former life as soon as possible.


We had come into town, and while we were walking along, were chatting as usual. On this occasion I was talking about my past, and speculating as to what it might have been. "I have to say, Gemma, I can't wait to find myself and to return to being the person I was before all this happened. Just think what it will be like for me to be able see my family and my friends again, and for my life to return to normal, just as it was before I got myself into this situation."

"Why?" Her voice was sharp, startling me. She sounded like a schoolmistress reprimanding a student. "Don't you feel at home here, Chris? Here with us? I can't imagine you leaving us now. As far as I'm concerned, *we* are your family now. You have a good life here, don't you?"

"Why yes, Gemma. Of course I do. Of course I have a good life with you and your father, but…"

"Well then. Let's hear no more of such talk. No point in depressing yourself. Better just to forget your past now, and start afresh."

What she had just said was unsettling enough, but I was even more alarmed when she promptly removed my hand from her arm and walked off, leaving me stranded. Was she punishing me for expressing my hopes by leaving me standing there on a crowded sidewalk, not knowing where I was, and unable to move? It wasn't only unnerving for me to be abandoned like that, but to think that she was under the impression that I'd be living with her and her father permanently, was an assumption on her part that was highly disturbing, and I could feel panic rising in my gut...

"Right, Chris. Let's go, shall we?" Gemma came back and took my arm as though nothing had happened, and we continued with her shopping. How long had she left me standing there? I didn't know. Maybe not more than a few minutes, but I did think it peevish and unworthy of her, though, unkind even, to have behaved like that. Still, she was back to her normal, pleasant self now, and I certainly wasn't going to say anything. After all, everyone has their moments.

I was thoroughly confident now around the house and the large area of farmyard surrounding it. I washed the dishes, filled and emptied the washing machine, hung clothes out on the line, prepared the vegetables for dinner, set the table, fed Paddy and anything else possible for me to do. They were careful to make sure things were always in the same place, and by this time I made my way between the house and the barn without even thinking about it, there being certain focal points along the way, telling me exactly where I was.

It was a beautiful morning, and the sun was warm on my face as I made my way back from the barn with the eggs. I was thinking how well I was coping. Soon I'd be able to see exactly where I was going, of course, but in the meantime it was good to have the confidence to do the things I was doing, and to help Gemma and her father at the same time. Naturally, the more independent I became, the better it was for them, not having me rely on them for everything I did and everywhere I went around the house and farmyard. Obviously the last thing I wanted to be was any more of a burden on them than I already was...

"Chris! Can you hear me? Chris! Answer me. What happened?"

I clambered to my feet and felt my knees. They were wet and sticky, and hurting. "I... I don't know. What did happen?"

"You fell over the wheelbarrow, which of course had to be full of chunks of broken bricks, didn't it? I thought you must have knocked yourself out when you didn't answer me. Didn't you hear me asking you if you were all right? You had me really worried there. Come on. Let's get you inside. We need to take care of those cuts. They're bleeding quite badly.

You really must learn to make your way more carefully, Chris. I've watched you; you need to slow down."

"But I'm fine as long as everything's where it's supposed to be, and the wheelbarrow had to have been moved, or I wouldn't have walked into it. It certainly wasn't where it normally is, because I know this part of the yard like the back of my hand."

"Don't be silly, Chris. Of course it was where it always is. I'd have warned you if it wasn't. Don't I always tell you? Of course I do. As I said: don't always be in such a rush. You need to take your time."

We arrived back into the kitchen, where she sat me down. "Now you just sit there, and let me take care of this mess."

"I'm sorry. I can't think what happened. I don't understand. I was so sure I was on the right track."

"No need to be sorry. Just be more careful how you go in future, my dear. These cuts are quite nasty, and I think you might even be going to have some permanent scars there too."

"Maybe you could get me one of those canes for the time being, so I don't bump into things. That was pretty scary and unnerving, apart from being damn painful as well."

"I'm sure it was, but I don't think you need a cane, Chris. Normally, you do perfectly well around here, and when you're in town, you're with me. Besides, it would be hard for you to do your chores if you had one hand holding onto a stick, don't you think?"

"Well, look at it this way; it won't be long now before I'll be able to see exactly where I'm going, then neither of us is going to have to worry about things like this happening."

She didn't comment, and spent almost a half hour taking care of the damage, before deciding I needed a tetanus shot at the A & E, where I sat in silence while waiting to be called.

"My, this place has changed a lot since I was here last... but that was many years ago now," Gemma remarked.

I was still questioning why I should have so seriously misjudged where I'd been walking, and said nothing.

"Yes, I was always having to bring my dear little son here to A & E... He was always having accidents, bless him. I don't know why. Then one day he had such a bad accident, they couldn't save him, and he died."

"What! You had a son?"

"Yes, I did, and whenever I look at you, I can't help thinking of him. He was a lot like you in a way -- a very much younger version of you, of course -- and much like I imagine you were at seven years old too."

"That's how old he was when he died?"

"Yes. And he looked very much like you must have looked at that age too. Odd really, but his name was Chris as well – well, Christopher actually, but I called him Chris." She took my hand. "And now, when I watch you make your way round the farmyard, I find it hard not to believe you *are* him. He'd be about your age now too, and I'm sure would be very much like you in every way."

"That's a terrible thing to have happened to you, Gemma, but you say he was always having accidents. What sort of accidents?"

"Once he fell out of his pram, and we ended up here, of course. I don't know altogether; things just seemed to happen to him -- accident prone, I suppose you'd call it. Then one day he wasn't looking where he was going, and fell down the manhole out in the farmyard... Somehow the cover hadn't been put back properly... He never regained consciousness." She sighed. "And there was I, always dreading the day he'd grow up and leave home, and I wouldn't have him to look after anymore, but then he was taken from me anyway."

I found her hand and squeezed it. "I'm very sorry Gemma. I hardly know what to say..."

My name was called then, and the subject closed, and as it wasn't one I felt I myself should bring up, I said no more about it. If she needed to open up to me about it again, though, then of course I'd do my best to comfort her in the same way that she was being of comfort to me.

The result of my coming a cropper over the wheelbarrow was that I lost my recently regained self-confidence. I'd been so sure I'd been on the right track when I blundered into it, and I'd hurt myself badly too, so even though I knew I soon wouldn't have to bother about things like this happening anymore, the incident, in the meanwhile, made me so anxious and nervous that my every move became faltering, finding it necessary to feel my way with every step, afraid I was going to get it wrong again and crash into other things.

As a result, Gemma insisted on coming with me everywhere I went, telling me she needed to help me regain my lost confidence. It all impressed on me a fact of my life as it was for the moment: my lack of independence, something of which I didn't want to be reminded, no matter how temporary it was.

I began to notice a difference too in how she was treating me lately. When I first arrived here, she'd made every effort to make me as independent as possible, and as quickly as possible. Now, though, she seemed to be reversing the process, being too willing to help, insistent even, rather than letting me try to do things for myself. Yes, I did need her help on occasion, but not by her being overly attentive the way she was becoming. She needed, rather, to practise some tough love, and force me to be as independent as possible, and it wasn't happening. Things were reaching the stage, even, when I wondered how she could continue cope with me under these circumstances. What would I do, or where would I go if she did decide I was too much of a responsibility? How much longer, too, could I take being like this?

## CHAPTER 7

I wasn't sure how long I'd been at the farm. Time seemed to have lost any significance, and there was still no word from Mr. Cartwright, the ophthalmologist. Anyway, Christmas was coming up, so it must have been about three months, I think, and they were expecting family over the surrounding week.

Gemma was excited. "My brother and his wife and their two children will be coming. I haven't seen them for a good while, so I'm really looking forward to seeing them again. You'll like my brother, Chris. He's quite a bit younger than I am. I imagine he's just your sort of man too, friendly and outgoing. Has a good sense of humour as well."

I was excited at the thought of being able to meet another man closer to my own age, and was happy to help prepare the beds in the spare bedrooms, and with other preparations too, although helping to decorate the Christmas tree was obviously not one of them. Gemma said the decorations were at least a couple of generations old, and that she only ever used white lights, which she said looked more natural than coloured ones.

Christmas Eve arrived, and with it the family, who drove into the farmyard just in time for supper. There were introductions all round, and there being only four of them, and two of those children, I felt at ease, and it was great too that everyone was behaving quite naturally towards me as though I really was just another member of the family. By this time I almost felt I was.

"Chris, this is my son, Colwyn. A good old Welsh name." Gemma's brother, Henry, laughed. "We call him Col."

"Oh really! That's my name too... My God! I've just remembered my name! I can't believe it! Gemma! Did you hear that? I've just remembered my name! It's Colwyn! Same as your nephew here!"

"Wow! That's amazing! Any chance you remember your last name as well then?" Henry asked me.

"Yes. I do! It's Yeats. My name's Colwyn Yeats! Yes. Definitely. It's Colwyn Yeats. I'm sure of it! When I heard the name Colwyn, I just knew that was my name too. Then my last name came as well... I've remembered who I am at last! It's come back! That's extraordinary! My brain's finally starting to unscramble itself! It's come back at last! I can't believe it!"

"Well, well! This is quite a breakthrough, I must say, and I think we should all celebrate, don't you?" Mr. Atkins put a glass of wine in my hand, and clinked his own against it. "Okay everyone. Raise your glasses to Colwyn Yeats, and all he was, and what he will be again soon -- the very best of luck, son."

"Thank you. Thank you. I'm still having a hard time believing it, though. After all this time, I've actually remembered who I am! It's amazing, isn't it? That it should have come back to me just like that, when you mentioned the name Colwyn, Henry. You've no idea how excited am... No... That's not true. Of course you know how I feel... Well, now at least I can start this ball rolling, and get myself out from under your feet at last, Gemma. I'm sure your patience must be near to running out at this point, don't you think?..."

There was no response.

"Yes, well... Henry, I have to say I only wish you all had come to visit sooner! What a difference it would have made to Gemma here if I'd remembered my name earlier! I don't think Job himself could have been more patient than she's been with me these last months, so..." I raised my glass. "A very special toast to Gemma. Gemma, thank you for bearing with me and all my problems. Here's to a very special person."

There were congratulations from Henry and his wife, Joan, and Mr. Atkins, although I still heard nothing from Gemma, nor did she come up and give me one of her frequent hugs, but that was all right. This was a family reunion after all, and there were more exciting things for them to be celebrating than the fact that I, a stranger, had finally remembered my name. Her brother and his family had only just arrived, and there was news to be exchanged, so the momentous fact, to me at least, that I'd just remembered my real name at last -- that I had an identity and was no longer an official John Doe -- wasn't discussed further.

For me, though, it was naturally all I could think about, and for the rest of the evening I concentrated hard, trying to discover what else I could remember, scarcely listening to what the others were talking about. I couldn't come up with anything else, though, but it was a start, and now, of course, I'd be able to find out who Colwyn Yeats really was.

That I had to wait, though, until the end of Christmas, when the American Embassy would be available to do the necessary search, had me as tense as a piano wire. After all, my whole future depended not only on regaining my sight, but recovering the lost 'me' as well, the prospect of remaining in my current state for the rest of my life being a future which didn't even bear thinking about. Looking forward now, therefore, to returning to my former life and being reunited with my family, was now producing an almost unbearable longing, and filling me with an excitement in which I allowed myself to revel, wallow almost, without restraint.

In the meantime I did my best to enjoy Christmas with my new friends, a happy, family Christmas in which presents were exchanged, and I received an iPod from Gemma and her father.

"I'm sorry I can't give you and your father anything, Gemma. If I had the money, I'd be only too happy to buy you great presents; I can't think of anyone more deserving."

"Don't be silly, Chris, my dear. We're not expecting anything, as you well know. Just having you here with us is all we need."

Monday arrived, and while I was out collecting the eggs Gemma called the embassy. When I returned, she had disappointing news. "I'm sorry, Chris, but I'm afraid all I got was a recorded message saying that it being holiday time, unless it's an emergency I'll have to wait until after the New Year when the regular staff will be back. So there's nothing for it, I'm afraid, but another wait, my dear." She patted my arm. "Never mind; it's only a few more days."

The suspense was excruciating, but there was, of course, nothing to do, but wait.

The holiday season finally came to an end; Henry and his family departed, and Gemma, needing to return to work, left before I woke that morning, having assured me the previous night that she'd call the embassy as soon as she could after arriving at work.

A day never passed so slowly, so when I heard her car coming into the farmyard, I rushed out to meet her.

"I called them on the dot of nine this morning..."

"Yes! Yes! Gemma... So who am I after all this? Where's my home? My family? Come on! Out with it! I can't wait!"

"Well..." She took hold of my hand and squeezed it. "I'm truly sorry, my dear, to have to tell you this, but they called back just before I left this afternoon, and told me there was no record of anyone by that name in the United States, or even Canada for that matter -- at least, not that answered to your description in any way. They'd checked all resources at their disposal, but were sorry they couldn't be of any further use in trying to find out anything more about you. Without a passport or other means of identification, and no report of you being missing, there's nothing they can do. They think you probably made a mistake, and that the name that came to you wasn't yours at all -- just a fluke. I really feel awful having to disappoint you like this, Chris. I mean Col … Oh! To heck with it! As far as I'm concerned, you're still Chris to me, and always will be... And, by the way, they very kindly checked the UK records too, but came up with nothing there either."

Devastated, I'd stopped listening. Wasn't I American after all, or even British? Where did I come from then? What nationality was I? Indescribably depressed by the news, and by having my high hopes dashed so decidedly, I took myself off to my room.

"Why?" I kept asking myself over and over. "Why is it that no-one's looking for me, or even reported me missing? Don't I have any family or even friends? Who on earth am I then? These days, with all the electronic media and other resources, people just don't go missing without their disappearance being noticed!"

I'd been so sure that my real name was Colwyn Yeats, and even if I'd mistaken Henry's son's name for my own, where did the 'Yeats' come from? Nobody had suggested that name!

Not knowing the answers to these questions compounded my misery, and leaving me wishing that I'd not remembered my name -- or whoever's name it was that had come to me. The only thing preventing me from falling all the way into a dark pit of depression was that very soon now I'd at least have my cataracts removed. Then, if nothing else, I'd be able to start doing my own research, and hopefully find out everything for myself -- although if even the American Embassy had failed to find out who I was...

--------------------

*I woke to find myself lying against the door to the for'ard cabin. How long I'd been there I'd no way of knowing, although I could still hear the rumble of thunder in the distance, so it couldn't have been that long. I lay there for a few minutes, gathering my wits, then sat up slowly, checking myself over. My hand had a painful burn on it, as did my arm, although nothing that wouldn't heal quite quickly. What had happened to my shirt and life jacket, I didn't know; they'd vanished, although the cotton crew-pants I'd been wearing at the time were still on me. Other than that, I seemed to be still in one piece; the boat wasn't sinking, and there was no water seeping in through any cracks or holes in the hull that I could see, so the grounding system had done its job. The bonding system, however, hadn't, and for that I had to thank Callahan* and his failure to get it thoroughly checked out -- I was very lucky not to have lost my life. I was grateful, at least, that the boat was in salt water, not fresh, or I would definitelyy have been killed.

I pulled myself to my feet, but feeling light-headed, grabbed hold of the nearest bunk for support, then lay down on it, and almost immediately fell asleep. When I woke up, it was starting to get dark, and, feeling better now, I climbed off the bunk, and stood up. I no longer felt dizzy, but shook my head to clear away the cobwebs making it feel thick, as though I had a hangover. My eyes too were playing up, seeing everything as though through a misty veil, and I blinked to clear them, but the veil remained.

Still feeling not quite myself, and unsteady on my feet, I climbed up on deck to check for any visible damage to the boat in the way of cracks or holes in the hull. Although Gascoigne and Callahan had removed all the boat's electronics, the VHF antenna had been left in place at the top of the aluminium mast, being useless without any communication equipment attached to it. Now though, bits of it were scattered all over the deck, so it had at least done its job as far as serving as a conductor was concerned. As for the rest of the boat, it would have to wait until daylight as I'd no lighting on board, not even a flashlight with which to check it out.

Although it wasn't possible to inspect the outside of the boat, the morning showed no hull damage from the inside, and there were still no signs of leaks, so my craft was still seaworthy, which was something to be thankful for, if little else.

On the down side, I was still drifting, and could see that the coastline was gradually receding -- the squall that had come through with the thunderstorm had contributed to this --

and I hoped a south-westerly wind would come up again soon, and allow me get back on track, fear of losing sight of the coastline again now uppermost in my mind, especially as the filmy mist clouding my vision had not only failed to go away, but had become thicker, starting to leave me as though looking through lightly frosted glass.

"All I need now," I told myself, giving an ironic laugh, "is for this mist to get to the stage where I can't see where I'm going, and I'll be in big trouble." It really was no laughing matter, though, and I sighed. Was there anything else that could possibly go wrong with this disastrously ill-fated voyage?

Over the rest of the day I watched helplessly as the coastline dwindled in size to become a pea-sized spot of land resting on the horizon. If a wind didn't come up soon, it would disappear altogether.

Night fell, and as there wasn't anything I could do to either steer the boat in any direction, or protect either it or myself, I crawled back into my bunk. The last thought on my mind before I fell asleep was that as I had no running or masthead lights to indicate my presence to other shipping, if a tanker were to run me over in the dark, one consolation would be that I'd never know much about it.

I woke to the sound of the halyards slapping against the mast; the wind had come up, creating quite a swell, but when I opened my eyes, I found I could no longer distinguish any shapes around me, everything shrouded in a fog so thick that all I could see was a solid, dirty-grey blur. I groped my way up on deck, only to find that the sky, the sea, everything on the boat, even the boat itself, had all melted into this one grey amorphous mass as well, and the shoreline, even if it were still visible otherwise, was also lost in my dense fog. All I could be *sure of was that it was daytime. Now I was truly in great danger.*

*In which direction the coast lay, I'd no idea. For all I knew, I could be headed back out into the Atlantic, and as I couldn't tell from which direction the wind was blowing, I didn't know in which direction I'd need to head the boat once I hoisted the sails. Even that proved impossible, though, as I couldn't see to hoist them.*

*In complete despair now, I went below, and lay down on my bunk. There wasn't anything I could do to save myself or the boat. I was at the mercy of Mother Nature, and I buried my head in the pillow and cried, something I'd not done since the day I'd witnessed three of my men being blown apart by a roadside bomb in Afghanistan.*

--------------------

Every day I fetched the mail from the box at the end of the driveway, and on this day, there was a business letter that felt like the sort I might expect to receive from the hospital. I passed my fingers over the logo on the envelope, convinced I could feel the raised letters, NHS, on it. It had to be my appointment with the ophthalmologist at last, and I waited impatiently for Gemma to come home and read it to me.

"I'm so sorry, my dear, but you shouldn't try to second guess yourself all the time like this; you only end up being disappointed. You got the 'N' right, but it's from the National Farmers' Union for my father."

Several weeks had passed since my disappointment over the failure to find out who I was, and I was doing my best to come to terms with that. Maybe if Gemma tried again in a while, news of me would have finally surfaced. I told myself to be patient, but time was passing, and with still no word from the ophthalmologist either. I'd been under the impression that he was going to give me priority. Didn't he realise how important this was for me?

"Gemma. Do you suppose we should call his office to see what's going on? Mr. Cartwright told me it would be treated as an emergency, and I don't even know how long it's been now. I'm actually getting more than annoyed with him at this stage. Surely he must know how hard it is for me, and knowing it's so easy for him to give me back my sight, and make my life bearable again. I'd say it's downright callous even, wouldn't you?"

"Sometimes these things take longer than expected, my dear. I'm sure he'll make the appointment as soon as he can. It could be that he's been overburdened with life-threatening emergencies. At least he knows your situation doesn't come into that category." She took my hand and squeezed it. "I know you're being as patient as you can, Chris, but hang in there; I'm sure it can't be that much longer… In the meantime, you know I'm always here to help you my dear."

"Yes, Gemma. I know that, and you mustn't think I don't appreciate it, but it's not fair on you either, having to do things for me that I should be doing for myself, and not having me help out around here the way I should be -- not just helping you either, but your father as well. Think how much I could do for him around the farm if I could see."

Several more weeks passed, during which time I'd probably been rather too vocal about not hearing from Mr. Cartwright, so was immensely relieved when Gemma was able to tell me that a letter had at last arrived from his office. Struggling as I'd been to come to terms with still not knowing who I was, and that my overall amnesia showed no signs of going away, this was a tremendous boost to my morale -- nothing could have lifted my spirits more, it being even more important to me than knowing who I was. That problem, for the moment, could wait. Remaining blind, couldn't.

"Oh Chris! Shall I open it?"

"Yes, of course! Go ahead. It has to be my appointment to have my cataracts removed finally! Great! When is it then?"

There was silence.

"Gemma? What's it say? When is it? Come on. Out with it. It better be soon after all this. I can't go on like this much longer."

Gemma took my hand.

"Well? What is it? There's nothing wrong is there? Don't tell me it's not my appointment after all. I don't think I could handle waiting any longer for it."

"Oh dear! Oh dear! My dearest Chris. I just don't know how to tell you this. Oh dear. If I could keep this from you, I would, but I can't. The letter's addressed to you, and you have every right to know what it says."

I put out my hand, reached for one of the dining chairs, and slumped down onto it. "What? Read it then."

"This is what it says, '*A further review by Mr. Cartwright of his examination regarding your eyes, regretfully reveals that the damage is beyond repair, other areas, apart from the lenses, being found to be irreversibly compromised. This being the case, the removal of your cataracts would yield no positive results, so surgery is not recommended. We regret, therefore, nothing further can be done to restore your sight'."*

Kevin's dire predictions swirled though my brain. He'd been right after all. I was trapped, dependent -- now permanently -- on the help and goodwill of others, locked in a body that could neither see, nor knew who or what it was, its world defined by its remaining senses.

Convinced I was of no use to myself or anyone, I found it hard to bring myself to do anything after that. I was bereft, and grieved for the loss of my sight, something equally precious to me as a loved one. Paddy, the only creature I knew to truly understand me, would even sneak upstairs, and lie on my bed close to me. He at least knew what I was going through, and I hugged him to me, like a child clutches a favourite toy.

Gemma, however, remained remarkably upbeat, no doubt for my sake, and did her best to console me, but nothing she could say to me helped. Hope and high expectation that everything would soon be alright, had gone; she couldn't bring it back, her love and encouragement not enough to allow me to hold it together -- in my present state anyway.

--------------------

*Another night passed, and I was woken by the sound of waves breaking on rocks. I wasn't sure whether to be pleased or petrified, as the closer I got to it, the louder it became. I went up on deck, and although I couldn't see* anything, the depth of the greyness surrounding me told me it was early morning.

I groped my way for'ard, clinging onto the rails with both hands, feeling the salt spray on my face. Within minutes the boat began pitching violently in the surf, every now and then giving a bone-jarring shudder as she bottomed out on the sea bed. There was a violent jolt, followed by an immense crack, and the rail to which I was clinging, fell away, catapulting me into the air.

--------------------

Some weeks had passed, and I was beginning to question Mr. Cartwright's revised opinion. If the man had made a mistake the first time, perhaps he was wrong this time as well, and I refused to accept his latest decision as final.

"Gemma, I simply cannot accept what Mr. Cartwright said. This is my life we're talking about, and he can't just write me a cold, impersonal letter giving me a life-sentence like this. Anyone would think he was writing to tell me I needed a new prescription, or something. It borders almost on the unethical for him to dismiss me like this. I need to meet him face to face -- talk it over with him. Maybe he could recommend I see a specialist, and get another opinion."

"My dear Chris, Mr. Cartwright *is* the specialist, or consultant, as we say here, and although my father and I aren't poor, we can't afford to pay for you to go privately to another one I'm afraid, my darling. Besides, Mr. Cartwright is one of the best anyway."

"I do need to see him, though, Gemma. I can't just lie down and shrug it off. I need to hear him say it... tell me to my face." My voice trailed off, and I turned my head away, not wanting Gemma to see I was choking up yet again.

She put her arms round me. "All right, my dear. Let me phone and make an appointment for you."

"Can you do it now, please?"

"Well, it's too early now; his office won't be open yet, but I'll call from work this morning, all right, my dear?" She smoothed my back. "I'm so terribly sad to see you go through this, my love. If I could do anything to put everything to rights, I would. You know that, don't you?"

"Yes. I know you would."

That evening, as soon as she arrived home, I asked her about the appointment.

"It's too bad, my dear, but he left only yesterday for his vacation, and won't be back for a month. His secretary has made an appointment for you, though, the nearest slot being three months down the road -- I've got the exact date here somewhere -- but she did say that if Mr. Cartwright considered it an emergency, then he'd most likely see you sooner."

"Another three months?" I sank down onto the sofa and put my head in my hands.

Gemma had sat down beside me on the bench outside the kitchen door, and put her arms around me. "Chris, my dear. My father and I are so worried about you. You're not eating, and you must know that in the time you've been with us we've grown to love you so very much. You've added a glow to our lives that was sadly missing. We believe now that you truly belong here with us – that you are ours. It's time to face up to the truth: no-one has been able to trace who you are, or where you come from; you have no money, and you have lost your sight. Will you please, please, my love, for your own sake, if not ours, give up the battle against the inevitable, which is consuming you, and allow yourself to settle down here permanently as part of the family? As I said, I feel already as though you're my son come back to me after all these years, and my father finds such great pleasure in your company too. So, my dear, will you not learn to live here with us for always? Nothing could make us more happy... Please, my dearest Chris... You must know how much we love you."

My mind was a blank. There was no ability left in me to battle against anything, including Gemma's pleas., and I nodded.

She patted my hand. "My dear Chris. Here you'll always be loved, and we'll see to it that you feel as much at home here with us as you would have with your own family -- maybe even more so. After all, there's no guarantee at all, you know, that your previous existence was a happy one, is there?"

"Thank you." My voice must have shown as little enthusiasm as I felt. Yes, it was immensely kind of her, and yes, she'd shown nothing but love and concern for my welfare ever since she'd so generously taken me in -- and she could have been right; maybe my previous life hadn't been a happy one. Maybe, even, it had been so horrendous that it was the very thing that my brain had chosen to hide from me!

Now I was being offered a whole new start in a loving environment, and a chance to make the most of the faculties that I still had remaining. How ungrateful could I be? After all, without Gemma, first of all I'd now be dead, drowned, and secondly, without her I might have lived out the rest of my days in that dreadful psychiatric unit, or somewhere equally frightening. What other option had I anyway, but to accept? Where else could I go even if I'd wanted to? On top of everything else, as she'd pointed out, I didn't have a dime to my name.

Yes, I had to accept, and in accepting, it was up to me to learn to be a loving and responsible member of the family. I couldn't turn around and become a morose and unhappy individual that they would eventually come to hate, ruining their lives as well as my own. No. My acceptance demanded that I reciprocated with equal generosity, and I owed it to them now to do my best, and with this thought I finally resigned myself to my new existence.

I did try, but I had my moments, quite frequently venting my anger and frustration, but Gemma was understanding, ever-forgiving and caring. There was no question she loved me as a mother loved a son, and she carried out her role with the greatest patience and concern. She also continued to call me Chris. Colwyn Yeats, to her mind, never existed other than in my imagination, and now I had my doubts about it myself too. It took all I had, though, to pretend all was well with the world -- my world.


It was yet another day when I was to be found sitting on the bench outside the kitchen door, gazing into my fog and listening to all the sounds of the countryside. It was one of those days in early February, when Nature teases Pembrokeshire with a few warm days, just to remind everyone what it can be like when the rain-laden gales of winter fail to funnel up the valley, eating into the bones, and killing plant life with its salty breath.

Unusually, there were footsteps coming towards me across the farmyard. Gemma was at work, and Mr. Atkins had gone to attend to some sheep out in the meadow where lambs were already making their appearance. I stood up. Two sets of footsteps were advancing upon me, and soon they were standing in front of me.

"Hello there! Are we ever glad to have come across you! Not too many people around in this neck of the woods at this time of year, are there? We're hiking the Coastal Path, and seem to have lost the trail somewhere along the way, and were wondering if you could you direct us back onto it."

I gave them a broad smile. "Hi there! Care to sit down a minute first? Take a breather? Great to have some company! It can get pretty quiet here. It's warm today too, so how about a beer? "

I motioned towards the bench behind me. Nothing would cheer me up more than to have the chance to chat with someone from the outside world. After all, I rarely had company other than that of Gemma and her father, and I needed someone to take me out of myself, make me forget, and stop my brain from whirling around in never-ending circles like a ship on full-steam-ahead without a rudder.

The bench shuddered as the men sat themselves down on the old boards.

"Now that sounds like a friendly offer. What say you, Jim? A beer?"

"Wouldn't say no."

I retreated to the kitchen, and reappeared with two bottles and an opener. "Do you need glasses?"

"No, bottles are just fine... But this is cider. I suppose you wouldn't happen to have beer, would you?"

I held out my hands, and they returned the bottles to me.

"Guess I goofed. Sorry about that. These new premium ciders have bottles that feel exactly like the beer ones. Maybe you should come in and check for yourselves... I tend to muddle them up. Sorry."

They were friendly men, and, beers now in hand, they kept me company for well over an hour, seemingly interested in hearing me talk, and asking me lots of questions, that I was happy to answer when I could. When it came to those about where I came from and things like that, though, I drew a blank, of course, and they commented that it must be weird not to be able to remember one's past.

They stood up. "Well, time to get moving, Chris. It's been great to chat with you, and thanks for the beer."

"Sorry I can't direct you to the Coastal Path after all that. You may see Mr. Atkins out in the field though. He'll be able to tell you."

"No problem." They shook hands with me, and went on their way.

My hearing had become more acute of late, presumably making up for deficiencies elsewhere, and as they walked out of the farmyard, I heard the one say, "Damned nuisance he's blind as well."

It seemed an odd thing to say. "You can say that again," I muttered. "You're damned right it's a damned nuisance." I even felt slightly annoyed after what I considered to have been a friendly encounter, and was standing there, thinking about the remark, when another part of their conversation reached me.

"... using the poor sod like that."

"Well, so are we, if it comes to that."

I shrugged, and returned to my bench, resuming my vigil over nothing whatsoever, while the ship in my anxious brain revved up again to full steam ahead, still rudderless, once again forging ahead in its endless circles, going nowhere. Baby lambs were bleating in the distance.


My confidence in negotiating my way around after the wheelbarrow incident, had long-since returned, and as I now knew the layout of the farmyard well, continued with my chores, such as feeding the chickens, collecting the eggs, and throwing hay over the fence for the steers, a great help to Mr. Atkins. Gemma downloaded a selection of music for my iPod, and while they watched TV in the evenings, I listened to audio books and music. I found the guitar music especially comforting, and listened to some of it over and over again, it seeming to bring an extra pleasure to me.

It was at this time that the day of my appointment with Mr. Cartwright, the ophthalmologist, arrived. Although Gemma considered it all rather pointless, I was still excited about the prospect of talking to him. It was as though my meeting with him would somehow cause him to change his opinion, and tell me that everything was going to be all right after all.

The appointment was for that afternoon, and it was arranged that Gemma would come home from work after lunch, pick me up, and drive me down to his office. For some reason, though, right after breakfast that morning, I developed a severe headache. It was unusual for me, but, as Gemma suggested later, it was probably because I was all tensed up about meeting with Mr. Cartwright.

As with everything else in the house, things were always kept in the same place so that I knew what was where, and it was no different with medications, so on this occasion I went to where the headache tablets were always kept. This time, however, for some reason or another I ended up with Gemma's sleeping pills, and as the shape of both types of capsules was identical, I couldn't tell the difference, and took two of the sleeping pills by mistake. As a result, when she came back home to pick me up, she found me dead to the world on the sofa, the dose for these being one capsule only.

Not knowing what had happened to me, she'd sent for the paramedics, and I ended up in the A & E instead. All I knew of the whole event, apart from the fact that I'd missed my appointment with Mr. Cartwright, was that the next day I felt like I'd been on a bender.

Gemma patted my hand. "I can't believe you took the wrong pills, Chris, my dear. I've checked, and the headache ones are exactly where they're supposed to be. You really should be more careful, and as a result, you've gone and missed your appointment with Mr. Cartwright, and now I suppose we'll have to wait again for another meeting with him."

The other appointment never came. When Gemma called to reschedule it, the message came back that although Mr. Cartwright understood my concerns, he was strongly of the opinion that all an appointment would do would be to further depress me by hearing him reiterate what he'd already told me, so didn't recommend it.

The second July since my arrival in the country came and went, and Gemma was happy. I continued to make every effort to be a contributing and good-natured member of the household, and to be as contented with my life as possible, given its constant ups and downs. To my frustration, though, it always seemed to be when I was on one of my ups and coping reasonably well, that a down –in the form of an accident of some sort or another --would come along to destabilize me, often causing me to hurt myself sufficiently to need hospital treatment.

Each event succeeded in destroying my budding confidence too, in that my accidents always seemed to happen right after I'd regained my confidence after a previous one, making it so that I was becoming increasingly dependent on Gemma's loving care and help, something she seemed not to mind at all, even when my accidents meant her having to cart me along to A & E, something that was happening ever more frequently.

Gemma was convinced that it was all due to my getting over-confident, and becoming careless, so she was constantly warning me to slow down, with the result that I became ever more hesitant and nervous about going anywhere without her, turning to her for help which, with her never-failing kindness, she was always ready to give me. It depressed me to be like this, but I assumed this was how it was for everyone in my situation, and supposed I should feel grateful that I had someone like Gemma to be there for me; there had to be many who had no such support.

On the latest occasion I'd had quite a serious accident, though, that was causing me a great deal of anxiety because of the additional burden I became to Gemma.

There was a covered drain hole in the farmyard. It was one of my points of reference, because, when I stepped on it, the cover rattled. On that day though, when I stepped on it, my foot went down the hole beneath the cover, which, instead of sitting properly in its frame, had been resting on the side of it. When I fell I heard a crack, and knew I'd broken something. Unable to get back to the house, I had to lie there until either Gemma or Mr. Atkins came to rescue me. I tried calling the latter, but he was too far away to hear me, so I was very lucky that Gemma found she wasn't needed at work that day, so happened to be back home within a few minutes of my fall.

She called the ambulance, and while we waited, she made us a cup of tea, and told me that it was that same drain that her young son had fallen into with such tragic results. She patted my knee. "I couldn't bear to lose both of you."

Hours later I arrived home, a cast up to my knee, having broken my ankle. As the hospital had told Gemma it was too dangerous for me to try to use crutches, I was wheelchair-bound for the following six weeks and in the full-time care of Gemma, who took time off work to look after me. I hated her having to do this, and worried constantly about being such a burden on her, the stress adding to my misery and feeling need to apologise for all the trouble I was causing her.

"My dear Chris, there's absolutely no need at all to keep saying sorry. You weren't to know the lid of the drain wasn't in its proper place. I can only think that one of the cows somehow managed to unseat it. Never mind, my dear. Don't worry; we'll soon have you back on your feet again. In the meantime, you know I'm only too willing to take care of you."

She continued to fuss over me, assuring me that I was no problem at all to her, even getting me into the farm van, and wheeling me around the village, despite my protesting that I would much prefer to stay at home.

"No indeed! I'm not leaving you alone at home in this state. I'd be worried sick about you. Besides, you need to get outside and get some fresh air, my dear. It's not good for you to be stuck in the house."

For me, though, it was embarrassing to have to sit there while Gemma cheerfully explained to everyone what had happened, and how she was caring for me -- and for me to need to keep agreeing that I was indeed most fortunate to have such a wonderful person as Gemma to look after me. I had to say the tone of her voice seemed to indicate that she in no way suffered from her burden. On the contrary, she appeared to be bearing her cross with surprisingly cheerful fortitude, and I continued to wonder at her amazing patience.

## CHAPTER 8

Gemma had invited to Sunday dinner some new arrivals in the village. They were a man and his wife, somewhere about Gemma's age as far as I could gather, and their daughter, who was home after recently graduating from university. Her name was Anne Foster. Anne and I were seated next to each other at table, and, over a typical Sunday dinner, were soon chatting away.

"What did you get your degree in?" I asked her.

"Geology and botany."

"I'm interested in geology too... I have the feeling I had something to do with it in my past life; I seem to know quite a bit about it. Are you going into paleobotany then?"

"This is great! I usually have to explain to people what that is. The answer is yes. I've always been interested in fossil plants."

I nodded, and our private conversation continued throughout the meal. On every level we seemed to find an interest, and it was the most pleasurable and stimulating experience I'd had since all this happened to me.

When it came time for them to leave, Anne had a suggestion. "Maybe we could go out some time, and go where we can see some of the more spectacular geological formations

… Oh! That came out the wrong way, but you know what I mean."

"Of course I do, and I'd like that. It would be great."

"Oh Anne! Are you sure? You will be careful where you take him, won't you? Our coastline can be so very dangerous."

"Gemma! Please! *Be careful where Anne takes me*? I'm not a five-year-old, you know! She's asked me to go out with her, not offered to baby-sit me!"

"You don't have to worry, Miss Atkins. Of course we'll take care. It's no problem at all. Chris is no different from any of the visually-impaired students we had at university … *You're* all right with it, aren't you Chris?"

"Of course I am. The only problem I have with this at all, is that it'll be you who'll have to take me out, rather than the other way round, but that can't be helped, and I'm sure you knew that already, didn't you?"

Anne laughed. "Of course. Nowadays that's often the way it is anyway, and I don't see anything wrong with it at all… I'm game, if you are. How about next Saturday, then?"

"Sounds great by me. I'll look forward to it."

"I'm not at all sure this is a good idea, Chris. I wish I knew where Anne plans on taking you. What if you were to fall?"

"Gemma, will you please stop fussing over me. I'm a grown man, and I need to do this. You yourself have said I have to face challenges, so you already understand that if I don't face them, I'm going to be forever stuck around the house here, being even more dependent on you than I already am, and I'm sure neither of us wants that. I need to get out and about, or that's what's going to happen."

"I'm just thinking of your welfare, Chris. I know you have to take on challenges, but at the same time I don't want you to try to take on things that you're not capable of doing, my dear. I don't want you to get hurt -- physically or emotionally, that's all. I care about you."

"You can't tell me, Gemma, that blind men don't go out on dates. That's ridiculous. Anyway, it's Anne who asked me, not the other way around... My God, Gemma! You're not trying to tell me she asked me out of pity, are you? I'm sure you're wrong. You have to be... Well, if she doesn't like what she gets, she doesn't have to ask me again, so I'm going to go, and that's all there is to it."

Nothing more was said, and I was looking forward to spending the day with my new-found friend, even though my anticipation was naturally mixed with a certain apprehension, not of the sort that Gemma was worrying about, but going out on a date without being able to see was definitely new territory for me.

Saturday morning came, and I'd not long finished breakfast, when I became ill, vomiting.

"Chris, my dear. You look terrible. You go right back to bed, and I'll bring you up something to settle your stomach. It has to be your nerves getting to you again. I knew this wasn't a good idea from the start, and look what it's done to you!"

I felt so ghastly I could hardly make it up the stairs, and spent the morning being sick to my stomach, while Gemma first called Anne to say I wouldn't be able to go out with her, then wasted her own morning looking after me. On top of my disappointment, I now had an added guilt, as Gemma apparently had had her own plans to go out to lunch with some of her friends. I tried to insist that she go anyway, as there was no reason at all why she should hang around watching me throw up, but she refused, insisting that she needed to stay, to make sure I was all right. No amount of persuasion on my part had the slightest effect, so not only did I miss going out with Anne, but succeeded in spoiling Gemma's day as well.

I ended up spending the whole day in bed, and it wasn't until evening that I began to improve. What caused it I'd no idea, but as Gemma kept repeating, she was of the opinion it was just my nerves, although I could never have imagined myself as being the sort of man who'd be likely to be sick to my stomach on account of nerves, like some hysterical teenage-girl. Maybe she was right though, and, deep down, my lack of confidence had had its way after all -- a depressing thought to have to admit that my emotions could get the better of me. Whatever it was, though, I managed to ruin three people's day, and having to have Gemma stay home only served to impress on me how dependent on her I was, which depressed me even more.

The following Saturday, having no stomach upset this time, I was able to keep our new date, and we had a great day together. Anne was understanding in the best possible way, and even persuaded me to go for afternoon tea in a delightful little tea room, accepting with a laugh, my apology for not paying.

"I wish you wouldn't worry about it Chris. It's fine. I like going out with you, and I'm enjoying our time together a lot."

"You mean you'd like to do this again then?"

"I'd love to, although I don't think we should confine our outings to the study of geology, do you?" she laughed.

"My thoughts exactly." It was all so natural, so normal, and I was ecstatic. I'd met the challenge, and was successful -- even going into a public place to eat, and despite Gemma's worrying, my nerves didn't step in to ruin our time together.

When we arrived home Anne even gave me a kiss, before taking me back to the house. I couldn't have been more happy. I'd found a friend and some semblance of normality at last!

We went out several more times together, but then I heard nothing more from her. Nothing. I waited day after day for her call, but it never came. It appeared she was no longer interested, although I couldn't understand why. I'd enjoyed her company and our conversations so much, and she'd given me the strong impression that she enjoyed being with me too. I even thought we made a good couple -- that she truly liked going out with me -- and there was no doubting the tremendous boost she'd given to my confidence; she'd given me hope of a real life.

Now though, our relationship, such as it had been, was apparently over. That was it -- great while it lasted. It took little to flatten me, and I could only think that the reason she didn't call me anymore was because our outings together had finally caused her to come to the conclusion that not being able to enjoy doing the same sort of things with me that she could do with a sighted partner made her relationship with me boring and not worth continuing, so our going out together wasn't something she wanted to continue.

That she'd finished with me just like that, though, without any explanation, upset me a lot, especially as I was convinced of the reason why she'd done it. I was sad too to think that I'd managed to misjudge her so badly. I'd thought her to be a kind and understanding person, instead of which she'd simply dropped me, without even having the courage to tell me to my face.

My renewed confidence battered yet again, and my short period of happiness snatched away, I started to get bitter and mentally self-destructive, holding black, imaginary conversations with myself -- self-harm, but to my brain. I was beginning to hate myself, laying on myself every disparaging adjective I could think of, and, gorging on self-pity, and with nothing else to occupy my mind now that Anne had dumped me, it was taking over.

"You useless, colossal bore, Chris Whatever, or Colwyn Yeats, or whoever the hell you are!"

It was a Friday. Mr. Atkins was out on the farm somewhere, and Gemma was at work. As usual, she'd been most understanding and helpful following my brief relationship with Anne, and I'd accepted her motherly fussing with gratitude, even though I knew I was being more dependent on her than ever, not just physically, but emotionally now as well. I was even resigned now to accepting that I was *always* going to be dependent on her, but then, I already knew that this was how my life was going to be in future.

The phone rang, and I answered it.
"Chris? It's Anne."
"Oh Anne! It's you! I'm so glad to hear from you!"
"You didn't get my message then?"
"Message?"
"I called you nearly two weeks ago, Friday, at about six, to see if you'd come out sailing with my father and me on the Saturday. Gemma said you were out helping Mr. Atkins in the field, but she'd get you to call me when you came in. She didn't tell you?"
"No..."
"Chris?"
"It's strange that Gemma forgot to tell me... She *is* very busy though, so I suppose... Anyway, I'd have really liked

to have gone out with you again... I didn't like to call you... I thought maybe you had decided... Well, you know..."

"Oh no, Chris! Not at all! I've loved our time together... Actually, I didn't call you again until now for the same reason. I thought maybe you didn't want to come out with me, and that's why you hadn't called back. Then I decided to give it another try."

"You won't believe how glad I am that you have! I was thinking you'd dumped me."

"Ah Chris! I'm so sorry! That's too bad... for both of us. Nothing could be further from the truth. Anyway, how about coming out with us tomorrow instead? The tide won't be so convenient this time; we're not in a deep-water mooring, so we're dependent on it, but we could manage it if we leave early."

"No problem. What time do you want me ready then?"

"How about I pick you up at seven?"

"Great!"

"Right, see you then. Lovely! I'm so glad you want to come."

"I can't wait."

"Oh my dear Chris! I'm so very sorry. How could I have forgotten? It quite went out of my head. Do forgive me. Anne has called again then, has she? She must have been wondering why you didn't call her back. I'm really so sorry, my dear. I can't believe how I could have forgotten; old age must really be catching up with me."

"Don't worry, Gemma. You can't be expected to remember everything, and yes, she has called again, and has invited me out again for tomorrow -- early. We're going sailing with her father. Then I'm going to spend the rest of the day with her."

"Tomorrow? Sailing? Oh what a shame! And I'd planned a special surprise for you. I've even bought the tickets."

"Oh? Tickets to what?"

"Oh, it doesn't matter. No problem at all, my dear. I know someone who'll be glad to have them. It's a concert. I'll just give her the tickets… Not to worry. I don't know about you going sailing though. Is it a safe thing for you to be doing?… It'll be quite a responsibility for them, won't it?"

"I'm so sorry, Gemma. If I'd known, I wouldn't have said I'd go tomorrow. I feel bad now that I've upset your plan. but you say it's not a problem. Are you sure? So it's okay if I go with Anne, then, is it?"

But there was no answer, and when I got up early after setting my alarm, Gemma was still in bed, so I couldn't get to see her and clear the air, as it were, before leaving. Even so, this didn't prevent me from enjoying my day, because I discovered that I not only enjoyed sailing, but seemed to know plenty about the subject as well.

Mr. Foster, Anne's father, was impressed, so impressed even, that once out of the harbour, which he said was a tricky place in which to manoeuvre, he had enough confidence in me to ask if I'd like to try my hand at sailing the boat.

"We've just got the jib and the mainsail up. I don't use the genoa or spinnaker very often." We had just come about on a new tack, and he handed me the tiller. "Okay, you've got a straight run now. Let's see what you can do."

It all seemed so natural to me. I just knew that normally, I'd watch the leading edge of the sail for signs of luffing, but as I could also hear it when it luffed, and was more aware of the feel of the wind when I couldn't see what I was doing, I found it not that difficult to make adjustments so as to make the most of it. When I combined that with the pressure of the tiller in my hand, I found I could keep the boat headed up and on course.

Mr. Foster clapped me on the back. "Well, Chris. I can tell you: this isn't the first time you've ever sailed a boat. Are you enjoying it?"

"I think 'enjoying it' is a bit of an understatement, Mr. Foster; I'm in heaven."

When I arrived home I apologized to Gemma for having spoilt her surprise.

"No, no Chris my love. Don't you think anything of it. I told you not to worry, and that I'd be able to give the tickets to someone else. Anyway, I have another surprise for you instead. While you were out, I was at a loose end, so I made you one of your favourite sponge cakes. What do you think of that?"

It was true I loved her sponge cakes, but somehow wished she'd not gone to all the trouble of making it; it just had the effect of making me feel that much more guilty for having ruined her day.

"Thank you, Gemma. As they say: 'The way to a man's heart, etcetera'. And you certainly know how to make a great sponge cake."

Anne and I went out regularly after that, but, always mindful of my overwhelming debt to Gemma and her father, I made sure I didn't overstep the bounds, giving the impression that I was taking their hospitality and care for granted. Following the sailing incident and ruining Gemma's surprise concert, I also made a point of asking her first, before I arranged to meet up with Anne, and was always home by the time she returned from work. After all, she had a full-time job, and it wasn't fair for her to have to come home and start preparing dinner on her own, so it was something with which I always helped. I made sure, too, to do my other chores as well before going out, so assumed that if Gemma wasn't at home, it was fine for me to be out too. It was a system that worked well, I thought.

Anne and I had been out all day, leaving shortly after Gemma left home for work. We drove out to the Preseli mountains, and walked up to what Anne called 'Preseli top', the highest of the hills. The weather was perfect, and I could even feel the aura of space around us. There was little wind, and the only sounds were those of a hawk -- a buzzard, Anne said, circling above our heads -- and sheep. Nothing could have been more enjoyable, and we had a perfect day together.

On the way home, however, we got held up by an accident ahead of us, and it was almost an hour before the road opened again, which resulted in my arriving home late for supper.

I burst in through the door, apologizing for my lateness and full of excitement about my day. Gemma and her father were already eating dinner. I was so busy chattering on about the great time we'd had, and then about the accident, I gave them no chance to say anything, before I finally tucked into my dinner. I was hungry now too.

"You know, Chris, my father and I aren't running a boarding house here."

I almost choked on my mouthful, and put down my knife and fork. "Oh Gemma! I do hope I…"

"It's not good enough, Chris. You're getting less and less like a member of the family, and more and more like a non-paying lodger. You're off all the time with this Anne girl; we hardly ever see you anymore."

"Oh come on, Gemma! All the fellow's done is find himself a girlfriend, and good on him, I say. We can't keep him cooped up here forever." I heard Mr. Atkins get up and go out, leaving me to the full onslaught of Gemma's tirade.

"Well, I'm the one who has to do a full-time job as well as all the work around here, and as far as I'm concerned, if you want to spend so much time with your girlfriend, Chris, then maybe you'd be more comfortable going to live with her instead..."

"What! You can't be saying you want me to leave, Gemma. I just can't believe what you're telling me. How could you? Surely I haven't been such a disappointment to you! And how could I possibly ask the Fosters if I could live with them? Anyway, I thought this was my home, and that you love me as your son. That's what you always keep telling me, but now you're basically saying you no longer want me, and are ready to throw me out. I... I don't know what to say."

"It's not that *we* no longer want *you*, Chris -- not at all. Of course we want you, my dear. We love you, but I've had the feeling recently that you're no longer happy living here with us -- that *you're* the one who doesn't want *us*."

"How could I possibly have given you that impression? Nothing could be further from the truth, Gemma. Surely you must know I'm happy living here with you and your father! Am I not pulling my weight? I'm willing to do whatever I can anytime, and I thought I was good company too. I've tried to be. Am I becoming a burden? I know I seem to be forever having accidents, and keep needing extra help from you, but believe me; no-one is more aware of this than I am. Maybe you're finding me too great a responsibility after all. I'm so sorry. Obviously I try my best *not* to have accidents, and I can't understand why, despite everything, I keep on having them. As far as helping out is concerned, I'm perfectly willing to do more. Perhaps I could get a job -- bring in some money. There has to be some sort of work I could do, but you've never let me even look for one before. Maybe now's the time."

"Don't be ridiculous, Chris! You're not fit to go out to work, and what sort of work could you do anyway? There's nothing that I can think of. Besides, who's going to ferry you back and forth to a job? *I* can't, neither can my father. He's got his own work to do, without catering to *your* needs. And as far as being good company is concerned, you can't be good company if you're not here... No, the more I think of it, the more I think it's perhaps time for us to think of finding somewhere where you'll be happier."

"Gemma. Please, please. Don't do this to me. How can you talk like this? Though it makes me choke on the words to say it, you must know I've nowhere to go, even if I wanted to, which I don't. Move on where? You must know too, that, as I just said, I can't possibly ask Anne's parents to take me in. Besides, I've taken you on your word that I have a permanent home here with you. I've committed myself to that. Have you any idea what you're saying now that you're prepared to do with me? What you're putting me through? Have I really been so thoughtless that you feel I'm simply using you? You can't possibly think I don't know and appreciate every minute of every day how indebted I am to you: you saved my life; brought me into your home; feed me; clothe me; provide me with all the comforts of a home life, mostly at your own expense, and have continued to look after me, even after discovering that my disabilities are with me for the rest of my life. You've made me as happy as it's possible for me to be, and you can't think I'm not constantly mindful of all this."

"I'm sure the psychiatric unit would be willing to take you back."

"*The psychiatric unit*! Oh my God, Gemma! No! I'd sooner die than go back to that place after what happened to me there. Besides, I don't understand. What makes you think they'd be willing to take me back? I was found to be of sound mind. Have I done something to make you think I'm not? -- that I've lost my reason, or something?"

She came up and hugged me. "I don't *want* to send you back there, my dearest Chris. All I'm asking for here is a little more consideration. You need to spend more time home here with us. Your absences have been just too much. Unacceptable."

"You mean you want me to stop seeing Anne?" My brain was so confused, it was starting to shut down on me, refusing to think. I could feel it saying, "Accept the fact. Once again you've no options. You aren't in a position to decide anything for yourself. You're dependent". Maybe I *was* going mad.

"Are you listening to me, Chris?... I was saying, no, you don't have to stop seeing Anne, my dear. Just remember *we* are your family, and we need and deserve to have you here too."

I nodded. It seemed, then, that if I didn't want to be sent away, I was going to have to let Gemma decide if and when I could see Anne. At least, that was the way I was interpreting all this. My brain had stopped functioning in a rational way, what Anne and I had done, and where we had been earlier in the day, forgotten.

Thinking about all this in retrospect, which of us was to blame, I couldn't decide. One thing was sure, and that was that as far as I could see, it had come out of nowhere -- a bombshell. I tried, though, to come at it from Gemma's point of view. Perhaps I had indeed failed in my obligations. Another thing I was sure of too was that I couldn't share any of this with Anne, especially about the psychiatric unit threat, for fear she'd think I was hinting to go to live with her and her parents, and I couldn't put them in that position.

I could at least phone Anne for myself, though, so told her I needed to stay around the farm a bit more for a while, because I was beginning to treat the Atkins's home as though it was some sort of hotel, rather than my home, and Gemma had remarked on it.

"Give me a week or so, Anne. Hopefully things will have cooled down by then... I suppose Gemma has a legitimate gripe; I've had such a great time being with you that I've probably not been paying enough attention here on the home front."

"Don't worry, Chris. Given your situation there, with the Atkinses having taken you in as they did and all, it has to be pretty awkward for you. So, yes, I guess there's no option, is there, really, but to cool it for a while, given what Miss Atkins has said? Not seeing you, though, is going to be awfully hard, and I'm going to miss you so much, Chris. Anyway, okay. Give me a call when you think things have calmed down, and as I said: don't worry; I'll still be here... Can't wait to hear from you."

That week, without Anne, I'd no option but to stay at home. Mr. Atkins had little work for me to do, and I tried to pay special attention to Gemma, whose spirits, although there wasn't anything extra she wanted of me either, improved dramatically, even though she was at work all day. Just knowing I was there seemed to be enough to satisfy her, and when she arrived home she'd give me a big hug and a kiss, and chatter away to me, telling me all about her day as though nothing at all had come between us.

## CHAPTER 9

It was Fall again, and the big, old-fashioned stove had been lit, giving the kitchen a cosy atmosphere, and as the room was a real farm-kitchen -- huge -- we now sat in there most of the time. All the trauma of the psychiatric-unit threat was behind us; Gemma was happy, back in her motherly role, and my brain, truly shocked by the incident, had wavered back and forth before finally restoring its equilibrium once more. We were a family again, and there was no further suggestion that I wasn't a part of it.

Having been here so long now, I knew my way around well, and even found my way up to the end of the long driveway, where Mr. Atkins had set up a mail box -- American-style -- to collect the morning newspaper and whatever the mailman had delivered into it. There were fence posts every eight feet, and having already learnt the location of every shrub, gate and pothole along the way, I'd lately started to regain my confidence once more, becoming more independent, and having had only one accident recently, was also becoming less of a burden to Gemma, which was naturally a great relief to me, and, I was sure, to her too. I was learning finally to cope.

"Chris! Telephone! It's Anne." It was evening, and I was out in the yard, having just collected the eggs, and Gemma was calling to me from an upstairs window.

"Oh! Great! Tell her I'm coming. I'll be right there."

"Slow down, Chris, will you? Take your time. We don't want any more accidents, and I'm sure Anne will wait for you."

I got to the kitchen, put the eggs down on the table, then headed for the phone, which was on the other side of the room. The next minute I was on the floor, with the palm of my hand smack up against the old stove, where I'd reached out in an attempt to save myself from falling. I let out a yell as the searing hot door of the ancient fire-box burned into it.

By the time I'd removed it, Gemma was at my side.

"Christ! That hurts!"

"Cool water." She rushed off, and came back with a bowl of water, and stuck my hand in it. "I think we need to go to A & E with this right now, Chris. It doesn't look good at all."

She hustled me off in the car, my hand still stuck in the bowl of water, the phone presumably still off the hook, and I wondered if Anne had heard everything while waiting for me to answer. We drove along in silence.

"So what happened here then?" the doctor on duty asked me.

"I tripped over the…"

"He tripped over the vacuum cleaner, and fetched up against the door of the old stove in the kitchen. I keep telling him not to rush, but he will insist…"

"Why was the vacuum in a place where he could trip over it? Did he put it there himself, then forget?"

"No, I didn't…" I began again.

"No. I'm afraid that this time it was all my fault," Gemma explained. "You see, I was vacuuming, then needed to go upstairs for something. Chris was out collecting the eggs, so I didn't expect him back so soon, but then the phone rang and it was for him, so I leaned out of the upstairs window to tell him, completely forgetting I'd left the vacuum where he might trip over it." She put her hand on my knee. "I'm so very sorry, my dear."

"You do have to be extra careful about these things, you know, Miss Atkins, when you have a visually-impaired person in the house. As his carer, you should be more aware of the dangers. He could do himself some serious damage. As it is, his hand is quite badly burned here."

"Oh, but I *do* care! I spend much of my time caring for him! I just wish he'd slow down and be more careful about where he's treading, that's all."

"I see that this is the sixth time you've been here to A & E, Chris. The first time, you fell over a wheelbarrow, it seems."

"Yes, well, on that occasion he made a mistake about where he was going, and walked into it."

"Is that what happened, Chris?"

"Well, yes, I guess so, although at the time I was convinced I was walking where I usually walked... I obviously goofed."

"Then, I see you broke your ankle falling into a drain-hole, and, just some weeks ago you came here with a bad glass cut across the palm of your left hand. What was that all about?"

"He'd been washing up the dishes right after…"

"How about we let Chris explain what happened, shall we, Miss Atkins?"

"Yes, well Gemma was right, I'd been washing up the dishes right after she left for work, and had casually swiped my hand around the sink, looking to see if there was anything I'd missed that needed washing, and came across a shard of glass from a broken tumbler…"

"Come along now, Chris. Admit it; you were careless, and must have clipped the glass against the side of the sink." Gemma patted me on the knee again. "He does the washing up for me, you see . He's so very helpful, aren't you, my dear?"

"Gemma, I'm sure I didn't..."

"He has blackouts and forgets things sometimes, and I certainly wouldn't have left a broken glass in the sink! The last thing I'd want is for me to be the cause of any injury to him. The poor man has enough to contend with, without me adding to his problems. I'm just so very glad that, as it happened, I'd forgotten to take some important papers to work with me, and had to turn round and come home to fetch them. I don't know what would have happened to him otherwise. It was bleeding so badly, I found him up at the entrance to the driveway, trying to stop passing motorists."

"He couldn't dial 999?"

"The cordless phone wasn't in its cradle, and I couldn't find it, so I wrapped my hand in a towel and went up to the main road, hoping someone would stop and help me."

"I see… and that required quite a few stitches, and obviously put your hand out of commission for a while." He took hold of my left hand. "How does it feel now? No numbness? Wiggle your fingers for me… Okay, you're lucky; you appear to have suffered no permanent damage there. Can you hold, say, a fork, comfortably now?"

"Just about."

"Well, I can tell you, your right hand is going to be out of commission now for quite a while as well, and I see you already have some permanent damage to that. What happened there? What happened to your finger?"

"I don't know."

"He suffers from amnesia."

"Yes. Thank you Miss Atkins. I'm already aware of that. Right, well, you certainly seem to be accident-prone, Chris. Perhaps you should do as Miss Atkins says, and slow down a bit."

It was four hours by the time we eventually arrived home, me feeling sorry for myself, my hand encased in a polythene bag, my confidence once again shattered, this time by the doctor's admonitions as well.

"You sit there now, and let me get you a cup of tea. I'm sure you can do with one. It must have been quite a shock for you, and that does look really painful. Here, let me help you get your coat off."

"Thank you."

"That's all right, my dear." Gemma put her hand on my forehead. "You're quite warm. Poor Chris! Always in the wars, aren't you? Like the doctor said as well, I just wish you wouldn't rush so. You need to take things more slowly. If you hadn't been in such a rush, as usual, you wouldn't have fallen so heavily, even though the vacuum was in the way. It's your right hand too, and you're not going to be able to use it for quite a while, again as the doctor said. Never mind, my dear; you know I'm always here to help you." And she kissed the top of my head.

I sat there saying nothing. Gemma prattled on, but I wasn't listening. As usual, I was going to need her to do things for me that I should be doing for myself, and how much more of a burden could I be on her? Surely the time must come when she simply couldn't cope with me anymore, and the thought scared me.

As always, though, Gemma was unfazed by my need to rely on her yet again. As she did every time I got into trouble, she fussed over me like a mother hen over a chick, and there wasn't anything I could do but accept it, and continually apologize for being what must be a right nuisance.

"I'm sorry to have left you hanging like that, Anne. You must have wondered where I'd got to." It was the following day, and I'd called Anne as soon as Gemma had gone upstairs to get dressed for work.

"Left me hanging? What do you mean, Chris? I don't understand."

"For not answering when Gemma went to fetch me to the phone last evening."

"I'm still not with you. The last time I called you, you answered it. When was this, anyway?"

"Last evening, as I said. Around five."

"But I didn't call you then, Chris. Gemma must have mistaken me for someone else. Is everything all right. You sound a bit odd. Has something happened? You're all right, are you? You've got me worried now."

"Seems all this was for nothing after all then." I finished explaining what had happened.

"That's dreadful... I hope your hand isn't permanently messed up, is it?"

"I won't know for a while. I hope not."

Anne was silent for a moment. "I know, Chris. Why don't we go out somewhere? Gemma won't mind, surely, especially as you can't be of much help around there right now. Let's just go out for a quiet drive somewhere. How about tomorrow?"

"Great idea! Yes, let's do that. Let me just check with Gemma first though – make sure she hasn't got other plans for me. Hang on. I'll be right back," and I put the phone down. "Gemma! Are you there? I need to ask you if..."

"No need to shout, my dear, I'm right here. And yes, that's sweet of you to ask me first. Of course you must go out with Anne. You're no use to me here right now, anyway, are you?" she laughed. "And while you're at it, why don't the two of you go out for dinner as well... In fact..." She went off, then came back and shoved some notes in my hand. "I think it's time you treated your lady-friend, don't you?"

"But Gemma..."

"No buts, and I've given you enough to treat her very nicely too. Go on then; take it. Anne's still waiting there on the phone."

"Did you hear any of that?" I asked Anne after Gemma left.

"Yes I did. How very kind of her. It's obvious she cares an awful lot about you."

"Yes. She does. I'm very lucky."

The next day Anne arrived after lunch to pick me up, and I was ready at the door to meet her, all smart in my clean pants and shirt, my boots polished by Gemma's father, my hand in its polythene bag -- rather spoiling the effect. Before answering the door I turned to Gemma. "How do I look then? Am I okay?"

She came up and kissed me. "Of course you're okay. You're always more than okay, Chris, and right now, you're even more handsome than usual, if that's possible. Enjoy your day."

"Wow!" Anne greeted me. "You look great, Chris, doesn't he, Gemma?"

"Indeed he does."

"Okay, you ladies. As you well know, flattery will get you everywhere. I think, though, that my hand, stuck in a polythene bag like this, must look like a pickled dead thing from a science museum!"

Our afternoon couldn't have been better, and then, in the evening, Anne took me to an excellent restaurant nestled in a wood in the country somewhere, and it was good to know that I'd be paying -- although, as usual, I was beholden to Gemma for that.

It was peaceful; the service efficient and unobtrusive, and I managed well, if clumsily. We drank each other's health, and enjoyed the excellent cuisine.

"I've just got to say this, but do you know what a stunner you are, Chris?"

I grinned. "You know something Anne? I honestly haven't the vaguest idea what I look like. For all I know I could look like King Kong, and, strangely enough, I *do* remember what *he* looked like, and why I can't remember my own face, when I can remember his, I've no idea. It doesn't make sense."

"I'm going to describe you to you then." She lowered her voice. "There are some people at the next table looking at you. I think they're talking about you."

"There! I told you I look like King Kong. They must have recognized me."

"Oh Chris! Stop it! Anyway, so that you know, you've got great hair. Thick, dark brown and wavy. How's that for starters?"

"So did King Kong."

"I'm going to ignore that. You have fine, almost aristocratic features with a sexy mouth and a great nose."

"You mean a great -- meaning nice -- nose, or a great -- meaning huge -- shnoz?"

"Oh stop it Chris! I'm trying to be serious, so you can imagine yourself."

"These days I spend most of my time imagining myself, though mostly who and what I was in my previous life."

"Well, at least you can now imagine how you look from my description. Oh yes! And you have to know you have a smile to die for."

"Better keep a straight face then, hadn't I? Can't have you keeling over on my account."

She leaned over and kissed me. "Oh Chris!"

After leaving, we stood outside and listened to the sounds of the night and gentle rustling of the trees, the leaves taking on that dry, papery sound that comes with the Fall.

Anne kissed me. "The stars are really brilliant tonight, and because we're so far away from the lights of the town, they're filling the whole sky."

"Can you see Orion?"

"Yes."

"See his belt? The three stars in the middle?"

"Yes."

"See that glow just below his belt -- in his sword?"

"Yes."

"That's one of the most beautiful sights in the sky. It's the Orion Nebula." I put my arms around her, kissed her, and there in the wood, beneath Orion and the trees, I told her how much I loved her.

"You have to already know this, surely; it has to be obvious, but I love you too, Chris, so very much."

I arrived home to find that Gemma had gone on up to bed, but had left the door open for me. I appreciated that, and went to bed more contented than I ever remembered.

It was a few days later, and Anne and I had gone out again for the evening. I was now deeply in love with her, and after bringing me home we made love in the car, and not being able to see was, for once, unimportant, our bodies coming together in a perfect union, as though made for each other, her skin so soft and smooth, her touch so gentle, and in the early hours of the morning I entered the house in a state of euphoria -- and jumped.

"Hello Chris. You're home at last."

"You haven't been waiting up for me, surely Gemma! There's no need for that at all. I'm not some teenager, been off on a binge somewhere. I *am* a grown man, you know."

"I know I needn't have waited up for you, my dear, but I'm so glad I have. It's worth it. I'm delighted to see you look so happy at last."

"I am, Gemma, unbelievably happy. In fact, I'm what you might call 'euphoric' even! Anne and I had a terrific evening, and I can't wait to tell you, Gemma, but she loves me! She told me so, and I'm sure I've never loved a woman the way I love her. How about that? I almost can't believe it, but it's true. Great, isn't it? I've decided, too, to ask her to marry me... Gemma? Did you hear what I just said? I said I'm going to ask Anne to marry me."

"Yes, I heard you, my dear."

"So?"

"I'm just thinking about what you said."

"Oh? That's all you have to say? You're *thinking* about it? Aren't you glad I've found the woman that I want to spend the rest of my life with? You have to be! For once I've got good news to share, and can't think of anything better to be able to tell you. We're going to be married! It's fantastic Gemma. I feel great."

Gemma came up to me and took my hand. "Come, Chris. Come over here with me, my darling, and sit down a minute."

She led me over to the sofa, and we sat down, she still holding my hand, and I wondered what it was she was going to say, especially as her response to my news had not been in any way the one I'd been expecting.

"Well?" I said, when we'd been sitting in silence for all of that minute.

She continued to hold my hand, patting it with her other one. "Chris. my love. How can I say this? Have you thought this through? The last thing I want to be is a wet blanket, and, believe me, I have only your happiness in mind -- and Anne's too, of course -- but it's because I care for you so much, there are times when I feel I should speak plainly to you."

"Thought it through? Thought *what* through? What's to think through? I love Anne, and she's told me she loves me too. We know we can be happy together."

"But Chris! Think, my dear. Yes, you may love each other, and from seeing you together, I'm sure you do, but what, other than your love, have you got to offer a girl like Anne? You've no job, no credentials with which to get one -- at least a proper job -- no money... No memory of who or what you are. No identity even. And although I hate to point this out, since you sometimes lately seem to forget it, despite all the accidents you've been having -- which should surely serve as a reminder to you -- you are quite severely disabled, my dear, being blind, as you are. Do you expect Anne to care for you financially and, much of the time physically, like I do, throughout your married life? Don't you think it a bit selfish of you to take advantage of her love like that? Besides, for all you know, you could already be married, and without proof that you aren't, you wouldn't be allowed to marry -- not legally anyway. You could end up being a bigamist."

She patted my hand again, and stood up. "Well, it's time for me to go to bed; *I* have to be up early tomorrow, even if you don't." She kissed me on the cheek. "Do think about what I've said, my dear."

How could I possibly *not* think about everything she'd thrown at me? I made my way upstairs, and spent the rest of the night sitting on the edge of my bed, doing just that, thinking, and it made me about as depressed as it was possible for me to be.

Anne and her family went away for a couple of weeks after that, leaving me in misery, waiting for her to come back, but not knowing what we were going to have to say to each other now when she came home. Gemma's comments had hit a home run, and I simply couldn't work out for myself whether she was right or wrong. What, indeed, *could* I offer Anne, when it came down to it, other than my love? And having Gemma point out I was disabled was like having her punch me right in the solar plexus, even if she was right, which she was, of course. As far as being already married was concerned, she could have been right about that too, although it didn't feel to me as though I was. However, as she pointed out, without being able to swear I had no impediment, I couldn't marry Anne anyway.

We had been invited over to the Foster home for Sunday lunch. It wasn't the first time I'd been to their house, as Anne had taken me there on several occasions, so Gemma seemed surprised when she discovered I knew my way around and even able to show her where to hang her coat.
There was so much activity going on all around us, Anne and I weren't able to have a private chat, and I wasn't feeling talkative anyway, thinking about what I was going to say to her in view of Gemma's comments -- something that had, naturally, filled my brain to the exclusion of all else during her absence.

We had sat down to dinner, and I'd just picked up my knife and fork and located my plate, when it was whisked away from me.

"Oh Chris! I'm so sorry. I forgot... I'll just make this a bit easier for him," and Gemma went off with my plate.

"But..."

"No, no," she called out from the kitchen. "It's no problem at all, Chris. No problem at all... Here you are. You'll be able to manage it now."

I was mortified. As Gemma must surely have known, there was no reason anymore for her to carve my food up for me, and everyone else must have been equally embarrassed as well, for there was quite a silence, with only the sound of scraping of knives and forks on plates as people set about their meal. What made it worse was that we weren't the only visitors, there being another couple there as well -- people I'd not met before, and who didn't know me.

I was truly cross, and found it hard to carry on any sort of conversation for the rest of the meal, especially as it seemed clear to me that Gemma, by doing what she did, had taken it upon herself to illustrate to Anne what a responsibility I was, and what she'd be taking on if she were to marry me. In the doing, she'd ruined my visit.


"Chris and I are going for a walk." We'd finished our meal, and I was most grateful for Anne's suggestion, as I couldn't wait to get away from everyone else.

We walked a little way in silence. "I can't believe that Miss Atkins took your plate away like that. I know she worries about you, but that was a totally weird thing for her to have done, especially as you hand is fine now."

"Yes, it was, wasn't it? Do you think everyone else thought that too?"

"Yes, it was pretty obvious."

"I could have crawled under the table with embarrassment."

Anne gave me a kiss on the cheek. "It was Miss Atkins who should have felt embarrassed. We all felt for you."

We walked to a local park, and sat down on one of the benches. It was a warm day, people walking, laughing and chattering, dogs barking, and children calling out to one another in their play. Off in the distance, tennis balls clacked on clay, and nearby, water cascaded as though from a fountain. Way above, a plane droned its way to some distant destination, and we sat and kissed, and I put my hands up to touch her gently, first her smooth cheeks, then her eyes, then her hair.

"I love you so much Anne." I was stuck, not knowing how to express myself. "*You* don't think I'm a responsibility, do you?" I blurted out.

She kissed me again. "Oh Chris! What an odd thing to say! Is this because of what Miss Atkins did? You shouldn't let that get to you. She was just being overly attentive – quite unnecessarily so, too."

"You haven't answered my question."

"If you think about it, I suppose we can all be a responsibility in one way or another. We've all got problems of some sort, don't you think? Hang-ups or whatever, although they may not be visible to everyone, like yours is, and, anyway, your particular problem has to be more of a burden to you than to anyone else... So, in answer to your question: no, I don't think you're a responsibility at all." She stood up and grabbed my hand. "Come on, we're getting way too serious here."

I wanted so much to ask her to marry me, but Gemma's warning had served as an effective deterrent, regardless of what Anne had just said. Other things aside, I was still not in any position to provide for her financially, so, for the time being, the best thing seemed to be to simply enjoy our happy relationship just as it was.

## CHAPTER 10

I had to go in for a check-up a couple of weeks after our chat in the park -- just a to make sure that my hand was properly healed, and they took a blood test at the same time. I heard nothing back as far as the test results were concerned, and Gemma told me that no news was good news, which was definitely something to be glad about. Anne and her family had gone away again for a few days, and I was longing to have her back in my arms once more -- my Anne as I now thought of her. I missed her so much, and she'd promised to call me as soon as she returned.

At least three weeks passed, and although Anne should have been home well over a week by now, I'd still heard nothing from her, and was starting to get worried. I'd have phoned her, but Gemma had recently decided that as she and her father both had mobile phones, they no longer needed the old house-phone, and had cancelled it as being an extra expense they didn't need. This made it impossible for Anne and me to get in touch with each other, because unless she came round to visit me, we now had to wait until Gemma was home before being able to talk to each other on her mobile.

Because of the cost involved, I didn't like to ask Gemma for a specially adapted mobile phone for my own use, and Gemma had not offered to get one for me, so, still not having heard from Anne, I asked Gemma to phone her for me on hers, but all she kept getting, even after several days of trying, was Anne's answering machine.

"Can you take me round to their house, please Gemma? I don't understand; Anne and I are really close, too close for her to abandon me without saying a word. Besides, she isn't the sort of person to do such a thing. Something must be wrong. Did you leave a message for her? Can we phone again, and this time let me leave the message if there's no answer? I have to talk to her; I need to know what's happening."

Yet another week passed, and Anne still hadn't returned any of my messages. By now I was desperate to talk to her, convinced that something drastic had happened, so I persuaded Gemma to drive round to the Foster home again, where I waited in the car while she went up to the front door. They weren't there this time either, though, so we had to drive home again, none the wiser, although Gemma had her own thoughts on what had happened.

"It could be Anne thought better of the relationship, Chris, my dear... of what she was taking on if things got serious between you. It's possible too that her parents had a say in the matter as well. After all, if I were her parents, I'd be quite concerned that she was, well, how shall I put it? Thinking of spending her life with... and I'd consider it necessary to give her my opinion and advice."

"You already have... To me, most forcibly; and then you emphasized your opinion when you made a fool of me when we had lunch there -- in front of all those people."

"Chris! Please! I know you're upset that Anne would appear to have dumped you, but don't blame it on *me*. I want only the best for you, and sometimes you seem to forget your disab ..."

"Oh! So I'm to go through life being constantly reminded?"

"Where it's appropriate -- yes, my dear. You have to be realistic in your aims. I just don't want you to get hurt, my love. It hurts me too, you know, to have you suffer like this."

Time passed with still with no word from Anne since that time she went away with her parents, and once again I felt trapped and miserable, there being no way in which I could track her down by myself, and ask her why she'd stopped wanting to see me -- although Gemma was probably right in her assumption. That made me feel even worse, discovering my judgment of Anne's character and her supposed love for me was so faulty. She could at least have told me of her decision to my face. However, I told myself, I'd thought she'd dumped me once before, and been completely wrong, so maybe this time too, there was another valid reason for her silence. The only possible one I could think of at all was that something terrible had happened to her and her parents, and that they had met with some disaster while on their holiday.

"Gemma, I'm sure something must have happened to Anne. Is there some way we could find out if the Foster family met with some accident while they were away? Maybe they never made it home at all. Perhaps their neighbours will know something. I'm really scared that something's happened to her."

"Well, I suppose we could pop round there again to see, if you like, my dear... I know! I could pass by on the way home from work today, and see what I can find out for you. Would that help?"

"Yes, it would. Thank you. Right now I feel I'm in limbo, just not knowing, and worrying about Anne. The thought that she might have met with some catastrophe is eating away at me. I need to know... I haven't slept nights worrying."

Gemma put her hand on my shoulder. "All right, my dear. I'll make enquiries this evening and, with luck, we'll get to the bottom of this... Like you too, I sincerely hope nothing bad has happened, so, you're right; we do need to find out."

That afternoon I couldn't settle to do anything, waiting impatiently for the sound of Gemma's car. In the end she was late arriving home, but that I put down to her once again taking time to do something for me that I couldn't to do for myself.

"Well? Did you find out where they are? Are they all right? Nothing's happened to Anne, has it?"

Gemma took my arm and led me back into the house, and I waited while she put her things down on the table.

"Why don't you sit down, darling, while I get us a cuppa first, shall I?"

"Can't you just tell me? Is it a long story then? Not a bad one, I hope... Forget the tea, Gemma. Just tell me. I need to know."

Water poured into the kettle, and mugs clattered as Gemma retrieved them from out of the cupboard. "Well. I've learnt something, but it still doesn't answer the question as to why she's not contacted you, I'm afraid."

I was standing behind her, and put my hand on her shoulder. "She's all right then? She hasn't suffered any accident or anything? Well, thank God for that, at least... So what *did* you learn then, otherwise?"

"Well, they weren't home, so I couldn't talk to them, but I did go to their neighbour, and asked her if they were away, or simply not home at that moment. She told me that, as far as she knew, they were there, just as always. In fact, she'd seen Anne just yesterday."

"*Yesterday*! Did you ask the neighbour for any details? What was Anne doing? Was she all right?"

Gemma handed me my mug of tea. "Let's go and sit down, shall we? I've been on my feet all day, and need to take the weight off."

"But what did the neighbour say? Could she tell you anything. How did Anne look?"

Gemma plumped herself down on the sofa with a sigh. "Ah, that's better." Her shoes clattered to the floor as she kicked them off, and then she patted the sofa, indicating that I should sit down next to her.

"My dear, I'm awfully sorry, but it would appear that your Anne has found herself another partner." She put her hand on my knee. "I didn't want to have to tell you this, Chris, but you would insist on knowing what had happened, so I did as you asked, and I'm afraid that's the answer."

I said nothing.

"Sometimes, my love, it's better not to know the truth, but, as I say, you insisted, and now you know."

"No. It can't be. I don't believe it... No. It can't be true. Anne wouldn't do this to me. I know she wouldn't. The neighbour has to have gotten it wrong. Anyway, just because she saw Anne with another man doesn't mean to say he's her partner. No. It's just not true. I'm sure of it."

"My dear, what else can explain the fact that she hasn't called you? She came home from her holiday; she wasn't in any accident; she appears to be perfectly healthy, and she's been seen with another man... Maybe she met him while on holiday. Who knows? And I should be completely honest with you, but haven't wanted to hurt you any further: the neighbour saw her and her new partner in a full embrace in the car outside her house, and then again after he opened the car door for her to get out -- quite a gentleman he must be too; you don't see men opening doors for ladies much these days, I have to say."

I got up, put my untouched tea on the table, and went up to my room.


My life had become even more of a mental rollercoaster with this latest downer, and I was beginning to wonder how many more rides on it I could handle before I fell off it altogether. My loss of Anne and how she'd treated me left me utterly miserable, and my feelings of loneliness and isolation from society, unable to read, or simply break into a run and work off my anxieties, brought me crashing down.

As always, Gemma did her best to revive my spirits, but I was so unresponsive, I wondered that she continued to even try, taking me out as she did on daytrips here and there, when she could be relaxing, enjoying her Saturdays and Sundays off from her job.

I did do my best to show my appreciation for her efforts, although it probably didn't occur to her that driving me around the countryside, taking me to different places, meant nothing to me. She might just as well have driven me round and round the farmyard, as all it did was to impress on me even further how much I regretted not being able to see anything: the coloured patchwork-kaleidoscope of the fields, the changing moods of the sea, the blue-washed hills in the distance, the sunsets and the delicate pinks and creams of the hedgerow-flowers she liked to describe to me on our way. It was a regret that filled me with a longing like no other, a special ache.

I continued to work on the farm, and gradually my life resumed its normal routine, my spirits beginning their laborious climb back up once again, although I thought constantly of Anne, and longed for her company, despite what she did to me. It seemed that I'd now reached whatever equilibrium I was likely to reach in my life, and my confidence yet again rose towards a renewed sense of independence.

"Chris, I know how the ladies love you, and I have a friend who I know would be only too happy to see a handsome young man to cheer her day. Would you be willing to come with me to visit her this afternoon? I know she'd love to meet you."

I smiled. "Of course Gemma. It'll be good to have the chance to do something for you for a change, instead of it always being the other way round."

She hugged me. "I know, my dear... And I appreciate that. Can you be ready in about an hour then?"

"Sure."

We set off, and it took just over an hour to reach our destination, during which time Gemma chatted away, and, as I repeated to her, I was only too glad to be able to do something to please her for a change.

Eventually we arrived. There were the usual, familiar sounds, and the air smelled of that odd mixture of ozone, along with passing whiffs of cut grass, cows, fertilizer and silage, as it did out on the farm.

"She lives in the country too then?"

"Yes, here we are. She lives here amongst other people, which is better for her. It's sad, but she's been having some problems the last couple of years, so has been coming here off and on for treatment."

"Oh? That's too bad. What sort of treatment does she need then?"

"Just a minute, love, I need to sign the register for us... There. Shall we go in then?"

"Fine."

There was a slight delay before the door opened, and we went in. There was a strange, but familiar smell, a certain mustiness, but I failed to place it for the moment.

"Hello Chris! How are *you* this long time? How good to see you again. You look so well. A lot better than when you left us, I must say. Good on you. Are you coming back to stay with us again then?"

"*What*! Oh No! Gemma! Where are you? Gemma, come back. I'm sorry but…"

But Gemma had gone, and I was left standing against the wall in that terrible communal room. Never, ever, despite Gemma's peevish, and what I'd thought at the time, empty threat to me, had I imagined I'd ever be inside this place again.

I was terrified, my mind suddenly whirling around, trying to think of the real reason or reasons why she'd brought me here. Had she simply returned me, like an unsuitable pet from the pound? Whatever it was, it had to be something to do with her deciding that, because she'd had to work so hard to look after me, she'd simply worn herself out doing it and, as I'd so often thought might happen, I and my problems had now reached the stage where she couldn't deal with them any longer; I was too accident-prone, too dependent, too nervous, too sad over the loss of Anne. That had to be it, and I stood there, my hands starting to shake.

"Welcome back, Chris... Here. Give me your arm, and come with me and sit down. Mind the table. That's it. Make yourself comfortable, why don't you, while you wait. How about a nice cuppa? A cupcake too?"

"No! No thank you. Where's Gemma? I need to find her."

"Who's Gemma, Chris? Just you wait there now, while I get you that cuppa."

"Gemma! Don't leave me here! *Please*!" I shouted. "Gemma! Where are you? *Please, Gemma*!" I stood up, charging forward in my desperation to get out of the place, and, colliding with one of the other tables, sent everything flying off it. "Have to get out! I've got to get out of here."

I charged into a tray that someone was carrying, and it went crashing down too. Then I slammed into a wall, stunning myself, and slid down it, ending up sitting on the floor. My dark glasses had gone, and the brilliant afternoon sun, streaming in through one of the nearby windows, lit up my head like an enormous searchlight. I sat there, struggling for breath, my back up against the wall, my legs straight out in front of me.

"*Please*! *Please*, someone, help me get out of here!"

"Steady now, Chris. Please don't shout. Calm down. You must remember how it upsets everyone, and causes situations to arise... Come on now. Give me your hand, and let's get you back on your feet, and find you a chair... There now. Sit down there a bit, and calm down. Control yourself. We can't have you kicking off like that, or we'll have to restrain you, and I'm sure you wouldn't want that, would you? You could hurt yourself -- and others too, and you've created quite a mess as well. There's tea, milk, cakes and everything all over the floor, and we're having to comfort some people. You really frightened them with that outburst... Now. Tell me. What is it that's troubling you?"

"I n-need t-to s-see Miss Atkins."

Who's Miss Atkins?"

"She b-brought me here."

"Ah! Now we're getting somewhere. Have you been officially checked in yet, then? Maybe your Miss Atkins is in Miss Carmichael's office signing the necessary forms for your admission as we speak."

"B-but she t-told me she was b-bringing me t-to s-see a f-friend."

"Well, she was right, Chris. We like to think that we are indeed friends to our service users here. Let me find out if she's still here, or if she's left already. Miss Carmichael will know. No need to worry now, I'm sure. There you are... Nothing to worry about at all... Just you wait here now -- and no charging off again, okay Chris? Here, have this cup of tea. Someone's kindly brought you a cupcake too. Homemade."

I shrank back into the chair, more than ever convinced that Gemma had brought me here and left me because she could no longer cope with me any more than Anne had been able to. That had to be why she'd not told me where we were going either. She must have persuaded the authorities that I was mentally incompetent or suicidal, and managed to get them to take me back here, to section me again, and tricked me into coming, and now my violent outburst had more than likely convinced them that Gemma's judgment was accurate.

The prospect was so dire my whole body shook uncontrollably. I was completely traumatized, and now in a full-blown panic, my heart was beating so fast, it scared me even more. I sat there shivering, tea and cupcake ignored. What if Kevin was on the loose again? What if he, or someone else, came at me with a razor-sharp knife again? I didn't trust them here at all. But as I'd already discovered when I slammed into that wall, there was no escaping from this place, and I sat there alone in my solitary prison, the Tower-of-Babel communal room of the psychiatric unit again.

Then someone tried to drag me to my feet, someone who obviously recognized me, because he was shouting. "It's Chris! He's back! Come on Chris. Come on!"

"Oh there you are Chris! I noticed you having a good time a while ago. Good for you! They really like you here, don't they? Was that the same game you used to play with them... I happened to see someone else I know too, so went to have a chat... I knew you'd be just fine on your own for a few minutes, knowing pretty much everyone here as you do... So, shall we go to see my friend then?"

Gemma took my arm, expecting me to stand up and go with her, but I sat there, still struggling to catch my breath, and completely disorientated because the last thing I remembered was being dragged to my feet.

"Chris, are you all right? What's the matter?... I'm so sorry to trouble you," she called out to one of the carers, "but Chris here seems unwell. Do you suppose you could see what's the matter with him? He's acting very strangely, and I'm so worried that he's having some sort of seizure, or something."

"Oh! You must be Miss Atkins then. You're the person who brought him in, are you? We were wondering who it was. He was looking for you earlier." He took my hand and felt my pulse.

"His heart's in overdrive, and he's deathly pale, poor man. Looks almost like he's gone into shock for some reason."

"Why d-didn't you... t-tell me... where we were c-coming? S-surely you m-must... must have known how I ..." The feeling of suffocation was intensifying, my breaths coming in big heaving sighs. It was my worst panic attack ever.

"Chris! For Heaven's sake! Get control of yourself. What's wrong with you? Anyone would think I'd brought you back here to stay, and gone home without you!"

Someone put a hand on my shoulder. "It's all right, Chris. It's all right. I remember you now. You were with us a while back, weren't you? It might be hard for him to control his feelings right now, Miss Atkins. He's obviously in the throes of a serious panic attack for some reason. Amnesia, you must understand, can often cause those suffering from it to be overly anxious and agitated. You must realise that, for Chris, life can be disorientating and confusing, and we do need to be understanding and caring about his fears, legitimate, or not... and for him, it must be especially difficult to cope with, given that he can't see either. Something must have happened here just now to set him off, although I've only just come in, so don't know what it could have been -- we're really short-staffed today."

"My dear man. Believe me, I do nothing *but* care for and understand him. I took him in. He's a much-loved member of my family, and I love him dearly, and do the absolute best I possibly can for him. It's no easy task, you know, for someone like me to take care of a man with the physical and mental disabilities such as those Chris suffers from, and although I work full time as well, I spend the rest of my days, and sometimes nights as well seeing to his needs, and you can see for yourself what's happened here now, when I left him for just a few minutes. All I did was go and have a chat with someone. One would have thought that here, at least, he'd feel at home, but he must have forgotten that he lived here for a while."

"I'm sure you do do your best for him, Miss Atkins... Are you willing to go with Miss Atkins to see her friend first -- before you go home, Chris?"

"S-so I *am* g-going home then?"

"Of course you're going home, Chris. As Miss Atkins has just said, your home is with her, not here."

Gemma put her arm around me. "Yes, of course it is Chris. My, my! All this panic about nothing." She patted my hand. "I don't know. What am I going to do with you? All this fuss..."

"How about it if give you something to settle your nerves a bit, Chris? You're obviously pretty agitated right now... Tell you what; I'll give it to you, and leave it up to you as to whether you take it or not. Is that okay with you? We can't force medication on our visitors,." The carer laughed, then went away and returned with a couple of pills which he dropped into my still shaking hand. "You can swallow them with your tea, right here, if you want." He handed me the cup. "Don't drop it now, will you?"

I put out both my hands. "Th-thank you."

"Not at all, Chris... I just talked to someone else, Miss Atkins, and she told me that Chris became so agitated with the patients who recognized him and wanted him to join them that it took two male members of staff to physically restrain him until he calmed down and stopped struggling with them. She said he seemed to be scared stiff of them all for some reason – probably the reason why you found him so agitated. Well, I must be off... Several staff members off sick today, so we're stretched rather thin, as I think I mentioned... You take care now, okay Chris? And do come and see us again, won't you? We're always happy to see our former service users. 'Bye for now."

"Chris! What on earth was all that about? I bring you to see a friend, and the next thing I know you're behaving like a mad man. And this is certainly not the place to go berserk like that, shouting at those poor people. Anyone would have thought they were trying to attack you! You're lucky I *didn't* decide to leave you here! I really don't know what to make of you sometimes." She smoothed my hand.

It was obvious that she had no idea what effect all this had had on me -- my fear that she was going to abandon me here -- so how could I explain? Still overwhelmed by the severity of my panic attack, and mortified too that she should have blurted out my problems so bluntly and loudly like that in front of everyone, I didn't answer.

Then she took me to meet someone who, it turned out, had gone out for the day with her relatives, so we left; and although she chatted cheerily all the way home, I said nothing: that because I'd gone ahead and swallowed the pills I'd been given, and was grateful for their effect.

Nothing more was mentioned about the trip to the psychiatric unit, but I still couldn't help wondering why Gemma had not told me where we were going, so I could have prepared myself. I suppose, though, that looking at it from her point of view, there was really no reason why she should think that visiting the place would upset me. After all, all that was well in the past, and she'd never have put me through purgatory like that intentionally. Besides, I decided, looking at it from any normal person's point of view, the idea of someone going to visit a psychiatric unit with the intention of seeing one of the inmates, and ending up being incarcerated there oneself was ludicrous -- preposterous even, when considered rationally, but maybe I was becoming irrational, paranoid, and even that possibility was enough to scare me.

## CHAPTER 11

I was sitting on the sofa in the big kitchen, half listening to some music. Gemma had gone to work, and Mr. Atkins to market with some sheep. I'd done my chores: made the beds, washed up, and put some clothes in the laundry that Gemma had left for me, and was bored. Without much mental or physical stimulation, I was led, as usual, to wondering what sort of life I used to lead. I'd been told I was in fine physical shape when found on Druidston beach, but could tell that I'd deteriorated considerably since then. I'd asked Gemma if it would be possible for me to go to a gym somewhere, but the problem, she told me, was getting me there and back, which I understood, of course. Even so, it was depressing for me to feel my body getting soft, the work Mr. Atkins had me do, not sufficiently strenuous to keep my muscles toned, and, unable to run, I suspected that if I were put on a treadmill, I probably couldn't run a quarter mile even. I was getting flabby.

I wasn't expecting anyone, so was surprised to hear a car come into the farmyard, and went to the door. I could tell by the sound of the engine that the car didn't belong to anyone I knew, so stood there, waiting, as a woman's footsteps approached.

"Chris? It's your social worker, Miss James."

. "Oh hi! Come in, won't you?" I held out my hand, and she shook it

Soon we were seated opposite each other at the big table. "I'm sorry to have been so long in coming to check on you, Chris. We're so stretched nowadays, what with the cutbacks. How are you doing?"

I was surprised. Her voice had mellowed from that of the woman who had spoken to me so coldly that day, when she'd told me I was going to be sectioned. Maybe her tone had softened because she'd heard of my experience with Kevin. Even so, it was hard to be more than merely civil to her. "I'm fine, and count myself very lucky to be here. Can I get you a cup of tea or coffee?"

"Coffee would be nice, thank you, Chris."

I went about making some filter coffee for her, and could tell she was watching me to see how I coped with the task.

"You really seem to be making yourself at home here, Chris, and coping well. I see you know your way around."

"Yes, well the Atkinses are kindness itself, and Miss Atkins, in particular, devotes so much of her time to caring for me, I sometimes wonder how she continues to manage it."

"Ahem... Chris. I have to ask you: everything *is* going well here for you, is it? You say Miss Atkins devotes much of her time caring for you, so she's been treating you well, has she?"

"Yes, of course! As I said, she's kind, but also especially caring, because I do seem to have more accidents than the average person, but then I suppose that's to be expected in my situation, isn't it? And whenever I end up doing damage to myself, she's definitely the most loving and helpful person anyone could hope to find."

"Yes, the hospital contacted me about that. That's the reason I'm here. Their records show that rather a lot of your accidents seem to require visits to the A & E department, and one of the doctors has expressed concern over the frequency of those visits. Would you like to tell me a bit more about the occasions on which you've needed the services of the A & E?"

"I don't understand why they should be concerned, but I do appreciate it, of course, that they'd think enough of me to send you here. I assure you, however, there's absolutely nothing to be concerned about."

"Tell me about these accidents anyway. Let me be the judge as to whether I should be concerned, or not, yes?"

"Okay. Well, the first one happened when I got overconfident, and one day slammed into an iron wheelbarrow full of rocks -- hurt my knees rather badly, but Miss Atkins was great about it. Still have the scars though."

"May I see them?"

I pulled up the legs of my jeans. "Sure. Why not?"

"That must have been quite a tumble you took; those are nasty scars. And Miss Atkins took you to A & E as a result then, did she?"

"Yes, she was worried that they'd get infected, so yes, we did end up there -- got a tetanus shot at the same time."

"I see. They must have taken quite some time to heal."

"A little while, yes. In the long run, though, it wasn't so much that that bothered me, but my lack of confidence afterwards. That went down the drain for a while, but Miss Atkins was really great about helping me get it back."

"And how did she do that?"

"She insisted on going with me everywhere, until she was satisfied I was okay on my own... I have to say I didn't think it was always necessary -- perhaps better to let me recover my confidence in my own way -- but she insisted, which just goes to show how much she cares about my safety."

"What made you trip over the wheelbarrow in the first place?"

"Well, naturally I wasn't expecting it to be where it was, and was convinced it wasn't where it should have been, but I was wrong."

"And how do you know you were wrong, Chris?"

"Well, Miss Atkins told me it was where it always was, so I was wrong... Would you like another cup of coffee?"

"No thank you. Tell me about the other accidents."

"Well, there was the day I managed to put my foot down a drain hole and broke my ankle," and I told her about that.

"And the other accidents?"

So I told her all about the various accidents I'd had where I ended up in A & E "They're pretty much always due to my making mistakes in judging where I'm walking. I guess I'm just not very good in remembering exactly where things are, even though I always think I'm right at the time, and it's always when I'm particularly confident about where I think I'm going that I seem to get it wrong, and then, of course, I manage to do even more damage to myself...Why all the interest in my goof-ups anyway?"

"Well, we don't want our patients to come to any harm, and I'm wondering if you might be safer in a more protected environment somewhere -- that's if we can find a space for you."

I stood up. "Oh no! Please don't take me away from here! I'm at home here! So I have accidents. I wish I hadn't told you now. Better the odd accident than have to go back to somewhere like that terrible place you sent me last time!"

"It wouldn't be anywhere like that, Chris. The people wouldn't be suffering from mental problems. I'll need to have a talk with Miss Atkins about this, though. What if you had an accident while she's out? Have you had any accidents while you've been left on your own?"

"Well yes, but on each of those occasions so far, I've been lucky. For one reason or another, Miss Atkins has happened to come home right after I've fallen, or whatever, so has been able to take me to A & E straight away. She's lost quite a number of days' work as a result of all my accidents, and I have to say I do feel guilty about that, but as far as taking me away from here is concerned, I do need to learn to cope on my own, you know, and I do try my very best to do that. Please don't deprive me of what little self-confidence I *do* have. Besides, I'm sure I'm happier here than I could possibly be anywhere else."

"Well, we'll see. Anyway, can you read Braille yet? And I'll give you a phone number to call if you find yourself having any more accidents."

"No. I can't read Braille, and I don't have a phone."

"You don't have access to a phone! Why not?"

I explained about the removal of the house phone because Mr. Atkins and Gemma had mobile phones, and no longer needed the land line.

"We can't have that at all. You need to be able to call for help. You can't keep on relying on Miss Atkins to fortuitously arrive home in time to come to your rescue. I must certainly talk to her about that." She stood up. "Right, I must be off. I'll be round to see you again. Thank you for the coffee."

"You're welcome." I followed her to the door, and stood there while she returned to her car.

As the door clicked open, I heard her talk to another occupant. "I'm going to insist we get him…" The door closed. What, I wondered, was she going to insist she got me? A phone? Braille lessons?

## CHAPTER 12

As usual, Gemma was at work, Mr. Atkins out on the farm, and I was alone in the house. I'd finished all my chores; Paddy and I had been up to fetch the mail, and I was sitting on the sofa listening to Julian Bream and John Williams playing together. Things were going well, and Gemma had been more contented lately than in a quite a while, and after my experience at the psychiatric ward that awful day, she'd taken great pains to let me know how much I meant to her, and -- as she told me far more often than I really wanted to hear -- how like the son she'd lost I was. All this helped me wobble back onto an even keel once more, although I'd not yet summoned up the courage to ask her if Miss James had spoken to her yet. I assumed not, as there was no mention of my getting a phone or Braille lessons.

Surprisingly, I'd not heard anyone arrive, so jumped when there was a knock on the door. I waited for someone to come on in, but it was followed by a silence, which was unusual; people normally, if they bothered to knock at all, opened the door and came right in.

I went over and opened it. "Hello?"

"Hi! I've come to see Colwyn Yeats. Is he here, please?"

I was so surprised I simply stood there with, I am sure, my mouth open.

"Is he here please?" the man repeated. "I need to talk to him. I'm his brother."

"You're my brother? *My brother*? My God! I can't believe it! You've found me at last!... I can't believe this is happening. Is this actually for real? It's really you? You don't recognize me then? Have I changed that much?"

"Col? Oh! Col! Yes! I see now; it *is* you, bro! And yes, you *have* changed a bit. Must be the sunglasses, and you're thinner." We gave each other a hug, but I was too embarrassed to ask him his name. Maybe he'd get around to saying it, without my having to ask. "Well, give Marjorie a hug too, bro. Or are you so overwhelmed at seeing us?"

He'd said, "*I've* come to see..." so I hadn't realised she was there.

"Oh I'm sorry Marjorie. How are you? Do come in! I can't believe you've found me at last!"

Marjorie gave me a kiss on the cheek. "Hi Col. I'm very well, thank you. How are you though, this long time?"

"Well, now you've finally found me, I'm fine." I shook my head. "I'm sorry; you've got me in a complete I-don't-know-what here. I still can't believe you've found me! It's been so long! Do come on in," I repeated, but in fussing to let them in, bumped into Marjorie who had stopped in front of me. "Oops. Sorry." I moved to one side and bumped into my brother.

"Col? Are you all right?... What's going on, bro?"

While I made us all some tea, and found some of Gemma's sponge cake to go with it, I began telling them everything, including the news that had my brother not told me, I'd have had no idea who they were. For a while that, plus their discovery that I couldn't see them, seemed to dampen the reunion a bit, until my joy at their having found me lifted the atmosphere more to where it should be, although it still seemed oddly strained on their part -- not surprising really, seeing that my brother not only had to discover that I was blind, but that I'd not even known what my own name was, let alone his, which was "Tim" he told me.

The shock of their arrival sent me off yet again on my emotional rollercoaster, and after having experienced a welcome calm for a number of weeks, I was now racing upwards to a high level of agitation again.

We were still sitting around the kitchen table, me asking innumerable questions, and now too hyper to even listen to the answers, when Gemma arrived home.

I leaped up. "Gemma! Guess what! My brother, Timothy, and my sister-in-law, Marjorie are here! They've finally found me, and have come to take me home -- to take me home! Can you believe it? At last I'm going home! It seems totally unreal after all this time! And I was right! My name *is* Colwyn Yeats after all!"

I heard Gemma sit down on the sofa, but when she made no comment, I went up to her, found her hand, and squeezed it "Oh! I'm sorry, Gemma." I gave her a kiss. "I'm so sorry. How thoughtless can I get! Here you are, just come home from work, and here I am, greeting you with the news that I'm going to be leaving. I'm sorry. I could at least have waited a bit before dropping it on you like this the minute you come in through the door... although, you *would* have wondered who the visitors were anyway, wouldn't you? And so I'd have had to tell you anyway.

"It's almost impossible to realise that I'm actually going home at last, Gemma -- home to my family... I'll come to visit you often, though, and you must come to visit me too... Tim tells me I'm an oceanographer, a graduate student no less, and I come from Rhode Island. I can't imagine why the Embassy couldn't find me; it should have been easy enough, given all their resources... Well, I guess that doesn't matter now. My brother's found me... And they're going to take me around a bit first, before we fly back -- it's going to take a while for me to get a new passport anyway."

"So when will you be leaving us then, Chris?" Gemma's voice was emotionless, but when I tried to hug her, she pushed me away roughly. "How can you leave me now? After all I've done for you, Chris? How could you? You can't leave me! *This* is your home."

"But Gemma! This is my brother -- my own brother! Surely you wouldn't have me reject my own family? Surely you understand! You *must* understand! I'm me again! I'm Colwyn Yeats, and I belong with them."

"But *I'm* your family now. You can't simply abandon me like this! What'll I do without you? And you still haven't told me when you're walking out on me."

"Please, Gemma, please don't say that. Please. I'm not walking out on you. It's not like that. We've both known that I'd most likely be found at some point, and at that time I'd have to leave. We've both known that... And Tim says we have to leave tomorrow."

"*Tomorrow!*"

"Yes, we do have to leave tomorrow, I'm afraid, Miss Atkins. I've been searching for Col for a long time, and I simply can't afford to spend any more time here now I've found him."

"Gemma. You must know how much you mean to me, and I promise, I *will* come back. I'll *never* forget my life here. I'm so sorry to have to leave you like this after all you've done for me, but don't you see, I *must* go. It's only right. You wouldn't deny me my blood family would you? But I'll come here to visit as often as I can... Gemma?"

But there was no answer.

My brother and Marjorie were staying at the local inn that night, and left soon after, the atmosphere having become chilly and unwelcoming, and leaving me embarrassed and sad about the distress I was causing Gemma. I kept telling her how sorry I was, but she'd have none of it, refusing to speak to me, so in the end I gave up.

"Well, I think I'll have an early night. It's been a long day, even if it's been an exciting one, so I'll say goodnight." And I went upstairs to my room, knowing I was so looking forward to the morning, there would be little chance of sleep.

I'd been in bed for about three-quarters of an hour, listening to a talking book, when there was a knock on the door.

"Chris. Can I come in please?"

I switched on the bedside light. "Of course you can, Gemma." I sat up, and she came over and sat on the side of the bed.

"I didn't wake you, did I?"

"No, not at all. In fact, I think I'll be hard-pushed to sleep at all tonight -- I'm way too excited about what's happened. I'm still finding it difficult to believe it even."

"That's why I've brought you some chamomile tea. I must apologise for behaving so badly, my dearest Chris. It was inexcusable of me. It's just that I'd arrived home after a hard day at work, as you said, and had driven home as I always do, looking forward to seeing your face." She smoothed my cheek. "You should know, if you don't already, you do have such a lovely face, my dear; so gentle and kind, and so very intelligent. And I do love it so... And I'm not surprised at all to learn that you were working for your PhD. You must imagine how I felt, though, to come home only to be told that you'll be leaving me. It was more than I could cope with. Even so, I'm so embarrassed by the way I reacted, especially in front of your brother and his wife."

"Well, I'm sure they'll forgive you for that, Gemma. You can't be blamed. It had to have been a terrific shock to you, and I wish it could have been softened somehow. It's been a shock for me too, but obviously not in the same way as it's been for you... Look at it this way though, Gemma. At least they could be left in no doubt that you liked having me live here with you," I joked.

"Small consolation... Oh dear. I'm going to miss you so much, my love... Miss you so very much."

"Well, as I said, this doesn't mean we'll never see each other again. We'll visit each other often, okay?"

"It's not enough, I'm afraid. My son is to be lost to me all over again."

I'd no answer to that, so said nothing, and after a minute, she kissed me goodnight, and left.

I think I must have been asleep only a couple of hours after she left, when I woke up, my stomach in turmoil. I barely made it to the bathroom in time, but that wasn't the end of it: I spent the whole night on the bathroom floor, vomiting every few minutes, and when Gemma came to wake me in the morning, I was still there, my head propped against the toilet.

"Chris! What is it? How long have you been like this?"

"All night, I think. What time is it?"

"It's eight o'clock. You're usually up by now, so I came to look for you." She took my arm, and I hauled myself to my feet. "Let's get you back to bed."

"But my brother will be here in another hour to pick me up. I need to get ready."

"My dear Chris! You're not going anywhere today. You're way too ill. It's those old nerves of yours again, making you sick every time you get worked up over anything."

I collapsed back onto my bed, and she held my hand, smoothing it with her thumb.

"But…"

"No 'buts' about it. I refuse to let you out of the house like this."

It was true; I felt terrible -- drained from vomiting all night. It was rather like the time I was intending to go out with Anne for the first time, but this was far worse. Perhaps Gemma was right, and nerves had been the cause. Fortunately the worst seemed to be over now, but she was also right in saying that travelling anywhere in my present state definitely did seem out of the question.

"You stay there, and I'll bring you something to drink. You must be dehydrated." She left the room, and returned, handing me a glass. "Here, drink this." It was sparkling water.

My brother, of course, turned up at nine o'clock, as scheduled, and was upset, even annoyed, that I wasn't in a fit state to travel. He tried to urge me to make the effort anyway, but with Gemma adamant I shouldn't go, I left the two of them to argue it out. Naturally I cared, but raising the energy to contribute to the discussion was beyond me right then.

"All right, Col. We'll leave it for today, but we can't delay things too long. It took us a long time to find you, and our time is running short now. Our plane reservations…"

"I'm sorry. I don't know what happened. One minute I was fine, then…"

"Yes, well never mind about that now. Stay in bed today, and we'll make it tomorrow instead. One day's delay won't be too disastrous, I guess." He gave me a brotherly punch on the arm, and left.

I wasn't able to eat anything all that day, but, it being Saturday, and Gemma at home, she plied me with drinks, and, as usual, smothered me with care and attention. I began to feel better later on, but then it all came back that night -- leaving me spending another night in the bathroom, and this time it was even worse than the previous night. I felt I was dying. What was going on? Gemma was still convinced it was me and my nervous disposition that were to blame and, as I said, it seemed she was right. Maybe so much had happened to me, I was no longer able to cope with *any* form of stress, good or bad; I'd become allergic to it. I even gave it a name: 'adrenalin poisoning'.

Regardless of the cause, however, by the morning I was more ill than I'd been the previous morning, and again Gemma insisted I shouldn't leave the house. My brother, though, insisted I go, sick or not, and this time wouldn't take 'no' for an answer, but promised Gemma that if my condition showed any sign of worsening, they'd take me to the nearest emergency room.

"Do you mind if I use the bathroom before we leave?" Tim asked her.

"No, of course not. It's this way, down here," but he was already half way up the stairs.

"No. It's all right, Miss Atkins. I'll use Col's. I need to double-check he has everything anyway." He came back down a few minutes later. "Okay if I take this mug with us, please, Miss Atkins? Just in case we need it for Col."

"Yes. But let me wash it out for you first though."

"No problem. I washed it out in his sink already. Thanks anyway. Okay, Col, are you all set?"

"I just need my glasses. Can someone get them for me, please?"

"Where are they? I'll get them," Tim offered. "I didn't see them when I was up there, though."

"They're right next to my bed."

He disappeared upstairs again, then called down. "They're not next to your bed, Col."

"They have to be. It's where I always keep them. I usually put them on first thing, but what with everything this morning…"

"Can you think where else they might be? I've looked everywhere: under the bed, among the bedclothes, in the bathroom, down beside the chair. Sorry Col, they're just not here." He came down again. "We can't hang around any longer. You'll have to go without them."

"I can't. I can't stand bright lights. It's like someone's exploded a huge sun in my head, and it gives me a migraine."

"Miss Atkins. Can you think where his glasses might be?"

"No. That's something Chris takes care of himself. I've no idea."

"Well, I'm sorry, Col. You'll just have to shut your eyes. We'll get you some more."

"But…" I gave up. They were special-prescription glasses. What a damned nuisance I was all round! Now I was a whinger as well, and somehow or other I found myself stretched out on the back seat of their car, with a blanket and a pillow to keep me company.

And so I left Gemma and Mr. Atkins -- a peremptory farewell after so long in their care.


For some reason I expected us to be going on a long trip, such as to London, in preparation for our departure, but instead, we had barely travelled an hour -- if that -- before stopping.

"Here we are." Tim got out of the car, and came round to let me out.

"So soon?"

"Yes, we're staying here for a few days. We were going to take you on some trips locally first, but you're obviously not up to it right now, so we'll check in, and you can lie low till you feel okay again."

"Whatever you say. It's a relief that you're making all the decisions. My stomach's stopped churning finally too, and I wouldn't say no to some food."

"Well, I suppose we could have an early lunch. What do you say, Marj? Are you ready for a bite to eat?"

"Fine with me." Marjorie, I was discovering, was a woman of few words. Half the time she was so quiet I couldn't even tell where she was, or even if she was there at all.

"Here we are then. It's a nice hotel." Tim grabbed hold of my arm, and hustled me in through the door.

It certainly seemed like a good hotel -- plush carpets underfoot anyway. There was even a bellboy who took us up in an elevator, then out into a corridor. Then they all walked off without me, so I stood there, miffed at being abandoned like that, and unwilling to shout after them. Presumably they'd soon discover I wasn't with them, and come back to get me. They did.

"Oops! Sorry bro!"

The bellboy showed my brother and Marjorie to their room, and was ready to show me mine, but Tim butted in. "You can show *me* his room. I'll see to him." He was being businesslike, and super efficient, and talked as though I wasn't even there. Knowing I wasn't well, though, he was probably simply taking charge.

"Right you are, Sir." And they walked off, once again leaving me standing in the corridor.

Where either Marjorie or their room was I'd no idea, and was beginning to feel awkward and uncomfortable. I stood there, waiting, then, hearing heavy footsteps approaching, and the sound of someone trundling a suitcase along, I went to step out of the way, and almost fell into space. I put out my arms to save myself, and fetched up against a door jamb of an open doorway.

"Try adding more water to it next time, mate." And man and suitcase went on their way.

Eventually Tim came back. "You could have gone on into our room, instead of standing there."

"I would have if I'd known where it was."

"You're standing in the doorway."

"How the hell am I supposed to know I'm standing in the doorway? How am I supposed to know that's your room?"

Tim ushered me inside without commenting, and tired, sick, or for whatever other reason, I was beginning to resent what I considered to be my brother's offhand attitude towards me. I couldn't help being the way I was, and it wasn't fair of him to make me feel stupid, especially in front of others. Did I embarrass him, or something? Maybe the two of us hadn't got along well in the past, and Marjorie certainly gave no indication at being overjoyed at having found me.

Perhaps it *was* just that I was tired, and being oversensitive as a result. I stood there. The room was incredibly bright, as though someone had turned a floodlight on me from just a few feet away, and it invaded my eyes and my brain with its diffused glare to the extent that I had to put my arm in front of my eyes to cut it out. I missed my glasses.

"Fantastic view! You should see it."

"Should I? Well I can't, and that's all there is to it. And this bright light's killing me."

"Sorry... Well, shall we go down for lunch then? Are you ready, Marj? Tell you what, Marj: Col and I'll go down to the restaurant, and we'll see you down there, okay?"

There was no answer, but presumably Marjorie had heard, because Tim took off, carting me along with him, and we were finally seated in the restaurant.

To me it seemed as though Tim was definitely feeling awkward about having me with him, and that made me feel even more uncomfortable. The sooner I was back home in the States, the better. I just hoped my whole family wouldn't behave in such an offhand way. Tim seemed edgy as well, and kept popping off to make phone-calls, and these, as far as I could make out, must have been ultra-private calls, otherwise there'd have been no reason why he couldn't make them from the table, in front of me. It wasn't as though he'd no cell-phone either, because it rang on several occasions while we were waiting for our food to arrive, and each time he disappeared out of my hearing range to answer it. It was all making me as edgy as he was, especially with silent Marjorie being nothing more than a presence.

"You want a drink, Col?"

"No thanks. I'll wait till my stomach has settled. I don't think I could take another bout of whatever that was... I don't like to have to say this, Tim, but I need to tell you. Please don't walk off and leave me again, like you did back there in the corridor. It's disorientating to be left standing, not knowing where you are, and afraid to move."

"What? Oh sure. No problem, bro."

"How did our parents react when they heard you'd found me?"

"Well, excited naturally."

"What did they say?"

"Well, I don't remember their exact words -- happy though."

"That's *it*?"

It was like getting blood out of a stone. Where was all the animation? The enthusiasm? The interest even? I was beginning to wonder if they were even glad they'd found me. Maybe, even, they'd only recently bothered to start looking for me. Maybe Gemma had been right, and my other life, my real life, hadn't been a happy one, so what was I going back to? I was afraid to think of the possibilities, so gave up, but by now had become so agitated that I managed to knock over my glass of water, the contents landing in my lap, causing me even more embarrassment, what with waiters coming and mopping everything up. I wanted to crawl under the table, and disappear.

Lunch over, Tim told me he had some business to attend to, but that I could go for a walk with Marjorie if I wanted. I decided I'd prefer to go to my room and catch up on some sleep. Besides, I heard no word of encouragement or enthusiasm from Marjorie at the prospect of going for a walk with me.

"Excellent! Good idea." It was almost as though he was relieved to get rid of me, and we went up to my room, which was where, I'd no idea. I didn't even know the floor and room number, and forgot to ask. Tim unlocked the door.

"Right, here you are then. In you come."

I stepped inside.

"Right then. See you later," and he left, shutting the door behind him.

I found the bed, and lay down, and did the best thing possible: I fell asleep.

It was still daylight when I woke up, feeling refreshed and altogether calmer. It had probably been all my fault earlier, not being well, and I made the decision that nothing would now interfere with my new-found freedom, the joy of being reunited with my family, and the relief of finally being on my way back to my own home and my own loved ones. In addition, any fears that my previous life could possibly have been an unhappy one, faded away.

I thought about Gemma and her father, and obviously felt regret there. That I'd managed to add what Gemma had called 'a glow' to their lives, was gratifying, but then for me to have summarily taken that pleasure away by leaving them with no time to adjust to the idea that I was going away, certainly made me feel guilty, although, as I'd tried to tell Gemma, they should have known and been prepared for me being found eventually. Even so, I'd done my best by promising to visit them frequently, and had invited them to visit me too, so there wasn't much else I could have done under the circumstances. Right now though, I wanted to concentrate on my own happiness at being back with my family, and so put them out of my mind for the moment.

I got up, found the bathroom, took a shower, shaved and dressed, and at the end was even feeling slightly less scared about my future life, although my career as an oceanographer -- even though I couldn't remember it -- was clearly over, which gave me a jolt of grief again about having lost my sight forever; and I wondered what I *would* be able to do, to achieve, if anything, now that the cataracts, and whatever the other damage was, were there to stay.

As Gemma had so rightly pointed out, I had no job, nor any prospect of getting one that was worth getting, at least not in the near future. I'd have to learn new skills for that, Braille even. My spirits sank again at the idea, but I brushed all negative thoughts out of my mind, and went over to the window; today was definitely not a day to be indulging in negative thoughts.

Although Tim had bought me some regular sunglasses, without my prescription ones the light from the window was still way too bright, flooding my whole head, and giving me an instant headache, so I drew the curtains, sat down, found some music on my iPod, and relaxed. I was hungry now, and would be ready for my supper when Tim came for me.

I didn't know how long I'd slept, but as it was still daylight, it couldn't have been that long, and I continued to sit there, listening to my iPod. After what must have been at least an hour, though, going by the amount of music I'd listened to, I was still waiting for Tim to come to fetch me. Where was he? I was getting really hungry now too, so decided to use the phone next to my bed to ask for a call to be put through to his and Marjorie's room.

"Could you please put me through to Mr. and Mrs. Timothy Yeats please?" There was silence, and I waited. Perhaps they were out somewhere.

"Hello, Sir. Are you still there?"

"Yes, I'm still waiting. Never mind. It doesn't matter. They're probably out at the moment. They should be back soon though."

"It's not that, Sir. I'm afraid I'm having trouble finding them. What's their room number?"

"I don't know, I'm sorry. They checked in earlier today."

There was another silence. "I'm sorry, Sir, but there's no-one of that name staying at this hotel. Are you sure you have the right hotel?"

A lump rose in my chest. "Stay calm," I told myself, "and think rationally." But I couldn't. All I *could* think was that I'd somehow been tricked; Tim wasn't my brother after all, which would explain his offhand attitude towards me and his inability to answer questions about my parents and their reaction to my being found. What about all those phone calls too that he'd made and received, and which I'd not been allowed to listen to? Marjorie had acted strangely as well. Who was she? Had I been kidnapped for some reason?

The possibility took hold in my head, and this, accompanied by the fear that their intentions regarding me were therefore obviously not good ones, led me to the conclusion that the one thing I needed to do now was to escape and get help before Tim and Marjorie, or whoever they were, returned and carried out whatever they planned to do with me. The problem was that I'd no idea where I was, let alone how to get back to the farm, especially with no money.

One thing was certain, I needed to get out of this room, but what would I do once out in the corridor? How could I go anywhere? Maybe someone passing by would help me.

I went to the door, opened it, and stepped out into the corridor, listening for footsteps or voices, but it was silent and empty, and I turned to go back in, remembering that the best thing for me to do, of course, would be to call the front desk for help. What I'd not realised, though, was that the door was one of those that closes on its own unless held open, and before I could stop it, I heard it click shut, leaving me stranded outside. Tim had taken the key-card too, so there was no way for me to get back in.

I stood there with my back to the door, panic rising in fear that no-one would come along soon and show me where the elevator was so I could reach the front desk safely before my kidnappers returned.

For well over a year I'd been living in the quiet countryside, sequestered, protected, dependent, with people to look after me. Now I'd been kidnapped by strangers and thrust, all on my own, into a strange place, with no-one to help me, no idea where I was, or what dangers I faced, yet having to make decisions and be responsible for myself. I was terrified, and stood there in the silence of the corridor too scared to move in any direction.

It seemed like an eternity to me, before I heard the quick footsteps of a woman approaching. As she passed me, I asked her if she'd please show me to the elevator, but she must have thought I was up to no good, skulking there in the corridor, leaning up against a door, because she broke into a run, and her footsteps faded into the distance, leaving me once more in the silence, surrounded by the smell of polish and bleach.

I felt myself all over. Had I dressed properly? Did my clothes look odd because Tim had packed them, and had got them mixed up? Had I spilt food down myself? Maybe my white shirt had ketchup on it. Had I even had ketchup? I couldn't remember. I felt my face. Had I shaved properly? It felt okay. Would I look like some kind of idiot if and when I finally arrived at the front desk? It was a risk I was going to have to take, and I waited in quiet desperation for someone to come.

After several more agonizing minutes I heard a trolley approaching in the distance, and a door being opened. I followed the sound, feeling my way along the wall, banging into a side table on the way, and heard the person leaving the room and shutting the door.

"Please, could you please help me? I need to find the elevator," I called out.

"Ze wat?"

"The elevator?"

"I not know how you say, eleevaater."

"The thing that moves people up and down from one floor to another." I gesticulated.

"Oh! Ze lift."

"Yes, the lift. Would you take me to it. Please... Now?" I said encouragingly.

"Ah yes! We here now. Which floor you like?"

"Where the front desk is, please. All I needed was to end up on the wrong floor, and be lost -- "As if you're not already lost!" I told myself. Within a few minutes, however, and with the help of someone else in the elevator, I made my way to the front desk, and by this time was in a high state of panic.

"Can I help you, Sir?"

"Yes, please." I paused to get my breath which, because of my agitation, made me sound as though I'd been running a marathon. "I rang a while ago and asked to be put through to Mr. and Mrs. Timothy Yeats's room, but was told there was no-one by that name staying here."

"That's correct, Sir. Are you sure you have the right hotel."

Only now did it occur to me that Tim had told me nothing, so I didn't know which town I was in, let alone which hotel. Not wanting to sound like a character out of a comic strip by asking, "Where am I?" I blurted out with confidence, "Yes, I'm positive." After all, we'd arrived here earlier that day, and unless someone had somehow transported me out of the hotel while I was asleep, then presumably I was still in the same place. "My name's Colwyn Yeats. Have you at least got *me* registered here, please?"

"What room number are you, Sir?"

"I d-don't know," I stammered, almost in tears with frustration and humiliation.

She came out from behind the desk and took my arm. "Shall we go and sit down a minute, Sir, and we'll see if we can sort this out. Can I get you a cup of tea?" She was pleasant, and I was immensely grateful for it, and we sat down in the hotel lobby, surrounded by seemingly a host of people coming and going with great activity. It reminded me of the communal room in the psychiatric unit, making me even more agitated.

"No, but thank you anyway." I'd reached the stage where I was afraid that if she walked off and left me for whatever reason, she too would disappear, so now she was there, right next to me, I didn't want her to leave. I was ready even to beg her not to leave me. Besides, I'd no money with which to pay for a cup of tea.

"Now... I have the register here. Let me see. When did you check in Sir?"

"Earlier today."

There was silence.

"Bear with me a minute, Sir. This is a large hotel, but I can find no record here of a Colwyn Yeats having registered here…"

"But…" My panic rose even higher, my heart beating faster, and I was now hyperventilating, gasping for air.

"Oh! Hang on! Here we are, Sir! But you arrived here yesterday, not today! You arrived just before lunch -- yesterday."

"*Yesterday*! But…"

I was opening my mouth to ask her the names of the two people who registered with me at the same time, when a hand clapped me on the shoulder.

"Col! Here you are! Where the blazes…? You frightened the life out of me! How did you get here for God's sake?"

The clerk stood up. From the tone of her voice, it was obvious she was annoyed with Tim, but remained polite. "This gentleman here was most concerned…"

I'd no way of telling what sort of sign Tim gave to her, but it must have been something to indicate I wasn't in my right mind, because the next thing she said was, "Then I think perhaps it would be wiser, Sir, not to leave him on his own again under the circumstances…" She put her hand on my arm. "I'm so glad all is well, Sir," and left.

I wanted to scream. The last thing anything was, was 'well'. "What the hell's going on?" I shouted at Tim.

"Quiet Col! Everyone's looking at you."

"I don't give a shit who's looking at me! Where the hell have you been? Who the hell *are* you? And how come I appear to have slept for over eighteen hours?"

"For Christ's sake stop shouting, Col! Calm down! Come back up to your room, and I'll tell you." He took hold of my arm, but I shook him off.

"I'm not going anywhere with you. I don't trust you, and I want to stay where other people are around. I feel safer that way, and if you don't hurry up and explain everything to me right now, right here, right this minute, starting with who the hell you are, I'm going to yell for the police at the top of my voice."

"I suggest you do no such thing, Col. They already believe here that you're suffering from a mental problem. Start shouting for help, and it'll be an ambulance that comes to pick you up, not the police."

I was speechless, and now cowed, deflated and defeated too. Tim took my arm again. This time I didn't resist.

"Now, as I said, calm down, and we'll go into the restaurant, find a table away from everyone else, and have some breakfast," which we did. Where Marjorie was, I didn't know, and, at this point, didn't care either. I'd been reduced to silence, and beyond even asking any more questions, let alone expect reasonable answers. Whatever was going on, there wasn't anything I could do about it. As it had been for so long now, I was at someone else's mercy. What was the point of asking any more questions? I sat there, my hands in my lap, appetite vanished, and when the food arrived, consumed mechanically whatever it was I'd been given, not even tasting it.

"Right," Tim began, once the food had been eaten. "I realise that from your point of view everything must seem highly suspicious, and for that, I'm sorry. That's my fault, and I assure you there's a simple explanation for all of it. First of all, you'd been so sick when we left the farm, and were so tired after not having slept for two nights, as well as having undergone some pretty traumatic experiences with us arriving and all, I decided the best thing for you would be to make sure you had a good sleep, which I did."

"You could have asked me first."

"Yes, in hindsight I probably should have done. I'm sorry, Col." He put his hand on my shoulder. "To be honest, though, you looked as though you were in no state to make any decision for yourself, so I just went ahead and made it for you."

"Why aren't you registered here?"

"Actually, I am. We are, I should say… I know this sounds sort of cloak and daggerish, but given my line of work, I need to travel undercover, using a pseudonym, so I wouldn't have registered as Timothy Yeats."

"You could have told me."

"Oh Come on, Col! Give me a break! So you can't remember what I do for a living! Well, I can't be expected to keep remembering what *you* can't remember! Anyway, I'd planned to fill you in on what you wanted to know, after you'd had a good sleep. It would have been fine if you hadn't gone and got your knickers in a twist, and started wandering around the corridor… You did have a good sleep, didn't you?"

I nodded. "But why did you leave me for so long? What did you think I was going to imagine when you left me all that time without telling me anything?"

"For your information I *did* call in to check on you -- several times in fact, but when I looked in on you at eight o'clock this morning, you were still fast asleep. You must have woken up right after I left. Maybe the sound of the door closing woke you. I don't know. So I left you again for another hour or so, in which time, of course, you woke up and your imagination went into overdrive. In retrospect, I suppose that, given your experiences over the past year, that was to be expected. I'm sorry you got all antsy."

"Well, thanks for that, at least."

"Oh lighten up, will you? I'm doing my best."

"What's with you and Marjorie? Don't you get on, or something?"

"Ah yes. Well... I suppose that's pretty obvious. Things haven't been going well lately, and we had a row. That was one of the reasons you got left longer than you should have been this morning."

I tried to do as Tim said, and lighten up, but was still feeling shaken. "Sorry to hear that. Did you make up? Where's Marjorie now?"

"Gone off on her own, I'm afraid... Gone back home."

"That's too bad," I lied. I was relieved. Marjorie seemed a bit of a drag anyway. Tim and I would probably be better off on our own. "So what now? Have you sent for a new passport for me yet?"

"Ah, yes! That reminds me. Good thing you mentioned it. I've got the form here for you to sign, and we need to get a new passport photo taken. We should do that this morning. In fact, it's getting on for eleven now, so why don't we get going?"

"Ready when you are. Oh, by the way, can I have my room key, please, and what floor and room number is it?"

"It's 503, which means it's on the fifth floor, and is room number three."

"Yeah. I *am* capable of figuring that out, believe it or not. And the key?"

"If you don't mind, Col, I'd prefer to hang on to it myself. Besides, you can't go anywhere without me, so you don't need it."

"That's not the point. I don't like the idea of being kept prisoner in my own room."

"There you go again, being paranoid. Right, here's your key. Take it. You won't know how to use it anyway -- you have to insert it a particular way."

"I know," I snapped. "I'm not completely helpless, you know." I shoved the key back at him. "Oh, take the damn key. I'm fed up with the whole thing."

Tim stood up. "Right. Time to go I think. Come on. Just sign the passport application first."

This I did. It was the first time I'd written anything, let alone my signature, in so long that it must have looked very strange, especially as my lost index finger made it even more difficult to write.

As we left the hotel, I stopped.

"What's wrong now?"

"I've just realised; I haven't a clue where we are. What town are we in?"

"Tenby."

"Really? I've been here before."

"You have? When?"

"Gemma brought me here not long after I went to live with her and her father."

"It's a very pretty town." Tim took hold of my arm. "Come on. We can't stand here all day."

"Yes, Gemma told me it was pretty too."

We went to have my photo taken, and on the way out of the store Tim slapped me on the back. "You're still a helluva a good-looker, Col, if it's any consolation to you, and you don't half get some looks from the women."

"Yeah. Sure."

"No! I mean it."

I said nothing. Whatever might have been in the past, was gone. I now considered myself damaged goods. If Anne hadn't wanted me, then nobody would, and I felt another jolting reminder of the reality of my situation.

"I thought we could go on a boat trip this afternoon," Tim announced on our way back to the hotel.

"Great! What sort of boat trip?"

"There's a boat tour by Zodiac around one of the islands that might be nice. It's for viewing seals and seabirds, but the feel of the wind and sea air would be good, don't you think?"

"That's your best suggestion yet."

So we went on our tour, and I sat there, the wind in my face, the sound of the surf racing past, and was rocked by the gentle rise and fall of the RIB as it slid over the Atlantic rollers. I listened to the hundreds of seabirds and to the sound of barking seals, and there were cries of delight from the other occupants as we come across what Tim told me was a pod of dolphins. It was the best tonic I could possibly have had, and by the end of it, my brain was once again back on an even keel. Not for the first time, though, I wondered how many more mental roller-coasters I'd be able to ride before losing my sanity altogether. That I was reaching the limit as far as what I could take, was becoming increasingly evident to me, and I was in dire need of being able to settle down and remain in a stable environment, once and for all.

## CHAPTER 13

We had finished breakfast, and Tim had brought me back up to my room.

"Why have we come back up here? I thought we were going out somewhere. Is it raining, or something?"

"Okay. Sit down here, please, Yeats. We need to talk." Tim's voice had taken on a startlingly different tone. It was straightforward, crisp and businesslike, and he most certainly had not called me 'Yeats' before.

I did as I was told, panic starting to arise yet again. "What's up now, then? Why the sudden formality? Please, no more surprises. I don't think I can survive any more."

"I'm afraid you're going to have to. There's no way around it."

"So what's happened now?" I could already feel my breakfast starting to churn in my gut.

"It's rather a long story, I'm afraid, and it's not over yet, unfortunately, but we need your help to finish it."

"We? Who are 'we'?"

"The CIA and MI6."

"*The CIA and MI6!* What the... ? Oh no you don't!" I started to get up, shaking my head, but Tim put his hands on my shoulders.

"No. Sit down, please. I need to explain to you. You have to hear this."

I sat down again, and let out a big sigh. "Okay, what do I need to hear? Go ahead. Get it over with."

"Thank you... Well, for starters, you should know that ever since the beginning of this year we've been aware of who and what you are, and where you've been. We've also known much of what you've been going through, and have been monitoring the situation. Being aware of your psychological profile, however, and knowing that in the past you've proven yourself to be a courageous, sensible man, capable of holding it together when the going gets tough, we're convinced that when we explain everything to you, you'll be capable of going the necessary extra mile for us.

"I have to tell you that seeing the bounds to which you've been pushed, first in Afghanistan, and now by these other circumstances, we're surprised you've remained as sane as you have; your strength of character is nothing short of phenomenal, and you have every right to be proud of yourself."

I put my head in my hands. "Yeah, yeah. I haven't the vaguest idea what you're on about, but go on then, explain."

"First of all, I should say that from our own point of view your being blind and suffering from amnesia have actually played into our hands, but we're hoping now to jumpstart the latter by filling in your background. If we fail in that, then we hope you'll be willing to co-operate with us anyway. Are you willing to help us?"

"Depends on what you want from me. I take it, for starters, you're not my brother then. I had wondered; you haven't given the impression of being particularly brotherly towards me."

"Yes, I apologise for my un-sibling-like attitude. I've been under immense pressure myself as well, especially during these last few days, but I'll get to all that in due course, and no, I'm not your brother. You don't actually have any siblings."

"Do I even have a family?"

"Yes, your father, Dr. David Yeats, has been told you're in safe hands, but hasn't been apprised of the details."

"Why? Because he'd kick up a fuss if he knew?"

"Well, he'd have had no say in the matter anyway, and all this is between the CIA and MI6. No information regarding you has been available to the public since we discovered your whereabouts."

"I think you'd better get on with the explanation, as I'm totally confused here, and getting more so by the minute."

"Right. First of all, do you remember why you were invalided out of the army?"

"No. I didn't even know I was ever in it, although people have said I've given that impression during some of my blackouts. Why was I invalided out?"

"You were going in to attempt to save one of your men who'd been wounded in Helmand Province, when an IED exploded nearby. You yourself weren't close enough to be hurt by it, but saw three of your men being blown to pieces. It's then that you yourself were shot at, and although wounded, you still tried to help your men, and had to be dragged away from what was a hopeless task. You have no recollection of this?"

I shook my head. "Perhaps it's just as well I don't."

"Well, you started suffering from post-traumatic stress disorder with sufficiently debilitating flashbacks after that, that you had to be let go, although you'll no doubt be pleased to know you left with an honourable discharge and a Medal of Honour for your bravery... All right. Next question: do the names Steve Callahan and Joe Gascoigne mean anything to you?"

"No. Who are they?"

"I'd rather hoped that the mention of their names might trigger your memory, but it seems that's not to be. And you've no memory of setting out with them to sail across the Atlantic from Marblehead, Massachusetts?"

"Nope."

"Hmm. Okay. Then I guess you can't tell us either what happened between then and being washed up on that beach."

"Sorry, no."

"All right then, I'll tell you everything we know, and at the end of that, hope you'll decide to help us catch these two guys, because they're terrorists, and we need to stop them before they carry out a plot they have to assassinate someone, and you're the only one left who can recognize them. So here goes…"

Tim explained to me briefly how I'd been set up by Callahan to make sure he, Gascoigne and another member of the crew arrived safely off the southwest coast of Ireland, where they were to be met by some co-conspirators, who'd ferry them to an isolated inlet on the Irish shore, after disposing of me by throwing me overboard.

"Christ!"

"Yes, well do you remember a man by the name of Bob Roberts? If you can't remember the others, then you probably won't remember him either, but I have to ask."

"No, I don't remember him either."

"All right. He was the other member of the crew aboard the sailboat you were skippering and navigating for them, but was an undercover member of the CIA, and until you set sail, had been feeding us with all the relevant information. We were hoping you could tell us what happened to him, because we lost all contact with him right after you set sail from Marblehead that day back in June, nearly eighteen months ago."

I held up my hand. "Heh! Hold it right there! This Roberts guy was one of you, and you all knew that they planned to kill me? Are you telling me that you lot were quite happy to sacrifice me to the cause?"

"I was going to get to that later, but guess I'd better go ahead and clear up that issue right now, as I imagine you probably wouldn't be willing to listen to anything else I have to tell you if I don't."

"You've got that right."

"Okay, do you remember being hit with a piece of lead piping the night before you left home for Marblehead?"

"No. It can't have done me any harm though, or presumably I wouldn't have made the trip. What happened?"

"When Bob discovered that the original skipper, also a member of the cell, was forced to back out, and Callahan had brought you in as a replacement, he informed us, and we instructed him to use whatever means necessary to stop you from going -- without eliminating you, that is."

"Oh! So you do have some heart after all!"

"Well, we figured that, given time, they would doubtless find a replacement amongst their own, without involving an innocent member of the public, but Callahan jumped the gun, and got you involved, something Gascoigne objected to strongly."

"So you're saying it was Bob Roberts who clobbered me with a piece of lead piping. Where did he hit me?"

"On your right arm. He was convinced he'd succeeded in breaking it, so was amazed when he found out you'd turned up the next day anyway."

"Would that he *had* broken it; it would have saved me from all this. I suppose, though, that with me already on board, there wasn't anything he could do at that stage to stop me going."

"We did set up another, contingency plan to cause you to back out, but you caught us out by setting sail before we could put it into effect."

"And how did you plan to stop me this time, or don't I want to know?"

"Well, I'd sooner not get into that, so let's go back to where I was. Right, so let me fill you in on what you wouldn't know, or would have known even if you could remember everything else -- unless, of course, you somehow found out what they were up to, in which case it's even more surprising that they didn't kill you as they'd planned to do.

"First Callahan. He'd become radicalized somehow, and had thrown in his lot with a terrorist group to which Gascoigne already belonged. We'd discovered that they planned to very publicly execute a highly influential member of parliament who was to be offered an award during an event to be held somewhere in Pembrokeshire, so we sent in Roberts to work his way into the cell to find out more. He managed to keep his cover, and was selected to accompany Callahan and Gascoigne on the mission."

"So why bother to sail across the Atlantic to Ireland? Why not just fly to the UK?"

"There were various reasons for that, including that Gascoigne already had a record, so would have had trouble gaining entry into the UK by legitimate means. Also, the rather hectic schedule of the MP and uniting that with an event to be held at an appropriate venue meant that the date hadn't yet been fixed either, so they planned to enter Ireland via boat at some isolated inlet, as I said, and hunker down until everything was in place, then, at the appropriate time, take another boat across to Pembrokeshire, where they could also land undetected. Unfortunately, it's taken much longer than expected for the scheduled event to be organized, which has held up things considerably."

"You're saying I willingly joined their crew then?"

"Yes, but obviously you weren't to know their true plan, and you're well known as a very capable skipper and navigator, so they knew they'd be in safe hands. Once you'd guided them to a designated rendezvous off the southwest of Ireland, the plan was to simply kill you, as I said. Why they didn't has been a complete mystery to us. However, whatever it was they did do to you, they must have been convinced you were going to die from it anyway, because nobody's come looking to finish you off in all this time... Obviously they didn't know what a good sailor you really are..."

"Mr. Foster said I had to know something about sailing."

"Mr. Foster?"

"Oh, nothing. That's another story: one I remember all too well, sadly... So for some unknown reason, instead of throwing me overboard, they presumably left me to perish at sea, but I didn't, and ended up being washed up in Pembrokeshire instead. That was pretty fortuitous. How come you didn't rescue me right then?"

"Well, we lost track of all of you once you set sail. As I said, we were expecting Roberts to contact us once he and the other two arrived in Ireland, but we heard nothing, and assumed you'd all been lost at sea, so it was quite a surprise when your Miss Atkins phoned the American Embassy right after New Year, giving the name Colwyn Yeats, and asking about you."

I held up my hand. "Whoa! Hold it a minute here! The embassy told you I'd been found? You mean they knew who I was, but didn't let on to Gemma! Why not? That's downright criminal! You let me languish for all this time, thinking no-one knew anything about me!" I stood up. "I've heard of some dirty tricks by the CIA, but this takes the cake. How could you just stand by and let me go through what I went through? All I can say is that it's a blessing I was at least living with someone who loved me and cared for me!"

"Yes, well. I admit we do bend the rules now and again, but this time wasn't one of them."

"What do you mean by that. I'm sorry, but I'm right pissed off, and you still want me to help you, after what you did to me?"

"The embassy didn't withhold any details about who you were, your date of birth, or where you came from. They gave Miss Atkins all those details. They gave her everything, in fact, to enable you to be sent home to the States immediately."

"*What*! You're the pits, man! I can't believe this! You can sit there, and actually lay the blame on some poor woman who not only saved my life, but took me in, and cared for me, despite all the trouble I caused her!... Well, all I can say is that you can go take a running jump, because I'm not lifting a finger to help you, and you can damn well take me back home right now! I'm out of here!"

Tim's voice was calm, ignoring my outburst. "You remember telling me shortly after I picked you up from the farm about the letter arriving from the ophthalmologist informing you that it would be impossible to remove your cataracts because too much other damage had been done?"

"What the hell's *that* got to do with anything? As you would know -- if you had any feelings whatsoever, which you obviously don't -- that was the worst day of my life, and why you would want to remind me of it now, other than to prove what a true bastard you are, I can't imagine. If I could see to do it, I'd give you the beating of your life, you damn bastard!"

"That's not what the letter said."

"What do you mean, '*that's not what the letter said*'? I gave you only the gist of it, but if you want me to be precise,

I can repeat the damn letter to you word for word; it's not something I'm likely to ever forget."

"You want me to repeat to you what the letter *did* actually say?"

"Sure. Go ahead. You're on a roll now, so rub it in. You're enjoying this, aren't you, you damned sadist?"

"Far from it. Contrary to what you may think, I do actually have feelings, and that's why it's as hard for me to have to tell you this as it is for you to have to hear it. The letter was to give you an appointment to have your cataracts removed three weeks from that date."

My shoulders sagged. "I find it hard to believe that even you would be cruel enough to say that to anyone, unless it were true. Tell me I'm right on that, because I can't take any more of what you're dishing out to me."

"No, I'm not lying. Remember two hikers coming to the farm one day, asking to be shown the way to the coastal path?"

I sighed. "You're flipping from subject to subject here; I can't keep up. You haven't told me about the cataract removal appointment yet, and as you must surely imagine, that information is of monumental importance to me."

"If you'll shut up and give me a chance, I'll tell you. So… The hikers. You remember them?"

"Yes."

"Right. They were MI6 men. We were mystified as to why you hadn't hightailed it back home to the States right after being informed about who you were by Miss Atkins, and we needed to find out not only why you hadn't left, but also why you hadn't just called the embassy for yourself, so we asked them to check you out. That's when they discovered you were blind as well. At that point, we gained access to the letter the ophthalmologist sent you, and found you had, for some reason, not turned up for your appointment either, and the ophthalmologist's office just assumed the reason for that was that you'd probably been found at last, and had returned to the States already, so they didn't follow it up.

"What I'm trying to tell you, Yeats, is that your Miss Atkins wasn't quite what she seemed to be. And please believe me; I know how you feel about her, and it really sticks in my craw to have to enlighten you. Oh! And if you need proof that Miss Atkins has known exactly who and what you are ever since that call to the US Embassy back at New Year, I can get you a copy of the conversation, which was recorded."

"I'm afraid that what's uppermost in my mind right now is that I've been unnecessarily forced to live like this all this time. Does this mean I can still have the cataracts removed then?"

"That's the good news in all this. Yes, you can. In fact, I have an appointment for you at the London Eye Hospital in three days' time."

I said nothing, but hid my head in my hands again. Tim put his hand on my shoulder and squeezed it.

"Why have you held back on this till now? It's been nine months since those guys found out about me. Why did you leave me to go through my private hell till now this minute?"

"Well, I'm sorry to have to admit that we've been guilty of serving our own ends on that score. We weighed up the pros and cons of leaving you in situ. The pro was that by then we'd found out where and when this MP was due to receive his award -- at a tattoo to be held at Pembroke Castle a month from today, to be exact -- and as Bob Roberts seems to have vanished, presumably killed, you -- as I said -- are the only one who can identify Callahan and Gascoigne. We need you to help us stop them, and you being conveniently located right there on the farm, and being looked after by Miss Atkins, was, from our own point of view the best possible place to hold you."

"So I'm conveniently warehoused at the farm, a dumb turkey, pecking my way around the yard, being fattened up for Thanksgiving... and if that was the pro, what the hell was the con then? And how the hell was I going to identify them if I was blind?"

"The con was that it meant you having to endure your handicap for those extra months, in Miss Atkins's care. Our intention then was to pretend to discover your whereabouts, come -- as we did -- to take you away from the farm, and have your cataracts removed in time for you to be able to help us catch these guys. Miss Atkins really played into our hands by deceiving you. At the same time, she appeared to be providing you with a safe and comfortable environment -- and you weren't to know any better, so ..." Tim's voice trailed off. "I'm not too proud of that part of it, I have to admit."

"I don't know what to say at this point. Too much to take in. And I was right; you *are* callous bastards after all...Why don't you just go ahead and tell me the rest of this sordid tale, but just one point, before you do."

"What's that?"

"I was the only one found at the wreck site. How do you know this Callahan and his buddy Gascoigne are still alive? After all, Roberts, you say, must be dead, because he's never contacted you as he was supposed to do. Maybe they all drowned out there somewhere, and I was the only one to survive."

"We don't know, for sure, but we have to go ahead on the assumption that they *are* still alive, having landed safely in Ireland after disposing of you and Roberts. All in all, it's a reasonable assumption, given the way the boat was found. If you'd all met with some disaster at sea, then, even though it ended up being wrecked on the rocks, there would still have been plenty of equipment lying scattered around on the shore, but there wasn't. There wasn't anything apart from the remains of the boat, and it was obvious that it had been meticulously stripped of everything, even its identification, so we're pretty much a hundred percent sure they escaped safely, no doubt met at a pre-arranged point by some collaborators not far from the coast of Ireland, just as Roberts told us they planned to do... No, it all fits. You can bet your life they're alive, and are all prepared to carry out their mission... So, as I said, the attack is scheduled for a month from now, as I told you, and we'd planned to pull you out about two weeks ahead of that. We needed to give you time to recover from your surgery before putting you in what could turn out to be a dangerous situation."

"I don't get it. Do I have an option here, or not?"

"Technically yes, but given your previous army record, we reckoned that, when faced with the facts, you wouldn't be the sort to chicken out."

"Well, why couldn't you have just told me all this back at New Year, got my eyes fixed, and asked me to stay on at Gemma's until needed. It would have saved Gemma from having me rely on her all the time. I could have been of such great help to them both, instead of being such a hopeless dependent. And although I shouldn't have to point it out, it would have saved me from a helluva lot of emotional distress as well as physical damage too."

"The problem there was your dear Miss Atkins, I'm afraid. We knew something was radically wrong with someone who would, first of all, not let on that she knew who you were. Then, later, when we discovered your vision problem, and that she hadn't taken you to get it fixed, we knew she must definitely have one oar out of the water. At that point we commissioned a psychological profile of a person who would do something like this, and it concluded that she'd obviously found in you someone to love and care for far beyond what is normal, and was willing to go to unforgiveable lengths to make sure you didn't leave her. This, unfortunately, reached the stage with her, where she also didn't want you to become so independent that you would no longer be in need of her constant care and attention as well, which is why she didn't want your cataracts removed. Sick, eh?"

"I've never heard of such a disease -- as it must be -- and find it almost impossible to believe. She was always so loving, solicitous and caring, especially when I goofed up, and ended up hurting myself. She was always having to take me to A & E, then keep doing things for me that I couldn't do for myself as a result."

"Yes, well, that all fits the profile, and brings me to why we've had to end up pulling you out now instead of later."

"And why is that?"

"You remember a Miss James came to see you fairly recently?"

"Yes, my social worker. Couldn't stand her, although I have to say she was a bit more sympathetic when she came out to the farm to see me."

"Well, Miss James raised the alarm, although the doctor on your last visit to A & E was concerned too about the number of accidents you were having."

"What do you mean, *'Miss James raised the alarm'*? What alarm?"

"When she found out about the number of times you'd ended up in A & E, then saw the various scars you have, and questioned you about them, she became suspicious that you were being abused."

"*Abused*! Gemma didn't beat me, or anything. As I keep saying, she was kindness itself, although I have to agree that those two things she *did* do were most certainly not the actions of a mentally healthy person."

"No, Miss James strongly suspected that your so-called accidents weren't accidents at all, but caused specifically by Miss Atkins to keep you, as I said, in a state where you constantly needed her help."

"We're entering the realms of fantasy here, aren't we?"

"Not really. As I said, it's all part of the profile. Similar situations can, and have, arisen with carers, although usually with children. It even has a name: Munchausen Syndrome by proxy. There was a case just recently, in fact, where a mother kept her child in a wheelchair so that he never learnt to walk. When found out, she explained that she wanted to make it so that he'd never leave her, and would always be dependent on her."

"You're saying that's what Gemma was trying to do to me?"

"I'm afraid so. Your Miss James raised such a stink about it, fearing that Miss Atkins would go too far, and end up killing you, that she threatened to make things awkward if you weren't removed from the farm at once. She was even more strident when she looked back in the records, and discovered that many years ago Miss Atkins had a child, a son, who also turned up at the A & E on a regular basis, and subsequently died when he was seven, although there was no suggestion at the time that she'd been the cause. He'd have been about your age now."

"Jesus Christ! Seems Miss James was right; I was a disaster waiting to happen. She knew what was going on then with your part in this?"

"No, nothing about our involvement at all, and given that you had apparently found a comfortable home at last, she'd been quite satisfied until she realised what was really going on where Miss Atkins was concerned, and that in the end, she could cause you to have an accident that could, as I said, lead to your death."

"This is all a bit much to take in. Discovering what Gemma appears to have been up to all this time, is stomach churning. No wonder I've been a physical and nervous wreck! If I think about it, there were so many times when I had my confidence shattered, making me realise I was never going to be in any way independent, no matter how hard I tried. It seemed that no sooner did I think I was coping well, than something would happen to knock me down again. It's hard to accept that all that caring was made possible for her by way of her own exquisite calculation and design. I have to say the revelation brings a sort of agony of its own."

"I have to tell you as well that Miss James was spot on with her fear that Miss Atkins might end up killing you; we nearly failed to get you out of there altogether... You know you were violently sick the night before we were to leave? Well, your Miss Atkins was so distraught at your leaving that she was determined that if she couldn't have you, then no-one would!"

"My God! What did she do?"

"Well, although I myself didn't suspect that she'd actually *try* to kill you, I did become suspicious when I found you so sick that morning, and against my better judgment, let her persuade me to leave you there for another day, which was a big mistake, because the following night she tried again. That's why I took the mug with me when we left, and it was found to have poison residue in it. Fortunately, she was short of a lethal dose, or you'd not be here now. She succeeded in making you pretty ill though, regardless, and it's because you've been so unwell emotionally and physically these last few days that I've refrained from dropping all this on you until I felt you were ready to cope with it. And I'm sorry if I've not been very good at attempting to play the role of your brother for you; as I said, this has all been pretty stressful for me too, although nothing, obviously compared with the mill you've been put through."

"Where is she now? In jail?"

"No. She has no idea that we cottoned onto her, and I'm afraid that if we took her to court, it would blow our whole operation, so we've just let her be. I doubt very much if she'll have such an opportunity again to display her sickness, and the authorities will obviously be keeping an eye on her. Oh! And by the way, you told your social worker that you'd been lucky, because whenever you had an accident while Miss Atkins was at work, she always happened to come back home in time to take care of you. Didn't that strike you as odd?"

"Perhaps it should have done, but at the time I was always in such a state that I was just relieved that she *had* come home in time to take care of me. Besides, you must remember, this woman was always telling me how much I meant to her, and how much she loved me, so why would it ever, ever occur to me that she was actually a wolf in sheep's clothing? Think about it: she saved my life; invited me into her home; did so much for me. How could I think anything bad about her?"

"Yeah. I guess in your unique situation... Well, anyway, I thought you'd like to know, she never actually did have a job, at least, not after she found out who you really were. She resigned from her post right after that, telling her employers that she needed to look after you full time, but presumably the real reason was so that she could also spend her time moulding you to fit the totally dependent individual she wanted you to be."

"I don't think I want to know any more about this. It's all gruesome beyond... To change the subject: you've got me thinking here about something else now. Why is it that Miss James took over a year before coming to check on me anyway?

Do they normally just abandon people once they've been conveniently farmed out?"

"My understanding is that you somehow fell in between the system's cracks, and it wasn't until the A & E doctor started asking questions that they remembered you, and dug out your file."

"Please don't tell me they're claiming now that lessons have been learned as a result! I'm fed up with being the subject of their damned learned lessons. Maybe I should start charging them for the privilege of using me to teach them."

Tim laughed. "Well, let's hope you won't be in a position again where they *can* learn lessons from you."

"True ...Well, in all this, you've not given me the opportunity to rejoice in its only positive aspect -- that you say I can have my cataracts removed! You're absolutely sure about this, are you? Because that's one thing I couldn't bear to hear wasn't true after all. I... ah... um..."

Tim put his hand on my knee. "Not to worry. I've made absolutely sure before letting you know. I'm not *that* callous. What with everything, you've had a pretty rough few years, and I have to say there aren't many who'd have come through it all as you have, but, as I said before, we knew you were made of tough stuff, and have relied on that."

"You wouldn't think me so tough if you'd have seen me sometimes."

"I said you were made of tough stuff, not a bloody saint."

I grinned. "I'm not? Gee, and there was I thinking... Okay. So where do we go from here? I wish my damn memory would come back."

"Well, we think your brain is probably blocking out whatever happened to you before you landed up on that beach a form of dissociative amnesia, probably exacerbated by what happened to you in Afghanistan. It's not rare, and can happen in combat, for example. In your case, though, you've apparently gone one step further and shut out everything that happened in your whole life before you wrecked the boat, not just the accident itself. We'll have to see about getting you help with that if it doesn't come back of its own accord. First though, we need to get your eyes seen to, so, as I said, we'll be going up to London for that as early as tomorrow."

"You're saying that within a week I'll be able to see again? It's hard not to just leap in the air and let out a rebel-yell of jubilation. If you hear any wild shouts in the night, you'll know I've finally succumbed to the urge. Right now, though, I think we should go get us a drink to celebrate, don't you? One thing I don't want to think about for the moment, is Gemma, although I imagine I'm going to have some sleepless nights reliving everything in detail, and trying to visualize how she achieved what she did. Hard to think she was even *capable* of such tortuous calculation; it must have occupied all her waking hours, playing on my emotions, and deciding when and how to bring me to my knees whenever she considered it necessary. Come to think of it, she must have been even watching me when I thought she was at work. No wonder she was able to come to my rescue so quickly!"

"I have to be honest Col; in some ways I'm surprised you didn't cotton on to what she was doing. Surely there must have been times when you questioned things she might have said, or done -- you being such a highly intelligent guy."

"*You* try waking up to find you've lost both your long-term memory and your sight in one fell swoop, and see how *highly intelligent* you'll act!"

"Yes, I guess you're right -- too busy trying to cope with your own problems to suspect she might have some of her own as well."

"You're damn right! I was trying to survive in a whole new and strange dimension, and didn't have a hope of figuring out that I wasn't the one to blame for being, as I thought, clumsy or thoughtless, or suffering from nerves, as she liked to tell me. When I think about it, I was a ready-made victim for her -- no-one could have filled the bill any better. In fact, if she'd searched the world for one, I doubt she'd have found it, but in her case, she found it lying on the beach -- a piece of jetsam, ready for the taking!"

Tim nodded. "Well, I certainly can't argue with that; you were basically dished up on a plate for her, weren't you?"

We were seated in a small alcove in the hotel's bar, beer in hand. "Why did you let the terrorists go ahead with their plot? Why didn't you stop them before they even left the States?"

"They're just small fry. We're after bigger fish. Other than that, I'm not allowed to tell you any more, I'm afraid. You're on a need-to-know basis. I have to ask you, though: you will help us catch these bastards, won't you? We literally can't do it without you, and chances are their target *will* get killed if you don't help us out. So, are you with us, Lieutenant Yeats?"

"So I'm back in the army then? Of course I'm with you."

Tim slapped me on the back yet again "No, you're not in the army; you were honourably discharged, as I said, but I knew you could be counted on anyway. Come on. Let me get you another beer, and have that celebratory drink, eh?"

## CHAPTER 14

It was three days since I'd had my cataracts removed. As I'd been unable to see at all for so long, and because both cataracts were removed at once -- an unusual procedure -- Tim insisted they keep me in hospital for these three days, so I could be monitored, as well as to make sure I didn't celebrate too wildly.

"So who's paying for all this then?" I asked when he came into the hospital lobby to pick me up.

"Ah! We have our sources," he laughed. "Nothing you have to worry about, though. How's it going? I see you have a newspaper in your lap there, so presumably all is well."

I looked up at him and grinned. "Hmm. So that's what you look like then, eh? Ugly s.o.b. aren't you?" and ducked when he pretended to take a swing at me.

I stood up, and started following him towards the entrance. It was strange being under my own steam in a strange environment, and not clinging onto someone else's arm. "You can't believe, Tim, how surreal it is, seeing everything again -- so clearly too. They said I might want to continue wearing sunglasses, though, but can you believe this? The new lenses in my eyes even have built-in UV protection! Amazing, isn't it, what they can do now?"

We reached the huge, sliding glass doors, and I looked out towards the street, where cars, buses and taxis were driving past, and people filled the sidewalk. I stopped and turned towards Tim. He was shorter than I'd imagined, and, surprisingly, almost bald -- obviously in good shape physically, though. "You know something, Tim? I've got to say this, because it's been on my mind ever since you told me about Gemma and all she did to me; I'm going to have to go back to see her some time. Can't wait to see her face, literally!"

"I find it hard to believe you even *want* to see her after all she did to you."

"Yes, well. I can't explain it properly, but, I think that seeing her is the only way I'm going to put her into perspective, if you see what I mean. I need to talk to her from a position of strength, and being able to see her and look her in the face will give me that. I can't ignore the fact either that she did save my life to begin with, even if she tried to end it when things didn't go her way. Also, despite being entirely at her mercy, there were times when I was as happy as could be expected under the circumstances."

"Well, I suppose I can't argue with that... Anyway, are you ready to step out into the big wide world again."

I walked out into the sunshine. "Sure. Let's go." And I put Gemma out of my mind.


Two weeks had now passed now since my vision had been restored, and I was still so enthusiastic about the whole experience that Tim found himself dealing with someone taking an almost childish delight in everything about him, remarking on this and that, reaching out and touching things, reading signs, and pointing out what to most people wasn't worthy of even a passing glance. I insisted on going to visit

London Zoo and the Tate Gallery as well as to a couple of plays, but although I'd have preferred to have gone on my own, Tim refused, telling me I was under their protection for the time being, so would have to put up with him as bodyguard.

I also had money in my pocket for the first time, and took great pleasure in paying for things, buying myself some new clothes, and getting what I called, 'a decent haircut'. Although I still didn't recognize myself in the mirror, I wasn't at all disappointed with what I saw. Ah! You're a vain man, Yeats, to be sure!

"My God!" Tim complained good-naturedly. "You're like looking after a five-year-old! And stop giving all the women the once-over, will you? It's embarrassing."

I laughed. "How much more time have we got before the big day then? A couple of weeks? You know something? I'm told I mustn't bend or lift weights for a while, but I've got a check-up this afternoon, and if I get the okay, I could certainly do with some sort of working out at a gym. Would that be possible, do you think?"

"Sure. A good idea. You look as though you could do with a bit of beefing up. It'll keep you out of trouble too, thank God; I'm worn out keeping up with you, Lieutenant Yeats!"

"Before I begin, though, I'd like to point out that we haven't yet celebrated my amazing recovery -- well, my visual one, that is -- and we have to remedy that. I'll let you decide where to go, though, as you must know London a lot better than I do."

Between the warmth and glow of the fire, the emotional turmoil I'd suffered one way and another, and the several neat Scotches I'd now consumed, I was beginning to ramble, and Tim let me go ahead, knowing that this was what I needed to do, and no doubt hoping it would cure my amnesia, which it didn't.

"You know, Tim, I've been going over and over in my mind the various incidents that brought me to my knees emotionally -- well, physically, they did that literally, of course -- and I'm thinking there's one thing that I could never forgive Gemma for, if it turned out that she was the cause of it."

"I'm surprised you could forgive her anyway, after what she did to you. What's this other thing, then?"

"If I'm right about what I'm thinking, then it would mean she destroyed the one thing that gave me hope and real happiness." I found it difficult bringing up the subject and talking to Tim about it, and downed my Scotch. "There was a woman I fell in love with, very much in love, and I'm sure she loved me as well. Her name was Anne. She was a university graduate, and lived locally. We got on perfectly – at least, I thought we did -- and I adored her, and what I'm thinking now is that I made the great mistake of telling Gemma I wanted to marry her."

"Gees! Given the way she felt about you herself, Col, that wouldn't have gone down well at all. What happened then?"

I sighed. "It was a lot more than, 'gees!' Tim. First she told me outright that I'd be extremely selfish by asking Anne to marry me."

"How come you'd be being selfish? In what way?"

I told him what Gemma's reaction had been.

"All I can say, Col, is thank God we got you away from this woman before she completely destroyed you! What a brutal thing to have said! Unbelievably cruel! Sadistic even, given that she knew she was the cause of the very reasons she gave you why you shouldn't marry this woman. And if she was willing to murder you rather than part with you, I'm sure destroying your relationship with another woman wouldn't have troubled her at all!"

"Anne was supposed to call me though, and I don't see how Gemma could have stopped her from doing that. I still can't explain that... although she did do away with the old house-phone, saying it was no longer necessary as she and her father had cell phones... I don't know. I'm trying to think back..."

"Maybe you should call this Anne, and find out her side of the story."

"Hmm. I'm not sure about that. It's so long now since I last talked to her. Surely she'd have found a way to contact me somehow, if she'd wanted to... It isn't as though she didn't know where I lived... I don't think I can do it."

"If you don't, though, you're forever going to be wondering what went wrong, and if our doting Miss Atkins had a hand in it... Maybe Anne still loves you."

We had a few more beers, most of the time spent in silence while I sat there and thought about Tim's suggestion. Did I want to open an old wound?

"I do still remember her phone number," I announced at last. "It's not one I'll ever forget -- even if I can't remember other things." I banged my fist on the table. "Okay. Yes. Why not? Why don't I call her right now. Find out..." I stood up, grabbed hold of the edge of the table, and stood there, swaying. "Oh!"

"Maybe tonight's not the best time to call, Col. You're drunk, and to my way of thinking, that's not exactly the ideal time to rekindle an old flame, is it?"

I sat back down heavily. "Maybe... Maybe you're right at that." I shook my head. "Not a good idea. I think I..."

"You think you what, Col?"

"I think I… I don't know… I…" I put my head down on the table, and was later told that it took the two hotel bouncers to carry me up to my bed.

## CHAPTER 15

I was nervous -- only natural, I suppose. After all, it certainly seemed as though Anne had simply dumped me, although if she had, it was still just as well I find out. "Anne? Is that you?"

"Yes, this is Anne Foster. Who's calling?"

"Anne. It's Chris."

"Chris! How *are* you?" Her voice was a mixture of excitement and polite reservation, as though she wasn't sure if she was pleased to hear from me, or not, so I thought I'd better plunge right in with my reason for calling in case she hung up on me.

"I'm okay, but I'm calling you because I need, for my own sake at least, to clear something up... Anne, why didn't you tell me you didn't want to see me anymore? I phoned you umpteen times, left messages even. Couldn't you bring yourself to talk to me? Why? I was desperate to hear from you. How could you have just dumped me like you did, without saying anything after all the great times we had together?... Well, anyway, I've finally got used to the idea that you don't love me anymore, so that's why I felt I could call you without getting too emotional about it. But I just need to know. It's been hard, you know."

"Wait a minute, Chris. Before you go on. What's this about phoning me, leaving messages and all that. I never received a single call from you!"

"What! But Gemma phoned you for me! I was standing right next to her when she did it, and when the answering machine came on, I left messages, begging you to call me."

"Chris. I swear, I never received any of those calls. Gemma must have got the number wrong, although how she could have done that so many times, I don't know. Maybe she put the wrong number into her contact list, or something."

"Gemma even drove me round to your house, but no-one was ever in. I thought something terrible had happened to you."

"I can't understand that. We haven't been away since, so you must have been very unlucky to find us out each time... Chris? Are you still there?"

"Yes, I'm still here, and I'm just thinking now that you're right, and that Gemma did phone the wrong number, although not because she'd got it wrong in her contacts list. All I know is that I left messages... Anne. Do you have some time right now? I think I need to do some explaining."

"Yes, of course."

"First of all, I know Gemma had a private phone-line somewhere. I thought it was at her place of work, but... but that's another story for now. Anyway, I now think she made a point of phoning that number each time, pretending she was phoning you."

"But what makes you think she'd do something like that?"

"It makes sense if she wanted to break up our relationship. I'm thinking now even, that she only pretended to go to your house too. I wasn't to know whose house it was that she went to when she left me out in the car. For all I know, she mightn't have been outside anybody's house."

I then explained all the things Gemma did to me, except about my real name, which Tim had told me to keep secret for the time being, and heard Anne gasp at each new revelation.

"You can tell me honestly now, too, whether something Gemma told me about you was true, or not... I can take it. She said she talked to a neighbour of yours, who said she'd seen you kissing another man outside your front door, and that happened quite soon after you dumped me."

"Oh Chris! No! That's not true at all!"

"Well, come on, Anne. Tell me. What *is* true then? You owe me that much, at least. Was the reason you didn't you phone me, just because you thought I hadn't phoned you? I don't get it. You'd promised to phone me when you got home, and you didn't... Still, I guess it doesn't matter now anyway... Anne? You haven't gone and hung up on me, have you?"

"No, Chris. It's just that all of what you've just told me has me wondering too now, and I want to ask you something, but don't know if I should, because Gemma said I wasn't to tell you. It's the reason I didn't call you. I'm sure it explains as well why she only pretended to call me for you, and even why she must have only pretended to take you round to our house as well."

"What the hell could Gemma have told you that was so secret I wasn't to know about it?"

"This is hard, Chris, because if she was right, I might be telling you something you definitely wouldn't want to hear, although the way I see it, if it *is* true, then you *should* know, especially if you meet up with another girl."

"I'm sorry, but what the hell are you getting at? What did Gemma tell you? If it concerns me, then you're right; I sure do have a right to know."

"Chris. When did you last have a blood test?"

"A blood test? Uh... I don't know... I think it was during that week you were away with your parents. Why? We heard nothing afterwards, and Gemma told me that no news meant the results were fine. Why? Weren't they? Is there something wrong with me?"

"Gemma phoned us and scared us to death. We were gutted, not just for you, but for me too."

"*Gutted*?"

"She told us your blood test showed you were HIV positive, and said that while she realised that I, of course, should know, she didn't want you to know, because she was worried about your mental state, and thought you had enough to deal with, without knowing that you were eventually going to get AIDS... Chris? I'm so sorry, but I didn't call you because I knew that, given what Gemma had told us, there was no way we could go on seeing each other, but as I couldn't think of any reason at all why I'd *ever* want to leave you otherwise, Gemma suggested that the best thing would be for me not to call at all... Oh Chris, darling! You've no idea how horrible it's been, not being able to phone or be with you! I've never been so miserable in my life! I've missed you so much! On top of that, we all went through hell waiting for me to be tested. Thank God, it came back negative, but it was a terrible shock all the same, and I've been just as worried about you too, wondering how you are. You don't know whether she was right, or not?"

"No, I don't, and that she might not have been lying to you is scaring the living daylights out of me. Are you going to be at home for a while?"

"Yes."

"I'm going to call the surgery to find out."

"But it's Sunday, Chris. They won't be open. You'll have to wait till tomorrow."

"I'm not sure how much more I can take to be honest, Anne. I've been driven pretty much to the edge. I have to think, though, that Gemma must have been lying about me being HIV positive, especially as you came back negative, which, given the way we were with each other, would surely have been impossible if I have got it. Now, though, I'm going to have to wait to find out for sure whether I have, or haven't... Sorry, but I'm not going to be much good at chatting after all this. Whatever happens though, I want you to know I still love you so very much, whether we can ever get back together again, or not."

"I love you too -- always have, ever since we first met."

"Listen, I'll try to get hold of the clinic tomorrow morning. I'll call you back as soon as I get the results. It may take them a while now to find them -- it's been so long. I won't call you before I get them though. I need to know before we talk again."

"Yes, I'd want to know first too. I do so hope it turns out well. Love you. And, by the way, I've not had any other partner since you -- no-one else has come even close to replacing you."

"The same goes for me too. I love you too, my darling. 'Bye for now."

"'Bye."

Tim came back, and could see I was once more in a mental turmoil.

"What's happened? You look like you've been clobbered. Did I do the wrong thing by encouraging you to call her?"

"No, it's not that. There's a possibility I'm HIV positive -- at least, that's what Gemma told Anne, which is why she finished with me... Can't say I blame her."

"Wow! You have me at a loss for words on that one." He walked over to the window, and there was silence, while I sat there, hands steepled under my chin, staring into space.

"You know, Col, I've been thinking here, and while I don't want to give you false hope, I bet you my bottom dollar that this is your Miss Atkins's doing; it has to be. That woman is capable of anything, and if she wanted to separate the two of you, can you honestly think of a more decisive way of going about it? My God! That woman's mind! She's as twisted as they come... Besides, although I don't know that much about it, I'd have thought they'd have picked up on something like that, before carrying out your eye surgery."

"I hope you're right, but it's going to be hell now waiting to get my blood-test results."

Tim came over, grabbed hold of my hand and pulled me to my feet. "Well, let's not make that wait a long one. Come along. You're coming with me right now, and we'll get this sorted out one way or another. We'll get you another test right now, and you'll know within an hour or so."

"You can do that? Okay, what are we waiting for? Let's go." And within a couple of hours, when we walked out of the clinic, I was able to forgive Tim all his sins against me, knowing I'd no signs of an HIV infection at all!

"Wow! Thank God for that! We've all been on tenterhooks since you called yesterday, hoping, and feeling so sorry for what you must be going through too, having to wait like that. Thank goodness you were able to find out so soon. It must have been purgatory for you... Hang on a minute; I need to let my parents know," and I heard Anne shouting, "It's all okay! He's fine!" She turned back to the phone. "And now, I hardly know what to say, other than it's absolutely the best news of any sort that I've heard since we parted all those months ago."

"Me too, obviously. Well, now we've got that out of the way, I have other good news that I'd wanted to share with you yesterday, but the HIV business got in the way… Anyway, sit down, because, as I said, I've got great news I want to share with you! Remember I told you that one of the things Gemma did was to lie to me about the letter from the hospital giving me a date to have my cataracts removed? Well, I've got my sight back already! I can see everything, and clearly too."

"*What*! Oh Chris! That's fantastic! How? When? When you told me what Gemma had done, I'd no idea you'd be able to have it fixed so easily and so soon too. I was even afraid that it mightn't be possible anymore after all this time, but that's the best news ever – well, apart from the HIV, of course! So all you need now is to get your memory back. Is there any news on that front yet?"

"No, but as I told you when we first met, the medics think my memory loss is due to some traumatic experiences I had before I was found. If I doesn't come back soon, I'm going to try to get help with that."

"This is all so intriguing! So you still don't know *why* you ended up there then?"

We had entered territory here in which, because of the CIA operation, I was forced to lie. "Still a mystery, I'm afraid."

"So what happens now, Chris? I can't wait to see you again. By the way, where are you phoning from? Are you back in the States already?"

I knew I couldn't see her until I'd completed this stint with the authorities, and couldn't risk her wanting to come to see me, so, knowing I was on a secure line that wouldn't divulge the caller's number, I told her that yes, I was back in the States. I hated lying to her like this, but couldn't afford to compromise the operation at this stage, so we chatted for a while about her life since our separation before finally agreeing to get together again as soon as possible.

For the first time in a very long time, I was full of enthusiasm and hope again, tempered only by the onus of being the only one in a position to foil an assassination attempt, and I wondered if the target of that attempt was even aware that he was indeed a target, and that the only thing that possibly lay between his life and his death, was me.

Under the circumstances it was just as well that I'd been spending as many hours as I was allowed, working out at a gym, being kept out of trouble so that now we were back in Tenby, both Tim and I were still in one piece, with me in as good a shape as possible, given the short time in which I'd been able to work on myself.

We were in the same hotel, Tim told me, and even in the same room that I'd stayed in right after leaving Gemma's, and I stood at the window, looking out over the sea. "You know, Tim, given the state I was in that day you took me away from the farm, not knowing who I was, and not being able to see either, it's no wonder you waited before unloading all the facts on me -- and although I didn't appreciate your comment at the time, you were right; the view's magnificent!" I looked around me. "So this is where I got locked out of my room when I went looking for you? I'm sure you can't possibly imagine what an unnerving experience that was. I came pretty close to losing it completely. When we came into the lobby a few minutes ago, I was looking around at it, bustling with visitors, just as it was on that day. It all looks so innocent now. It's hard for me to believe now just how much it terrified me then though."

I felt my stomach lurch, looking back over the cumulated horrors of my life in limbo, and straightened my shoulders. This was no time to be allowing myself to be affected by the emotional and physical devastation I'd suffered.

"It may surprise you to learn, though, that I actually do have one good memory of this town -- that day I came here with Gemma that I told you about. She couldn't have behaved better at that time. That had to have been before she became so attached to me. Come to think of it, I can't imagine why she *did* become so attached to me; I can't be that great to live with, can I?"

"Having had to put up with you myself for the last month has proved to me beyond doubt that she definitely had to have a screw loose -- can't be any other reason that I can see."

I grinned. "Okay, I guess I asked for that. Anyway, she took me into a fancy store here somewhere, and bought me some really good-quality clothes. I'd been wearing some probably awful-looking charity shop stuff up till then. After that, she took me to the beach and then to a great little café. We could go there again, if only I knew how to find it… That was one of my good days."

The following day was the day before the tattoo at Pembroke Castle, and Tim and I were sitting in the privacy of our room, having just finished tucking into a fine dinner, courtesy of taxpayers.

"Right. The guys you shared a beer with out at the farm that day will be here shortly, and we'll get down to business. We've been preparing for this ourselves for weeks now, so we're pretty much all set from our angle. What we need now is to get you up to speed. Incidentally, you've been given clearance to play whatever role is necessary, so, for now, you're one of us… Ah! Here they are." Tim got up, and let in the two men who had posed as hikers all those months ago.

I stood, then went up to them, smiling and holding out my hand in greeting. "Hi! I'm not sure whether I should be saying, 'Good to see you again', or not. Well, technically, I guess I haven't seen you before anyway. "

"Hi Colwyn! I'm Jim, and this is Tony. I have to say you certainly look a whole lot better than when we saw you last. Congratulations on everything."

"Thanks. And even if I still couldn't see you, I'd still recognize your voice… I got pretty good at that."

We all drew up chairs, and sat down. "Okay," said Tim. "Let's get started. First of all, let's cover what we *do* know at this point, and take it from there. It's tough luck, Col, that your memory's still failing you, because now you obviously won't be able point Callahan and Gascoigne out to us after all, so I'm afraid, pal, we're going to have to set you up as a decoy to bring them to you."

"Bring them to me? You're going to turn me into a sitting duck then?"

"Yes, you can put it that way. Right now, they don't know you're still alive, let alone that you're suffering from amnesia. They're going to be mighty shocked, I'm sure, to discover that you *are* still alive, and will immediately realise that as long as you remain so, you'll be a constant threat to them. You'd be far too big a loose end to leave hanging, especially as you knew Callahan quite well even before all this started, so they'll have no option but to eliminate you, and as soon as possible. To be honest, I still can't figure out why they didn't just throw you overboard instead of running the risk of you surviving. A huge mistake, that."

I shrugged. "Who knows? You say I knew Callahan already?"

"Yes, he was a grad student along with you, so you got to know him pretty well, so you're a particular threat to him, and always will be as long as you're alive, and potentially able to recognize him."

"How do you plan to set me up then?"

"Well, first of all, we need to let them know that you're there, so I've made arrangements with the announcer to ask the crowd to welcome you as a disabled American war veteran, whose birthday it is. I've made his introduction suitably melodramatic to get the crowd's sympathy. A missing index finger won't quite hack it, I'm afraid, so I'll give you a cane, and you can fake a rather dramatic limp."

"I've heard of actors putting a rock in their shoe to make it realistic. Perhaps I'd better do that; I'm not much of an actor."

"Whatever way you want to play it, Col."

"Aren't they going to smell a rat, though, if they find out I'm there? It's going to look like a mighty odd coincidence that I should miraculously turn up at Pembroke Castle on the day they've planned to carry out an assassination there."

"We've thought of that, but have decided that if you were there specifically to foil their plan, why would anyone advertise your presence so publicly like that?"

"Yes, but what if they think or, worse still, know I overheard what they were planning to do, and where, surely they'd see it as some sort of trap."

"We're going by something Roberts told us right before you set sail, and that was that, at that time, they had been given no instructions as to the exact location or even when the assassination was to take place, and that they wouldn't know these details until a few weeks before it was to take place, so no matter what you heard on the boat, you wouldn't have heard any mention of the date or of the tattoo at Pembroke Castle, and they'd know that. This being so, they'd have no reason to think that you were there to screw up their plan, because you'd have had no way of knowing when and where it was to be carried out.

"As I said, yes, they're going to be bullshit to see you survived, but you were aiming for Milford Haven in the first place, weren't you? As they already knew, you're an expert sailor, and they'd simply assume that, contrary to all their expectations, you eventually arrived there, and even decided to stay put or came back here again recently, although I don't think they're going to spend much time analysing all that. Their main thought, the minute they see you, will be how to eliminate you a.s.a.p."

"Incidentally, I know it's public knowledge now, but how did *you* first find out the when and where?"

"Can't tell you that, sorry."

"Okay. So... how do you propose to *stop* them from eliminating me, as you so kindly put it? I should hate at this stage to be yet again the subject of lessons having been learnt!"

"I'll get to that in a minute… Now, unless they're suicide bombers, the chances are they won't be using guns or explosives, which means they're probably going to try to get close enough to the target to inject him with something like ricin, then walk away."

"What if they *are* suicide bombers?"

"The entrance to the castle will be monitored; anybody looking in any way suspicious, will be given a body search."

"Won't syringes be found too if such a search is carried out?"

"Nothing's fool-proof, and we don't want to have so much security hanging around, checking every man that enters, that we frighten them off, so we still have to rely on you. The target won't be given his award until later in the program, and won't be making his appearance until just before then, when he'll be walking through the crowd to get to the podium.

There'll be plenty of regular police around, but not necessarily in the vicinity of the target."

"The police don't know about any of this?"

"No. Not specifically. They're always on the lookout at events like this anyway, especially if a celebrity is involved, but we don't want the place to look like it's the Queen that's visiting... Okay. Now. I've got my laptop here. Gather round and take a look at this virtual tour of Pembroke Castle... This is the Monckton Tower. See the wall here between that and the next wall, which is the wall of the Western Hall? Well, I'll be coming with you up onto the walkway along that wall, Col. The podium is going to be over on the grassy area near the gatehouse, so anyone standing near there can see you clearly. The walkway is also quite narrow, so anyone making their way along it towards you, or up the steps to get to it, will be relatively easy to pick out."

"Won't there be lots of people walking towards me on their way to take up a spot for themselves?"

"I'm going to keep you out of sight until everyone is pretty much settled, then add you to the mix. We'll get you over near the wall of the Western Hall. There's no access to the walkway from that end, so anyone coming after you will have to come up the steps to reach you."

He clicked on another tower. "Now this is the highest tower, the Keep, and it's seventy feet high. Tony'll go up there so he can see anyone making his way towards you, and will warn me. Don't worry, Col, I'll be right there at the bottom of the steps, ready to grab anyone fitting the bill, and Jim'll stick around near where the target will be, and keep his eyes open for any anyone in that area, showing any special interest in watching whoever's heading towards you... Right. Any questions? Jim and Tony already know their roles, so I won't go over that, but if you have any questions, Col, now's the time to ask them."

"What sort of weapon would they be likely to have on them then, if and when they do come after me? Presumably they won't be carrying spare syringes of ricin with them."

"Probably some sort of switchblade, or flick knife."

"Nice. Won't that be found in a body search, though?"

"Like I said, we can't search everybody. And there are non-metallic blades around now that are as strong and as deadly as steel if it comes to that.

"Getting off that track for the moment. I have to ask: who is, or was, Marjorie, by the way? Where does she come in?"

"Oh, she was just brought in to make it look more realistic to Miss Atkins that your family had found you. She's no longer in the picture... Right, the show starts at noon, so we'll be leaving here around 11a.m. to get us set up. Chances are that Callahan and Gascoigne will wait until the main influx of people to avoid special scrutiny, but we can't be sure of that, of course, so need to be prepared for them arriving at any time... Okay, that's it then. You and I, Col, will leave from here; Tony and Jim will be going separately. Let's hope this all turns out well."

"You ain't the only one, pal! I have to say I'd like to have at least something to show for everything I've gone through. All I crave now is getting back to having a normal life."

# CHAPTER 16

Tim came back from looking out over the scene for the umpteenth time. "Okay, Col, the place has pretty much filled up now, so let's get you out there, shall we?"

We climbed up onto the walkway, and made our way along it, wending our way through the lines of people who had already taken up their viewing positions.

"This should do it." Tim stopped and looked to make sure Tony and Jim were in place.

I turned and leaned over the parapet. "That's quite a drop down there, isn't it?"

"Yes, so don't go leaning over too far. Can't afford to lose you at this stage."

"Comforting to know you have my personal safety at heart."

Tim slapped me on the back. "Okay, I'll take up my position near the bottom of the steps now. Good luck."

I leaned on my cane. "I think I got a bit too realistic with putting that damned rock in my shoe. Hurts like hell."

"Too late now to remove it, so you'll have to live with it till it's over, buddy." Tim left me, and I stood there, surrounded by people peering over and between shoulders to get a good view over the large square in the centre, where the tattoo was to be held.

In the meantime I scanned the crowd below, hoping that I'd recognize Callahan and Gascoigne if I saw them, something that would save me from standing there as Tim's sitting duck waiting for them to try to bump me off. I couldn't see a familiar face anywhere, though, other than Jim's. I looked up. Tony was already peering out over the parapet of the keep. I couldn't see Tim, so just had to hope he was there somewhere, because without him there to waylay my would-be murderer, I was a dead man.

My heart was beating fast, but no longer as the result of a panic attack. At least my brain was now under control as far as that was concerned. I was nervous enough, though, to wish the tattoo would hurry up and get underway, so we could get this whole thing over with.

There was a sputtering and crackling as the announcer prepared to use the loudspeaker, swivelling the microphone around to get it to the right height, then blowing into it, before clearing his voice, and I cringed when he boomed out: "Ladies and gentlemen, before we begin, I'd like you all to join me in wishing a Happy Birthday to one of our American cousins, a disabled veteran of the war in Afghanistan, visiting us here today. He's also someone who, I should add, has a good old Welsh name: *Colwyn*. Lieutenant Colwyn Yeats, where are you? Can you put your hand up for us please?"

Tempted not to do anything, I hesitated before tentatively raising my hand. It was immediately seized by some enthusiastic onlooker next to me, who held it up high for me, shouting, "He's here!"

There was a burst of applause, and everyone began singing, *Happy Birthday to you,* at the end of which, I thanked them with a friendly wave. My face, I am sure, was scarlet with embarrassment, but my neighbours seemed almost proud to have me next to them, and tried to keep others from jostling me, making me feel even more awkward.

A band started to play, and I beat time to the music with my hand on my cane, trying to look nonchalant, while my nerves tingled with tension.

The weather was fine, the sun warm on my face, and I was grateful that its brightness no longer exploded in my head, giving me migraines, although they'd been right; I did still need to wear sunglasses. Under any other circumstance I'd have been happy to relax, but because I knew I'd recognize neither Callahan nor Gascoigne if they did come up to me, my nerves, as I said, were on edge, suspecting anyone making a move in my direction, and relieved to know that Tim was positioned to intercept them -- and for that we both still had to depend on Tony, up in the tower with his binoculars. I just hoped that whatever means he was using with which to communicate with Tim, worked!

The band stopped playing, and everyone, including me, applauded. This was followed by a lull, the only sound being the commands of the drill sergeant and the click of heels and rifles. It was in that lull, though that I became aware of another sound that came from within feet of me.

I'm still unable to explain or even describe the level of horror and fear that overtook me at that moment. All I knew was that it was a sound that filled me with an almost paralytic terror, every hair on my body tingling as though standing up straight like the hair on a dog's back, and I stood stock still, waiting for what I was sure was going to kill me.

I struggled to overcome my fear, and the desperate effort required caused it to turn instead into a frenzy of mental agitation in which I swung around to face the approaching sound, ready to fight for my life. Directly in front of me I saw, and recognized, Steve Callahan, and he was almost upon me!

He stopped, and now with no-one between us, we stared at each other. Steve was the first to move, and I saw the flash of the sun on the switchblade. I sidestepped, my cane flying over the edge of the walkway onto the grass below, the pain in my foot ignored. There was a jostling amongst the crowd, and I wondered for the moment where Tim was. Why had he let Steve pass him without stopping him? Because he was supposed to be protecting me, I was completely unarmed.

Steve came at me again with the knife, and this time drew blood on my chest before I was able to grab hold of his wrist, and clamp down on it; on it was my precious Panerai Radiomir watch. Fury, fear and the sudden and overwhelming mental assault I was experiencing, caused by the traumatic return of my memory, flooded my body with adrenalin, giving me a strength way beyond the normal, and Steve grunted and dropped the knife.

I kicked it over the edge of the walkway, and still gripping his wrist, tried to knock him unconscious with my other hand, but only grazed his chin. I had him backed up against one of the crenellations in the parapet, and was fully prepared to push him over the edge and onto the rocks way below, but he fought back, and pulled a syringe out of his pocket with his free hand. The fight then turned into a wrestling match in which I was desperate to avoid the point of that syringe and its deadly contents. Someone tried to come to my aid, but I yelled at him to stay away; he could get killed.

I had Steve leaning backwards over the parapet now, and tried to heave him over the edge, but he wriggled free by twining his legs around my knees and unbalancing me, forcing me to let go and to fall backwards onto the walkway, my head hanging out over the edge, my sunglasses flying off into space, leaving me dangerously dazzled by the sun. He swung around, syringe raised, and lunged, but I rolled out of the way, almost falling through the guard rail onto the grass below, but managed to scramble to my knees and seize hold of his legs, upending him so that he ended up flat on his back. I stamped hard on his wrist, and realised too late, that it was the one on which he was wearing my watch. There was a snap, and the syringe fell out of his hand. Someone reached out to take it. "Don't touch it!" I shouted.

The man pushed it out of Callahan's reach with his foot, then stood over it, allowing me to completely immobilize him by sticking my knee in his chest, while holding both his wrists down on the walkway, one on either side of his head, the one wrist showing the pinkish white of bone sticking through the skin, my watch, miraculously, still intact!

Steve tried to use his legs again to lever himself up, and kick me in the crotch, but I had him securely pinned down, blood from the knife-wound in my chest dripping onto his face.

"I can't breathe! You're... breaking... my ribs."

I kneed him even harder. "I don't care if I break every bone in your damn body! I'll kill you for what you did to me!"

"I can't..." Steve's eyes were starting to bulge, but I pressed even harder.

"It's okay Col, I've got him. You can lay off." Tim was pulling at my arm. I shook him off.

"*Yeats*! Enough, I said, and that's an order! We want him alive. *Let go, Yeats*! *Now*!... Give me a hand here, will you, constable?"

Hands grabbed hold of my arms, but I refused to release my hold on Callahan. The flat of a hand whacked me hard on the side of my face, stunning me, and together they pulled me off him.

I sat back on my haunches, silent, breathing hard, dazed. Tim put his hand on my shoulder, and I raised my own hand and clutched it.

"It's okay, Col. It's all over. Finis. You did it. You got him. Well done."

Tim helped me to my feet, and led me, limping and bloodied, away from the castle.

Just before the beginning of the fracas on the battlements, the band had struck up again, so apart from those standing on the walkway in my immediate vicinity, no-one was aware of what had happened, allowing all those involved in it to be able to leave the castle virtually unnoticed, and Tim to succeed finally in bundling a fuming me into the car.

"Where the hell were you? If I hadn't recognized that damned cough of Callahan's, and turned around, he'd have killed me for sure. I saw his face, and it all came flooding back. Then I saw the switchblade glinting in the sun, and I just lost it. I was ready to kill the guy. I would have done too, if you hadn't pulled me off him. It's pure luck that bloody cough of his triggered my memory. So, again, where the hell were you? I thought you were supposed to stop him before he got to me!"

"If you'll shut up for a minute I'll tell you where I was. Come on, Col, get in, will you?" Tim shoved me into the car and slammed the door after me, before going round and settling himself in the driver's seat.

For a couple of minutes we both sat there, breathing heavily, and staring straight ahead. "As I told you before, the police on duty were automatically on the lookout for any potential trouble," Tim started. "But what happens? Some damned off-duty cop sees me going after Callahan, and decides to become officious and stop me -- something about health and safety. The walkway was narrow; he was built like a tank, and refused to let me pass till I showed him my official card, all the time telling me, like a typical Brit cop, to *calm down,* while

I'm busy trying to explain to him that if he doesn't let me pass pronto, someone's definitely going to get killed!

"By the time I'd dug my badge out, and he'd taken his time reading it, meanwhile demanding that I be more explicit, you and Callahan were fighting it out. Once he finally got it into his head about the gravity of the situation, he then came with me, and he's the one who helped me drag you off Callahan before you killed him. Believe me, I nearly went crazy with this guy stalling, and not letting me pass. I could have throttled him."

Tim paused, panting, running his hands over and over again through his thinning hair. "It scares me to death to think of it, because, if you *hadn't* recognized Callahan, there'd have been nothing I could have done to save you. He'd have just shoved that blade in your back, and killed you. Believe me, I'm as shaken up as you are."

I looked at him, and realised that the adrenalin was coursing through Tim's body as strongly as it was through my own, both of us in a high state of nerves.

"Not much I can say in answer to that then. My own brain's still going round in circles, and I'm having a tough time dealing with it, so why don't you try to calm down yourself a bit, Tim, and go ahead and tell me what happened with Gascoigne. How did you get him?" I was breathless, the words tumbling out in agitation and excitement, and I tried to slow myself down as well. "By the way, as I said, it's Callahan's cough I recognized. That's what made me turn around. That cough of his nearly drove me crazy on the boat. Strange that it would end up saving my life. As soon as I saw the bastard, I remembered him. On top of that he was wearing my watch, which he'd stolen from me after knocking me out with some damn narcotic." It was now safely back where it belonged -- on my own wrist -- and I smoothed the face with my thumb. "My father gave me this for my twenty-first. Believe me I was ready to kill the son-of-a-bitch at that point."

Tim started the car, and we set off. "You nearly did kill him! And Gascoigne, yes, Jim told me he gave himself away by doing exactly what we'd hoped he'd do: while everyone else was watching the army drill, his head was turned in exactly the opposite direction, watching intently everything that was going on up on the walkway, and even gesticulating to Callahan, pointing towards you.

"With the crowd watching everything else going on, no-one else noticed, but it being obvious from his actions that it had to be Gascoigne, Jim was able to nab him while his attention was still directed towards you and Callahan. You, of course, were then able to positively identify him for us on the way out. I think you'd have tried to kill him too, if that cop and I hadn't been holding onto you."

He put his head back, and ran both hands through his hair again. "In the end a successful mission. Whew!"

"A bit more than just *whew* I'd say, and a bit too much luck involved to my mind, but yes, I suppose all's well that ends well, and an added bonus is that I've finally started getting my memory back, it seems... And would you mind putting your hands on the steering wheel instead of through your hair, Tim? Having got this far with my recovery, I'd appreciate living long enough to enjoy it. Incidentally, where are we going? This isn't the way back to Tenby, is it?"

"In case you haven't yet noticed, Col, your shirt is soaked with your blood. I took a quick look at it while you were still throwing a hissy fit back there at the castle, and it's a slash more than a penetrating wound, thank God, but we do need to get it seen to."

"Not the A & E yet again! They'll be expecting me to take up residence there at this rate! Well, they can take a look at my foot too, then. I wasn't expecting to be doing gymnastics with that rock in my shoe, and that hurts a lot more than the other. That's the last time I'm going to play that trick." I pulled off my shoe, and grimaced. It was swimming in blood.

"Let's hope it's the last time you have to."

## CHAPTER 17

It was a few days after the tattoo, during which time my brain, like a rusty wheel, started loosening up in fits and starts, remembering at first disjointed sequences of events, but gradually beginning to piece everything together like a giant jigsaw. Right now, Tim and I were seated in a darkened alcove of the hotel bar back in Tenby. I'd slept until noon, and was still struggling to come to terms with the return of my memory. I gazed at the flaming embers in the fireplace, watching mini firework displays of sparks flying up the chimney every now and then.

"Yes, if you don't mind, Tim, I do need to talk about it," I said at last. "That's the only way my brain is going to unscramble itself completely, and talking it all through will help me do that."

"Yes, well, as you can imagine, it'll help us too to learn what exactly happened on that voyage. As far as your private life's concerned, I can't help you much with that, of course, but feel free to bring up anything you like. You've certainly gone beyond the call of duty in helping us, God knows, especially with ending up bringing down Callahan on your own like that, so the least I can do is to help you regain some sense of mental stability. If I had my way you'd get another medal."

"Okay, let me start then with us leaving Marblehead. You mentioned that Bob had told you that Gascoigne had been dead against having me come on board as skipper and navigator. I can see now that that was probably why he was so aggressive towards me right along. We even got into a fight quite early on in the trip."

"I hope you won."

"Yes, I did. Going back to Bob, though, he definitely gave the impression throughout the whole time he was with us, that he was worried about something, and I can only assume now that it was because he knew what they intended doing with me, and could think of no way of stopping them without giving himself away. There was something else too: the day we were due to leave he didn't turn up, and Steve had to phone him to see where he was. You're more likely to know why that was than I, but maybe he was afraid right then that they'd rumbled him."

Tim made no reply to that, so whatever he knew, or didn't know, he wasn't letting on to me -- no doubt not on my 'need to know' list.

"You know what happened to him then?"

"Yes, I do," and I told him everything about the whole trip, including how they had thrown Roberts overboard, and how Gascoigne had cut off my finger, when I refused to take them to the coordinates where they were to be picked up."

Tim shook his head. "Poor old Bob. Not a pretty end to a fine career."

"I don't think he'd have suffered too much. I heard nothing, no shouts, no screams for help, nothing, so I'm pretty sure they must have drugged him first so I wouldn't hear anything. Perhaps he was dead even before he hit the water."

Tim said nothing, but got up and fetched us another round of beers. "Here." He pushed the bottle across the table at me.

"You know, Tim, I think the reason I went after Callahan so viciously was that, in a way, he was almost worse than Gascoigne. At least Joe was more or less above-board and consistent in his attitude towards me the whole trip. Callahan, was a complete weasel. It was obviously no mere chance that he'd discovered I was at a loose end after my research cruise had been cancelled, and it makes me furious when I think of his pretence of being so chummy and supportive." I drew a circle on the table with my beer bottle. "A right bastard. He just did whatever Joe told him to do, like an obedient sheepdog. I think that, given the chance, I could still quite cheerfully throttle the guy, and I hope he gets whatever's coming to him. Their original captain too, completely misled me, of course; they knew nothing at all about sailing, and I was virtually crossing the Atlantic singlehanded..."

I rambled on, telling Tim how I'd watched them strip the boat of everything, including its identification, before abandoning me, and all that had happened to me after that. I looked at my Panerai Radiomir watch. "They probably took that to prevent me navigating by the sun or stars... I wonder if Steve ever found out how valuable it is, though".

We sat in silence for a while, me still foraging in my brain for all it had hidden from me for so long. "You know you said you couldn't fathom why they hadn't ditched me in the Atlantic as well? Well, I do remember why that was," and I told him how Gascoigne had decided that throwing me overboard was too good for me, and had wanted me to suffer before finally succumbing.

"Well, he's certainly paid for allowing revenge to come before following orders. Serve him right."

I stood up. "My turn. What would you like? Time for something a little stronger, don't you think?"

"Why not? A double Scotch sounds good."

When I came back, I continued with my story until I came to the part where I lost my sight after the lightning struck.

I stopped. I hated even to think about what happened next, let alone express it out loud. "I need another drink. How about you?" I stood up. "No, I've got some money left; I'll get it."

I slid Tim's drink across the table to him, and settled myself down again, hands wrapped around my glass. The coal fire was sending out fingers of orange light across the darkened walls of the nook, and I held up my glass to look at the reflections through the amber liquid.

"I thought I was fine -- just had a minor burn on my hand and arm, and a sort of misty veil before my eyes." I stopped again.

"It's okay. Take your time."

"After that the mist became a dense fog, until after about three days all I could do was tell night from day, and that's how it stayed until the cataracts were removed... Not being able to see where I was going, I just had to let the boat drift, and that's when I ended up crashing onto the rocks near Druidston, where Gemma's dog found me. If she hadn't pulled me up the beach out of the way of the rising tide, and phoned for help, I'd have drowned for sure. That's what makes her subsequent behaviour so difficult for me to get my head around."

"How did you deal with your finger? That must have hurt like hell."

I nodded and looked down at where it used to be. "Yep. I used seawater to stop it getting infected. It worked, although apparently it was a bit of a mess after I'd got it covered with sand and seaweed on the beach." I rubbed the space with my thumb. "Seems to have healed over okay, no thanks to Gascoigne..." I sighed. "Joe knew exactly what he was doing when he cut if off; the one thing he did leave on the boat was my guitar, knowing I'd never be able to play it properly again... I was pretty good too, and that's something I'll really miss.

"I still find it hard to believe all Gemma did too. All in all, I really managed to hit the jackpot where human misfits were concerned, didn't I? I have you to thank you, though, for suggesting I call Anne. I'd never have done that otherwise; I was so convinced she'd dumped me... Well, when I come to think of it, it was, of course Gemma who convinced me of that by unloading on me all the reasons why Anne wouldn't want to spend her life burdened with someone like me, and then, when that didn't work, by lying to me, telling me Anne was having it off with another man! Poor Anne too! Telling her she might have contracted HIV from me!... I need another drink."

I started to get up, but somehow managed to get caught up in the chair, and landed on the floor. "Oh!"

I sat there, and Tim pulled me to my feet. "No, you don't need another drink. You've had enough, believe me."

I plopped down on a chair. "I want to call Anne... I want to ask her to marry me... You think she'll want me now, Tim? She says she still loves me... God, but I love her, Tim! How could Gemma have done that to us? I can't believe she did that!... I need another drink."

I stood up again, turned round, and bumped into a table. "Where did that come from? That table wasn't there before. Who put that table right there where I'd...?" I looked around... "Tim?"

I was desperate to see Anne again, but Tim insisted I go back to the States, not wanting me to let slip somehow that I'd been in the UK all the time -- even within a few miles of her.

"What's to say she wasn't at the tattoo as well?" I argued.

"If she had been, then I can't believe she wouldn't have recognized you somehow, even though she wouldn't have recognized your real name. You never got around to telling her what you thought your real name was, did you?"

"No. That all happened quite a while before I met her, and since you came into the picture, you've told me not to mention it."

"Well, I'm still going to insist you return to the States before seeing her. After that, you're off the hook, and free to go about your life again."

"Are you going back too?"

"No, I've been posted elsewhere, so this is where we part company, I'm afraid."


We were at Heathrow Airport, and I was leaving for Boston that morning.

Tim shook my hand. "Goodbye Col. It's been good to know you. I only wish there were more like you around. I know I can trust you to keep quiet about your latest experience." He grinned at me. "Wouldn't want to have to eliminate you after all…"

"Gee! Thanks! Am I going to have to spend my life looking over my shoulder in fear that you're going to come after me?"

"Only if we decide to put you to good use again."

I shook my head. "I have a feeling I ain't going to let that happen."

"Okay Col. Have a good trip -- wish you could invite me to the wedding…"

We parted, and a few hours later I was looking down at the grey Atlantic far below, its vast, white-capped rollers and the huge tankers reduced to picture-postcard size. I turned away. Would I ever be enthusiastic about making that voyage again in a small sailboat? It would take time before I'd feel comfortable doing that, that was for sure, and I wondered what other unseen dramas might be being played out way down there right now.

## EPILOG

It was New Year's Eve when Anne and I arrived, just after dark, in the White Mountains of New Hampshire, and checked into my favourite little B & B, hidden amongst the pine trees in Bartlett. The still, frosty air smelled of burning pine logs; the snow lay in ten-foot heaps along the path, and we stripped and sank down in the warm water of the old wine-cask hot-tub, a cloud of vapour rising into the frigid air around us. We lay there, snuggling up close, our naked bodies entwined, and gazing at the stars piercing the blackness of space above us.

"I hope Paddy won't mind staying with your father for a few days while we're up here. I'm so glad we were able to find him after Gemma ended up in that awful psychiatric unit. Sad, though, that Mr. Atkins died soon after she was taken away."

I climbed out of the hot tub, and held out my hand to help her out. "Come on. Let's get dressed, I want to show you something," and I drove us up onto the Kancamagus Highway, still open to traffic, and stopped the car -- my antique Corvette Stingray -- at one of the lookouts, surrounded by more great cones of snow. The air was numbing, clear, and silent, and in the background Mt. Washington gleamed in the moonlight.

We were alone in the wilds of New Hampshire, surrounded by a seemingly frozen-in-time tableau of solid-ice waterfalls, snow, glittering granite massifs, black silhouette-conifers and silver-barked birches.

I climbed out and opened the door for her. "Come on. Let's get out. As I said, I want to show you something." I took her hand. "Look up there." I pointed to the ebony vault of the sky and its myriads of stars. "See Orion?"

"Aah, Chris!" She put her arms around me, and we kissed. "How very far away we are from that restaurant in the woods in Pembrokeshire! You told me to look up then, and told me where to find one of the most beautiful sights in the sky, the Orion Nebula. I've never been able to look at it, or even think of it since we separated; it made me too sad. Never, *ever*, did I dare to hope you might see it again yourself, or that we'd get to see it again together like this."

I kissed her again, and tasted the salt of her tears. "It's beneath Orion that I told you how much I loved you, and now, beneath Orion again, I want you to know how very much I still love you, and to ask you to marry me. Will you, Anne? And I promise not to be dependent, except on your love for me."

"Yes, yes. Of course I will. I've never been so happy as I am at this moment!" She kissed me again. "Of course I'll marry you! Oh! I ache with loving you so much." And we held each other close.

"And if we don't get back into the warmth of the car right now, we're going to be two ice-statues standing here with beatific smiles on our faces, with Mt. Washington watching over us."

"At least it would be a highly romantic way to go!"

"I'm not ready to go that way yet, romantic or not, Mrs. Yeats-to-be."

## THE END